Ne
Weds!

Betty Neels Carole Mortimer
Penny Jordan

In this extra-special brand new collection,
these talented authors have created three very
different stories celebrating love and marriage!

There's nothing more exciting than a wedding!
Everyone basks in the happiness the occasion
brings, eager to see the bride walk up the aisle
and exchange vows with the groom. Then the
champagne starts to flow and the party goes
on into the night...

But the lead up to the wedding is just as much
fun and a lot can happen on the way to the altar.
Read on and share the excitement as three
couples make their journey from being nearly
(but not quite) weds to newly-weds!

Praise for the authors of

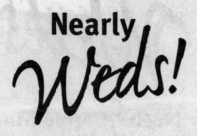

Nearly Weds!

Betty Neels

"Ms Neels uses animated dialogue and vivacious
characters to warm readers' hearts."
—*Romantic Times*

Carole Mortimer

"Carole Mortimer delivers quality romance with
an exciting premise and intense characters."
—*Romantic Times*

Penny Jordan

"Penny Jordan pens a formidable read."
—*Romantic Times*

Nearly
Weds!

Betty Neels

Carole Mortimer

Penny Jordan

MILLS & BOON®

*MILLS & BOON and MILLS & BOON with the Rose Device
are registered trademarks of the publisher.*

*First published in Great Britain 1999 by
Harlequin Mills & Boon Limited,
Eton House, 18-24 Paradise Road,
Richmond, Surrey, TW9 1SR*

NEARLY WEDS! © Harlequin Enterprises II B.V., 1999

The publisher acknowledges the copyright holders of the
individual work as follows:

MAKING SURE OF SARAH © Betty Neels 1999
THE MAN SHE'LL MARRY © Carole Mortimer 1999
THEY'RE WED AGAIN! © Penny Jordan 1999

ISBN 0 263 81561 7
108-9904

*Printed and bound in Great Britain
by Caledonian Book Manufacturing Ltd, Glasgow*

Contents

Contents

MAKING SURE OF SARAH

by

Betty Neels

Betty Neels spent her childhood and youth in Devonshire before training as a nurse and midwife. She was an army nursing sister during the war, married a Dutchman, and subsequently lived in Holland for fourteen years. She lives with her husband in Dorset, and has a daughter and grandson. Her hobbies are reading, animals, old buildings and writing.

Betty started to write on retirement from nursing, incited by a lady in a library bemoaning the lack of romantic novels. She has since become one of the most prolific and well-loved Mills & Boon® authors. She has written over 120 books, and over 30 million copies of her books have been distributed worldwide.

CHAPTER ONE

SARAH looked out of the car's windows at the flat, peaceful countryside of Holland, no longer listening to her stepfather's angry voice blaming everyone and everything but himself for getting lost. Her mother, sitting beside him with the map, had been ignored when she had pointed out the road they should have taken, but the main butt of his ill humour was Sarah.

He turned his red, angry face and said over his shoulder, 'You must have known that we had taken a wrong turning—why didn't you say so?'

Sarah said in her quiet voice, 'I don't know Holland. I came with you and Mother because you wanted someone who could speak French while you were in France.' She added before he could reply, 'If you had told us that you intended going back home through Belgium and Holland I would have bought a Dutch dictionary—so that I could have asked the way,' she pointed out in a matter-of-fact voice.

'Don't annoy your father, dear,' said her mother.

'He isn't my father; he's my stepfather,' said Sarah, and she wondered why her mother, after ten years or more, could bear to be married to him, and why she expected Sarah to think of him as her father. It had been mutual dislike at first sight, but her mother, who had managed to go through life turning a blind eye to anything which upset her, had steadfastly pretended that her ill-tempered husband and the daughter she had never quite understood were the best of friends.

Then, because she loved her mother, Sarah added, 'There was a road sign a mile or so back. It said "Arnhem, seventeen kilometres".'

'Why didn't you say so?' asked her stepfather furiously. 'Letting me drive miles out of my way.'

'I did. You told me not to bother you.'

He drove on then, muttering under his breath. Sarah turned a deaf ear, vaguely aware of her mother's conciliatory murmurs, uneasy now since he was driving much too fast. The road was narrow, with a ditch on either side and fields beyond; it stretched ahead of them with nothing in sight and the March day was drawing to a close. She thanked heaven silently that there were no curves or corners, and no traffic at all.

She had overlooked the ditches. Her stepfather, never a good driver, and an even worse one when he was in a bad temper, took a hand off the wheel to snatch the map from his wife's lap, and the car shot over the narrow grass verge and tumbled into the ditch.

The ditch was half filled with water draining from the fields, and the car hit the muddy bottom with tremendous force, its bonnet completely buried.

Sarah, flung hither and thither and ending up rather the worse for wear, still in her seat belt, was too shocked to speak, but it was, in a way, reassuring to hear her stepfather swearing, and then shouting, 'Get me out, get me out!'

Typical! thought Sarah, light-headed. What about Mother…? She came to then, scrambling round until she could undo the belt and lean over the seat where her mother was. Her mother was slumped over, her head against the dashboard, and she didn't answer when Sarah spoke to her. Sarah leaned over and found her arm and felt for her pulse—beating, she was relieved to find, reasonably strong. Her stepfather gave another shout, and she said loudly, 'Be quiet, do. Get out and help Mother, she's hurt…'

'You stupid girl. *I'm* hurt—my leg, my chest. Never mind your mother for the moment, go and get help. Be quick. Heaven knows how badly injured I am.'

'This is your fault,' said Sarah, 'and all you can think of is that you're hurt. Well, so is Mother...'

She wriggled out of her seat, and after a struggle managed to open the door of the car. The water, icy cold and thick with mud, came up to her knees, but she hardly noticed that. It was late afternoon and the sky was grey, but there was still plenty of light. She tugged at the handle of the door by her mother and found it jammed, so got back into the car again and leaned over to open it from inside. It didn't budge.

Frantically she managed to undo her mother's seat belt and haul her gently into a more comfortable position, relieved to feel her pulse was stronger now. There were rugs in the boot, but first she must turn off the engine, still running, and take a look at her stepfather. She hung over the back of his seat and managed to undo his seat belt and sit him up a little, not listening to his roars of rage.

And all this had taken only a few minutes, she realised, edging her way round to the boot and finding it thankfully burst open and the rugs easy to reach. She tucked them round her mother and stepfather and then scrambled up the bank and took a look. The flat countryside stretched round her, wide fields divided by ditches, a few trees, and not a house in sight. There was a clump of larger trees some way off. Perhaps there would be a farm there, but surely even on this quiet road there would be traffic or something, someone…

There was; still far off, but coming towards her, was a horse and cart. Sarah shouted then, and waved and shouted again until she was hoarse, but the cart didn't increase its speed. She didn't dare to leave her mother and stepfather, and watched it in an agony of impatience as the beast plodded steadily towards her. When the cart was near enough she ran towards it.

The man holding the reins halted the horse and stared down at her.

'An accident,' said Sarah. 'Police, ambulance, hospital.' And, since he didn't seem to understand her, she said it all again and added, 'Please, hurry…'

The man had a broad, dull face but he looked kind. He looked across at the upended car and then back at Sarah. *'Politie?'*

'Yes, yes. Please, hurry…'

He nodded then, thought for a moment, and broke into speech. It was a pity that she couldn't understand a word of it, but he ended with the word *politie* and urged his horse forward. Sarah watched the cart disappear slowly into the distance until the clump of trees hid it from view, and then she climbed back into the ditch.

Her mother was moaning a little, and Sarah tucked the rug more tightly around her and contrived to shift her legs so that they were free of the cold water which filled the front of the car. She tried to do the same for her stepfather, but one leg was at an awkward angle and she didn't dare to touch it. She made him as comfortable as possible and climbed out of the ditch once more, to meet a heartening sight: the blue flashing lights of a police car coming at speed.

The two men in it were large, reassuringly calm, and spoke English. She wanted to fling herself on a broad chest and burst into tears of relief, but it didn't seem the right moment.

'My mother and stepfather are in the car,' she told them, in a voice which shook only slightly. 'They're hurt. Is an ambulance coming?'

'It comes at once. And you, miss? You are not hurt?' the older of the two officers asked her.

'No, I'm fine.' She peered anxiously over the edge of the ditch to where the other officer was bending over her mother. She would have joined him, but the ambulance arrived then and she was

urged to stand on one side while the policemen
and the paramedics began the task of getting her
mother and stepfather out of the car.

They were hefty men, and made short work of
breaking down the car door, releasing her mother
and lifting her into the ambulance. Getting her
stepfather out was more difficult. His leg was broken and he was cut by broken glass, moreover he
disputed their actions, shouting and swearing.
Sarah was sorry that he was injured, but she
hoped that the men would put his uninhibited behaviour down to shock.

It was almost dark now. While they had been
busy, Sarah had unloaded their cases from the
boot and stood with them, waiting to be told what
to do next.

'You will come with us to the hospital,' said
the older constable. 'We will take your luggage
to the police station and tomorrow you may come
and fetch it.' He waved the ambulance away and
opened the car door for her. 'You have everything, passports, money?'

'Yes, I've put them in one of the cases. Where
are we going?'

'Arnhem.' He gave her a brief glance. 'You are
OK?'

Sarah said, 'Yes, thank you.' She was alive,

unhurt, although she was aware of aches and pains and wet and icy feet and legs; she was OK.

The hospital at Arnhem was large and modern, and the Accident Room was heaving with people. The two policemen set her down beside the ambulance, warned her to collect the cases from the police station in the morning and be ready to give a report of the accident, and sped on their way. She watched them go with regret; they had been briskly friendly—warning her stepfather that they would come to the hospital to see him in the morning, patting her on the shoulder in a kindly fashion—and now they had gone, siren sounding, blue lights flashing. Another accident?

Sarah followed the two stretchers into the hospital and presently found herself in a waiting room with a lot of other anxious people. Someone would come and report on her mother and stepfather, she was told by a busy nurse, taking down particulars and thankfully speaking English.

Sarah settled into one of the plastic chairs arranged around the room. Her feet were numb now, and she smelled horrible. A cup of tea, she thought longingly, and a nice warm bath and then bed. She was hungry, too, and she felt guilty about that with her mother and stepfather injured. People came and went. Slowly the room emptied.

Surely someone would come for her soon. She closed her eyes on a daydream of endless pots of tea and plates piled high with hot buttered toast and slept.

Mr ter Breukel, consultant orthopaedic surgeon at the hospital, finished his examination of Mr Holt's leg and bent his massive person over his patient. He studied the ill-tempered face and listened patiently to the diatribe directed at himself, his staff and everyone in general.

When Mr Holt drew breath, he said quietly, 'You have a broken leg; it will need to be pinned and plated. You have two broken ribs, a sprained wrist, and superficial cuts and bruises. You will be put to bed presently and in the morning I will set the leg. You will need to stay here until it is considered expedient to return you to England.'

Mr Holt said furiously, 'I demand to be sent to England immediately. How am I to know that you are competent to deal with my injuries? I am a businessman and have some influential friends.'

Mr ter Breukel ignored the rudeness. 'I will see you in the morning. Your wife will be warded also. She has concussion but is not seriously hurt.'

He waited for Mr Holt to say something, and

when he didn't added, 'Was there anyone else
with you?'

'My stepdaughter.' Mr Holt gave him a look of
deep dislike. 'She's quite capable of taking care
of herself.'

'In the circumstances,' said Mr ter Breukel,
'that is most fortunate.'

The Accident Room was emptying, so he could
safely leave the minor cases to the two casualty
officers on duty, but first he supposed he should
find this stepdaughter. Probably with her
mother...

Mrs Holt was fully conscious now, and complaining weakly. She had no wish to stay in hospital; she must have a private room, she wanted
her own nightclothes, her own toiletries...

Mr ter Breukel bent over the stretcher, lifted a
limp hand and took her pulse. It was steady and
quite strong. 'Your daughter?' he asked quietly.
'She was with you in the car?'

'Yes, yes, of course. Where is she? Why isn't
she here with me? She knows how bad my nerves
are. Someone must fetch her. She must find a
good hotel where I can stay for a few days until
my husband can return to England.'

'Mr Holt will have to remain here for some
time, Mrs Holt, and I cannot allow you to leave

this hospital until you have recovered from a slight concussion.'

'How tiresome.' Mrs Holt turned her head away and closed her eyes.

Mr ter Breukel nodded to the porters to wheel her away to the ward and went in search of the third member of the party.

The place was quieter now, and the waiting room was empty save for Sarah. He stood looking at her—such an ordinary girl, dirty and dishevelled, a bruise on one cheek and smelling vilely of the mud clinging to her person. A girl without looks, pale, her hair hanging in untidy damp streamers around a face which could easily pass unnoticed in a crowd. A girl completely lacking in glamour.

He sighed deeply; to fall in love at first sight with this malodorous sleeping girl, with, as far as he could see, no pretentions to beauty or even good looks, was something he had not expected. But falling in love, he had always understood, was unpredictable, and, as far as he was concerned, irrevocable. That they hadn't exchanged a word, nor spoken, made no difference. He, heartwhole until that minute, and with no intention of marrying until it suited him, had lost that same heart.

But he wasn't a callow youth; he would have

to tread softly, otherwise he might lose her. He went close to her chair and said gently, 'Miss Holt?'

Sarah opened her eyes and allowed them to travel up a vast expanse of superfine clerical grey cloth, past a richly sombre tie and white linen, until they reached his face.

She said clearly, 'Not Miss Holt; he's my step-father. Beckwith—Sarah Beckwith. That's a nice tie—Italian silk?'

Mr ter Breukel, aware that she wasn't quite awake yet, agreed gravely that it was Italian silk. Her eyes, he saw with delight, were quite beautiful, a vivid dark blue, veiled by mousy lashes.

Sarah sat up straight and pushed her hair off her face. 'I'm sorry, I fell asleep.' She studied his face, a very trustworthy face, she decided, as well as a handsome one, with its high-bridged nose and firm mouth and heavy-lidded eyes. 'Mother...?'

'I am Litrik ter Breukel, consultant orthopaedic surgery. I'm sorry there was no one to see you. It has been a busy evening. Your mother is to stay here for a few days. She has been concussed, but should recover quickly. There are one or two cuts and bruises which will heal quickly. Your step-father has a broken leg, fractured ribs, and he has been cut by glass. He must remain until he is fit to be sent back to England.'

'Do I have to arrange that?'

'No, no. We will see to that at the appropriate time.'

'May I see Mother?'

'Of course. But first I think you must be checked to make sure that you have no injuries. And you will need a tetanus injection and to be cleaned up.'

'I'm not hurt, only dirty and a bit scratched. And I smell dreadful…'

She went without demur to the Accident Room, where he handed her over to a stout, middle-aged woman with a kind face and a harassed manner. She spoke English, too. Sarah submitted to being cleaned up, her scratches and bruises dealt with, her injection given, to the accompaniment of her companion's pleased astonishment that she wasn't more seriously injured, and then, looking clean and smelling of good soap, she was handed back to Mr ter Breukel, who, eyeing her with all the delight of a man in love, thought she looked like some small girl who had been run through the mangle and left to dry.

He said merely, 'You feel better now? We will go to your mother.' And he led the way through

the hospital, in and out of lifts, up and down stair-
cases, and eventually into a ward with a dozen
beds in it.

Her mother had a corner bed, and was lying
back comfortably, but when she saw Sarah she
asked peevishly, 'Where have you been? I feel
terrible. I'm sure that I'm a good deal worse than
these doctors say. You should have been here
with me…'

Sarah said gently, 'I'm sorry, Mother. I fell
asleep…'

'Asleep? You must have known that I was lying here in pain? And your poor father…'

'Stepfather,' said Sarah.

'Yes, well—it is all very well for you, you
don't appear to have been hurt in the least.' She
added fretfully, 'I knew this would happen; you
always manage to annoy him.'

Sarah said nothing to that, and her mother
closed her eyes. 'Now go away and spare a
thought for your poor mother before you go to
sleep in a comfortable bed.'

Sarah bent and kissed an averted cheek, and
then was led away by Mr ter Breukel, who had
been standing just behind her, listening to every
word.

He made no mention of their conversation,

however, but walked her silently to the entrance, where she stopped and offered her hand. 'You've been very kind. Thank you. I know my mother and stepfather will be all right here. May I come and see them in the morning?'

He had no intention of letting her go, and for once a kindly Fate lent a helping hand; Sarah gave a small choking gasp. 'I'm going to be sick…'

There was a providential sink nearby, and she found herself leaning over it, a firm, cool hand holding her head…

Presently she gasped, 'Oh, the relief,' and then, aware of the hand, mumbled, 'How awful for you. I'm so sorry.'

'Best thing you could have done. You probably swallowed a good deal of ditchwater.'

He bent over her, wiped her face with his hand-kerchief and led her outside into the crisp March evening.

Sarah tugged on an arm to call a halt. 'Thank you,' she said again. 'I'm fine now.'

'You have somewhere to go? Money? Do you know your way about Arnhem?'

She looked away, searching for an answer which wouldn't sound like a fib.

'The police said I could collect our cases and things in the morning from the police station…'

'You know where that is?'

'No, but I can ask.'

'And until morning?' he persisted.

She opened her mouth to utter something mis-
leading but convincing.

'No, no. Let us have no nonsense. You have
no money, no clothes, you are extremely dirty and
probably hungry. You will come home with
me…'

He spoke pleasantly, but he sounded as though
he meant it. All the same, she said tartly, 'Indeed
I won't.'

Mr ter Breukel slid effortlessly into his bedside
manner. 'My dear young lady, my sister will be
delighted to meet you, and help you in any way
she can.' He didn't smile, but Sarah, peeping at
him, had to admit that he looked—she sought the
right word—safe.

'If you're sure I won't be a nuisance, thank
you.'

He nodded, walked to where a dark grey Rolls
Royce was parked and popped her neatly into it,
got in beside her and drove away.

After a moment Sarah asked, 'Will I be able to
arrange for Mother to go home soon? If she isn't
seriously hurt…'

'Shall we leave that for the moment? Time enough when you have seen the police in the morning. You will probably have to make a statement, as will your parents. Once the matter has been dealt with, arrangements can be made for you to return to England.'

He drove to the city's heart, where there were still ancient houses and shops which had miraculously escaped damage during the terrific battle towards the end of World War II, stopping presently in a narrow, canal-lined street.

The houses in it were old, narrow and tall, leaning against each other, each with a splendid gable. He stopped the car halfway down, got out and opened the door for Sarah. She got out and looked around her. She could have stepped back into the seventeenth century, for there was no traffic, no cars parked, only the rustle of trees lining the canal to break the stillness.

'You live here?'

'Yes.' He took her arm and marched her across the narrow pavement and up some worn steps to a handsome door flanked by long narrow windows on either side of it. He unlocked the door and urged her gently before him into the narrow hall beyond, its walls panelled, black and white tiles underfoot, a brass chandelier, probably as old as the house, hanging from the beautiful plaster ceiling.

As they entered, a door at the end of the hall opened, and a short, stout man came to meet them. He was accompanied by a large dog with small yellow eyes and a thick grey pelt, who bared awesome teeth in what Sarah hoped was a smile. Apparently it was, for he pranced up to Mr ter Breukel and offered his head for a scratch with reassuring meekness.

Mr ter Breukel obliged, exchanged a few words with the man and switched to English. 'This is Jaap; he and his wife look after me. And this is Max; he looks fierce, but he has the disposition of a lamb.'

Sarah shook Jaap's hand, then patted Max's woolly head and tried not to notice the teeth before she was propelled gently through a door into a high-ceilinged room with narrow windows and a hooded fireplace. She had no time to see more than that before a young woman got up from a chair by the cheerful fire and came to meet them.

'Litrik, you're late.' She lifted a face for his kiss and smiled at Sarah.

'Suzanne, this is Sarah Beckwith. She and her parents had a car accident this afternoon. They are at St Bravo's and she has agreed to stay here with us for the night. The police have all their things, and it is rather late to find a hotel…'

Suzanne took Sarah's hand. 'How horrid for you, and we'll love to have you; you must be feeling awful.' She cast a discreet eye over Sarah's deplorable person. 'Would you like a bath before dinner? Anneke can get your clothes cleaned up while I lend you something to wear.'

She took Sarah's arm. 'This is fun—not for you, of course, but I'm so pleased you're here. We'll find Anneke and I'll take you upstairs.'

She turned to her brother. 'Dinner in half an hour? You don't have to go back this evening?'

'No, not unless something turns up.' He gave a casual nod and smile and went to the fire, and Sarah, reassured by the matter-of-fact air he was careful to maintain, went back into the hall and up a carved staircase in a recess halfway down it.

A small, thin woman was waiting for them when they reached the landing.

'This is Anneke,' said Suzanne. 'Jaap's wife and a family friend for years and years.'

Sarah offered a hand once more and was aware that she was being carefully studied from beady brown eyes. Then Anneke smiled and led the way down a passage leading off the landing, opened a door and waved Suzanne and Sarah into the room beyond.

A charming room of pale pastel colours, deeply carpeted, with curtained windows a froth of white muslin. Sarah paused on the threshold. 'My filthy shoes…' She took them off and Anneke took them from her with a smile and said something to Suzanne.

'Take everything off and have a bath. Anneke will see to your things and I'll bring you some clothes.' She studied Sarah's small person. 'We're almost the same size. A sweater and trousers?' She gave Sarah a little push. 'Anneke's running a bath for you; I'll be back in ten minutes.'

Left alone, Sarah shed her damp and dirty clothes, laid them tidily on a towel so as not to spoil the carpet or quilt, and got into the bath. It was blissfully hot and delightfully scented. She could have stayed there for hours, but Suzanne, calling from the open door into the bedroom, roused her.

'I've put some things on the bed. Something is bound to fit, more or less. Dinner in ten minutes.'

Sarah, wrapped in a vast white towel, went to have a look. There was a heap of coloured sweaters, a couple of pairs of trousers, gossamer undies, slippers…

Dressed, her hair still damp and tied back in an untidy plait for lack of ribbons or pins, the trousers on the large side and the pink sweater she had chosen shrouding her person, she took a final look at her reflection. She looked as plain as always, she decided, but at least she was clean and smelling sweet.

She went downstairs and found Jaap in the hall, waiting for her. He led her with a fatherly air back into the drawing room and Mr ter Breukel got up out of his chair and crossed the room with just the right air of a polite host ready to put an unexpected guest at ease.

Suzanne, watching him, hid a smile. Litrik, impervious to the charms of various young ladies that his family, anxious for him to marry, had produced, was showing interest in this nice little creature with the plain face and the lovely eyes. And the pink sweater suited her very well...

Sarah, accepting a chair and a glass of sherry, happily unaware of Suzanne's thoughts, made polite conversation with her host and hostess, and, encouraged by Mr ter Breukel's artless questioning, said that no, she had never been to Arnhem before, had never been in Holland—only her stepfather had wanted to return to England by the night ferry to Harwich.

'Ah, yes—you live somewhere along the east coast? By far the easiest way to return.'

'He has a house near Clapham Common—that's London,' said Sarah flatly. And, since his raised eyebrows invited more than that, added, 'We—that is, Mother and Father, before he died, and me...' She paused. Perhaps it was 'I'. 'We used to live in a small village in Berkshire.'

'Delightful country,' murmured Mr ter Breukel, inviting further confidences.

'Yes, quite different from Clapham Common.'

'You live at home?'

'Yes. Mother isn't very strong...'

Suzanne asked, 'You're not getting married or anything like that?'

'No, we—I don't go out much.'

Mr ter Breukel said easily, 'One never knows what awaits one round the corner.' He knew, of course, but patience was something of which he had plenty. Having found her, he wasn't going to lose her by being hasty.

Jaap came to tell them that dinner was served; Suzanne took his arm and they crossed the hall to the dining room, with its panelled walls and oval table, the George the First Oak dresser along one wall, the oak Chippendale chairs. A pair of crystal candelabra stood on the dresser, and a silver and cut-glass epergne was at the centre of the table, which was set with lace mats and silverware— very plain, with a crest worn by time.

Sarah gave a quick glance around her and sighed with pleasure. Everything in the room was old and perfect and used—not taken for granted, but neither was it hidden away behind cabinet doors or packed in green baize, to be used only on very special occasions.

The food was good too, simple and beautifully cooked, enhanced by the plates upon which it was served; Delft, she recognised, and old, for they were patterned in pale lavender, not the blue one expected. Washing up would be a hazardous undertaking…

She drank the wine she was offered and Mr ter Breukel watched with satisfaction as the colour came back into her pale face. She hadn't been injured but she had been shocked, although she had done her best to hide that. A good night's sleep, he reflected, and tomorrow he would find the time to consider the future.

Suzanne escorted Sarah to her bed, after a cheerful goodnight from her host.

Sarah got into the silk and lacy nightie Suzanne had found for her and slid into bed, determined to make sensible plans for the morning; once she had retrieved their luggage and money and passports from the police, she reflected, she could decide what was best to be done. She would have to find out just how long her mother and stepfather would have to stay in hospital... That was as far as she got before falling into a refreshing sleep.

She woke to find Anneke standing by the bed with a little tray of tea and holding her clothes, clean and pressed, over one arm. Anneke beamed at her, nodding in response to her good morning, and handed her a note. The writing was a scrawl; it could have been written by a spider dipped in ink. With difficulty Sarah made out that breakfast was at eight o'clock and she would be taken to the hospital directly after the meal. So she smiled and nodded to Anneke, who smiled and nodded in return, before Sarah drank her tea and got out of bed. There wasn't much time; she showered, dressed, did the best she could with her face and hair, and went downstairs.

Mr ter Breukel and Suzanne were already at the table, but he got up to pull out her chair and expressed the hope that she had slept well.

'Very well,' said Sarah. 'Such a pretty room, and the sort of bed you sink into.'

'Good. You had my note?'

She buttered a roll. 'Yes. What shocking hand-writing you have. But I suppose all medical men write badly so that no one can understand, if you see what I mean?'

Suzanne turned a laugh into a cough, and Mr ter Breukel said gravely, 'I think that is very likely.' He gave her a glance just long enough to take in the delightful sight of her in her cleaned and pressed clothes, no make-up and shining mousy hair. Sarah, not seeing the glance, drank her coffee and remarked that he would be wishing to leave for the hospital and she was quite ready when he wished to go.

'Although I'm sure I should be quite all right to walk to the police station. Unless perhaps I should go to the hospital first?'

'Yes, that would be best. Everything depends on the condition of your mother and stepfather.' He got up from the table. 'You'll excuse me? I must telephone. Could you be ready to leave in ten minutes?'

She got into the car beside him presently; she had bidden Suzanne goodbye and thanked her for her kindness, and Suzanne had kissed her cheek, rather to Sarah's surprise, and said it had been fun. Sarah, thinking about it, supposed that for

Suzanne it had been just that, and she had liked
her... She liked the man sitting beside her too.

At the hospital he nodded a casual goodbye,
said that he would see her later, and handed her
over to a nurse who took her to her mother.

Mrs Holt was awake and complaining.

'There you are. I hope you'll arrange for us to
go back home as quickly as possible. I shall never
recover in this place. Tea with no milk, and nothing but thin bread and butter and a boiled egg.'

Sarah bent to kiss her. 'Did you sleep? Do you
feel better this morning?'

'Of course I didn't close my eyes all night, and
I feel very poorly. Have you got our things yet?
I want my own nightgowns; someone must do my
hair...'

'I'm going to collect them this morning; I'll
bring whatever you need here, Mother.'

'Have you seen your father?'

'Stepfather,' said Sarah. 'No, Nurse tells me
that he is to have his leg seen to this morning.'

'How tiresome.' Mrs Holt turned her head
away. 'Go and get my things; when you get back
I'll tell you if I want anything else.'

Sarah went through the hospital once more and,
because she was a kind girl, asked if she could
see her stepfather.

He was in a small ward with three other men, and she saw at a glance that he was in no mood to answer her 'good morning'. She stood listening to his diatribe in reply to her enquiry as to how he felt, and, when he had run out of breath, said that she would come and see him after he had had his operation. Only to be told that he couldn't care less if he never saw her again! So she bade him goodbye and started back to the entrance. Neither parent had asked where she had slept or how she felt.

Getting lost on the way out, she had time to think about her future. She supposed that some time during the day someone at the hospital would tell her how long her mother and stepfather would have to remain there. Mr ter Breukel had told her that someone would arrange their return to England, so it seemed best for her to go back as quickly as possible and look after the house until they returned.

She preferred not to think further ahead than that; life hadn't been easy living at home, her sense of duty outweighing her longing to have a life of her own. But her mother, each time Sarah suggested that she might train for something and be independent, had made life unbearable, with her reproaches and sly reminders that her father had told Sarah to look after her mother. Then, of course, he had had no idea that his wife would remarry—and to a man who was in a position to give her a comfortable life. And who had taken a dislike to his stepdaughter the moment they had met.

She found the main entrance at last, but halfway to it she was stopped.

A porter addressed her in surprisingly good English. She was to wait—he indicated an open doorway beyond which people were sitting.

Perhaps she was to be told what arrangements had been made for her parents. She sat down obediently; there was no point in getting fussed. She had hoped to return to England that day, but probably she would have to spend another night in Arnhem. Which should hold no terrors for her; she would have some money once she had been to the police station, and all she had to do was wait for someone to tell her what to do next.

There were a great many posters on the walls, and she was making futile guesses as to what they were about when the porter tapped her on the shoulder.

She followed him back to the entrance hall and saw Mr ter Breukel standing by the doors. Her smile at the sight of him—filled with relief and delight—shook him badly, but all he said was 'I'll take you to the police station,' with detached courtesy.

CHAPTER TWO

'CAN you spare the time?' asked Sarah anxiously. 'Don't you have patients to see?'

'I have already seen them.' Mr ter Breukel was at his most soothing. 'I shall be operating this afternoon. On your stepfather, amongst others.'

'How soon will I know when he can go home?'

'Probably later this evening. Ah, here is the police station.'

She was glad that he was with her. She gave a succinct account of the accident, and from time to time he was a great help translating some tricky word the officer hadn't understood. All the same it took a long time, and after that the luggage had to be checked, money counted, passports examined. She was given hers, as well as some money from her stepfather's wallet. He wouldn't like that, she reflected, signing for it, but she would need money to get back home. And supposing her mother travelled with her?

She explained that to Mr ter Breukel and waited for his advice.

'Does your mother have traveller's cheques in her handbag?'

The handbag was an expensive one from one of the big fashion houses, unlike Sarah's own rather shabby leather shoulder bag, and there were traveller's cheques inside, and quite a lot of money.

'Good. You can give the bag to your mother and she can arrange for it to be kept in safe-keeping until she leaves.'

Put like that, it all sounded very simple. But they went back to St Bravo's and suddenly nothing was simple any more.

Her mother's X-ray had shown a hairline fracture; there was no question of her leaving the hospital for some time. And there was no time to talk about it, for Mr ter Breukel had been called away the moment they arrived back.

Sarah unpacked what she thought her mother might need, and when that lady demanded her handbag gave it to her. Then she went in search of the ward sister, who told her kindly enough that it would be most unwise for her mother to be moved. 'And, since your father must stay also, they can return together when they are able to travel.'

Sarah went to see the other ward sister about

her stepfather then. He was already in Theatre, and Mr ter Breukel was operating. 'Come back later, about six o'clock, and we will tell you what has been done.'

So Sarah went out of the hospital and into the main streets. The luggage was safe with a porter, she had money in her pocket and she was hungry.

She found a small café and sat over coffee and a roll filled with cheese, deciding what she should do next. It made sense to find a tourist information office and find out about getting back home. Maybe not for a few days, but she would need to know…

It wasn't difficult to find, so she went inside and found that the girls behind the counter spoke English. She could fly, they told her, an easy train ride to the airport at Schiphol, or she could get a ferry from the Hoek van Holland or from Scheveningen to Harwich. They could arrange it for her.

Sarah thanked them, then asked if they knew of a small, inexpensive hotel. They went to a lot of trouble, and she left presently with a short list from which to choose. Now it was just a question of going back to St Bravo's, finding out about her stepfather, seeing her mother, collecting her case from the porter and moving into whichever hotel had a room vacant.

She went into another café and had a cup of tea and some biscuits, and then found her way back to the hospital. She went first to see her step-father, who was nicely recovered from the anaesthetic but whose temper was uncertain. He was propped up on his pillows, a leg in plaster under a cradle. In reply to her civil and sympathetic enquiry as to how he felt, he said angrily, 'That infernal surgeon says that I must remain here for at least two weeks…'

'I thought that once the plaster was dry you could walk with a crutch…'

'Don't be a fool. A broken rib has pierced my lung; it has to heal before I'm fit to be moved.'

'Oh—oh, I'm sorry. I'll tell Mother. I'm going to see her now.'

'And don't bother to come and see me. The less I see of you the better—if it hadn't been for you…'

No doubt he had told anyone who would listen that it had been her fault. She bade him goodbye and went along to see her mother.

That lady was sitting up in bed, pecking at her supper.

'It's so early,' she complained, as soon as she

set eyes on Sarah. 'How can I possibly eat at half past six in the evening?'

Sarah sat down by the bed and listened with outward patience to her parent's grumbles. When there was a pause, she told her about her stepfather.

'How tiresome. What is to happen to me, I should like to know? I've no intention of staying here a day longer than I must. You will have to take me home, Sarah. Your father—' she caught Sarah's eye '—stepfather can return when he's recovered. I can't be expected to look after him. Of course *you* will be at home, but I suppose you will need some help.'

She didn't ask Sarah how she had spent her day—Sarah hadn't expected her to—but told her to come the next morning.

'You must get me that special night-cream—and a paler lipstick, oh, and a bed jacket. Pink, something pretty. I don't see why I should look dowdy just because I am in this horrible place.'

'Mother,' said Sarah, 'this is a splendid hospital, and if you hadn't been brought here you might be feeling a lot worse.'

Mrs Holt squeezed out a tear. 'How hard-hearted you are, Sarah. Go away and enjoy yourself—and don't be late here in the morning. I want that bed jacket before the doctors do their rounds.'

Sarah stifled a wish to burst into tears; she was tired and hungry by now, and the future loomed ahead in a most unsatisfactory manner. She bade her mother goodnight and went in search of Sister.

Her mother was doing well, she was told; rather excitable and unco-operative, but that was to be expected with concussion. Sarah could rest assured that hospital was the best place for her mother for the moment, and that as soon as possible she and Mr Holt would be transferred back home.

'So you need have no more worries,' said Sister kindly.

Sarah began the lengthy walk back to the entrance. She must get her case and then go to one of the hotels. She had spent rather longer that she had meant to with her mother, and somewhere a clock chimed seven. She hadn't been looking where she was going and had got lost again. She stood in the long corridor, wondering if she should go to the left or the right...

A hand on her arm swept her straight ahead. 'Lost?' asked Mr ter Breukel cheerfully. 'We'll

collect your case and go home. Suzanne will be
wondering where we are.'

Sarah, trotting to keep up, and aware that everything was suddenly all right again, said, 'Well,
thank you very much, but I'm going to a hotel. I
went to something called VVV and they gave me
a list…'

Mr ter Breukel stopped so suddenly that she
almost fell over. 'Did I not tell you this morning
that you would be staying with us until we know
more about your parents? You must forgive me;
I have a shocking memory.'

'No, you didn't say anything.' She gave him a
thoughtful look. 'You can't have a bad memory;
surgeons must have excellent memories, otherwise they would put things back in the wrong
place!'

'That is a terrifying thought,' said Mr ter
Breukel, grave-faced, and he hurried her along to
the entrance. He found a porter to fetch her case,
opened his car door, ushered her in and got in
beside her.

'The hotel,' said Sarah. 'I mean, I can't impose
upon your kindness, really, I can't.'

He said briskly, 'I must tell you about your
stepfather, give you some idea of how long he
will be with us—and your mother, too. I'm a busy

man during the day, so our only chance to discuss this is in the evening. You do agree?'

'Well, yes…'

'Good. Are you hungry?'

'Famished,' said Sarah, without thinking, and then very quickly added, 'I had something to eat in a café.'

'Where?'

'I'm not sure exactly. It said "Snack Bar" over the door.'

'A roll and cheese and a cup of coffee?' He added gently, 'Sarah, you don't need to pretend with me.'

She realised with contented relief that he meant what he said. 'I know that, and I promise I won't do that. I *am* famished.'

Mr ter Breukel's handsome features remained impassive. A step in the right direction, he reflected. He cast a quick glance at her profile, which she didn't see. Her small nose had a slight tilt to it—most endearing…

What happy chance, reflected Sarah, had led them to meet again like this?

Mr ter Breukel could have told her, of course, but he didn't intend to. He had his own methods of getting information about visitors, and an intimate knowledge of the many corridors of St Bravo's helped.

Suzanne came to meet them as they entered the house. 'Oh, good, you're punctual. Oh, and you've got your case, Sarah. Jaap will take it up to your room, but don't bother to unpack it till later. Come and have a drink before dinner.'

Sarah, rather overwhelmed by this ready welcoming—just as though she had been expected to return, she thought—followed Jaap and her case upstairs and, despite Suzanne's invitation to go straight back down again and have a drink, fished around in her case and found the jersey dress she intended to wear. It was an unpretentious garment, in an inoffensive blue, and she didn't like it much, but it could be rolled up small and stuffed into her case and didn't crease.

She put it on quickly and tidied her hair, did her face rather carelessly and went back downstairs. She would have liked time to make the best of herself—she supposed Mr ter Breukel had that effect on any girl—but she was only here in his house so that he could tell her if any arrangements should be made for her mother and stepfather's return to England...

She accepted a glass of sherry, gave Suzanne an account of her day when she was pressed to do so, glossing over the bits that had been dull, and then ate her dinner, making polite conversation—the weather, the amazing ability of everyone in Arnhem to speak English, the delicious coffee.

Mr ter Breukel listened to her pretty voice, entranced; as far as he was concerned she could recite the multiplication tables and he would find it exciting. He made suitable replies in a voice of impersonal friendliness, and only as they were drinking their coffee in the drawing room did he begin to tell her about her parents.

They were sitting round the fireplace, she and Suzanne on the vast sofa facing it, he in a great wingback chair with Max lying over his feet. The room looked beautiful, the soft light from the table lamps showing up the magnificent bow-fronted cabinets with their displays of silver and porcelain, casting shadows on the heavy velvet curtains, and yet, despite the magnificence of its contents, the room was welcoming and lived in. And Mr ter Breukel was exactly right for it, thought Sarah; he fitted the room and the room fitted him.

You're letting your imagination run away with you, Sarah told herself silently, and sat up straight because he had put down his coffee cup and sau-

cer and now said briskly, 'Let me tell you what
has been done today—your mother is comfortable, but she is, if you will forgive me for saying
so, not an easy patient. She wishes to go back to
England, naturally enough, but I can't advise that.
She needs rest and quiet and to have time to resume her normal outlook on life; I have explained
to her that once she is home with your stepfather
she will need to feel fit herself.

'I operated on him this afternoon; he has quite
a severe fracture of the tibia, which I have put
together and put in plaster. He will be got up
within a few days, but there's no question of him
using the leg for weeks. He will be given
crutches, but he is a heavy man and not very co-
operative. So I think that their return to England
must be ruled out for two weeks at least.
Arrangements must be made so that they can
travel easily, and there must be some kind of nursing aid at your home. Your mother tells me that
she would be quite unable to do that. He'll need
physiotherapy, and of course the plaster will probably need renewing later on.'

He paused, but Sarah didn't say anything. She
was thinking with despair of the weeks ahead, at
the beck and call of her stepfather, who would
expect her to fulfil the duties of nurse as well as

the major tasks of the household. There was a housekeeper, and help for the heavy chores, but there would be the shopping and the ironing and the endless jobs her mother would want done… I mustn't moan, reflected Sarah.

'So I had better go home as quickly as possible and get things arranged.' She thought for a moment. 'I'd have to come back when they're ready to return—to help Mother.'

'That is, of course, one solution.' Mr ter Breukel gave the impression of someone giving friendly advice. 'But I wonder if you have given thought to remaining here and returning with your parents? It so happens that I might be able to offer an alternative solution.

'We have a great-aunt, living in Arnhem, whose companion has had to return to her home to nurse her mother; she may be away for several weeks. You might take over her duties until your parents are ready to leave the hospital. It is probably a job you wouldn't care to undertake—rather dull and needing a good deal of patience. On the other hand, you would have a roof over your head, be able to visit your mother and be here when they are ready to leave.'

'What a splendid idea,' declared Suzanne. She had visited her aunt that very afternoon and her

companion, Juffrouw Telle, had been there.
Moreover there had been no question of her going
home. But Suzanne had no doubt that if Litrik
said that Juffrouw Telle was going to nurse her
sick mother, then he had contrived something for
his own ends. Sarah, thought Suzanne with satisfaction, had done something none of the other
women acquaintances in whom he had shown no
interest had been able to do—she had stolen his
heart.

Suzanne said encouragingly to Sarah, 'Do think
about that, Sarah. Great-Aunt is quite an old dear,
and you would be able to see your mother every
day. I'm sure she would miss you terribly if you
went back to England.'

Sarah said, 'Your aunt—great-aunt—might not
like me... Besides, her companion might not be
ready to return when Mother and my stepfather
leave.' She added, 'Or she might come back
within the next few days.'

'Unlikely. Her mother will need nursing for ten
days at least,' improvised Mr ter Breukel
smoothly, 'and if you should have to leave before
she returns, then we shall have to find someone
else. In the meantime you would be helping several people, and I for one would be most grateful.'

Which reminded Sarah that this was a way in

which she could repay him for his kindness. And
there was no denying that it was a way out of her
problem.

Mr ter Breukel, watching her face, was delighted to see that his plotting and planning were
likely to be successful. He reminded himself that
he must find a suitable gift for Juffrouw Telle.
Middle-aged, patient and kind-hearted, she had
been with his great-aunt for years; she was almost
one of the family, and had been only too ready to
agree to his scheme. It gave her an unexpected
holiday, and the pleasure of sharing a secret
which held more than a whiff of romance...

Sarah didn't waste time weighing up the pros
and cons; the pros were obvious, and if there were
any cons she would deal with them later. She said,
'Thank you, I would be glad to help out until your
aunt's companion is able to return. And it is I who
should be grateful, for now I don't need to worry
about anything.'

For the next week or two, at any rate, she added
silently. And after that I'll think of something.

Suzanne said, 'Oh, splendid. I'll take you to
Great-Aunt tomorrow. In the afternoon? You'll
want to see your mother and stepfather first.'

Sarah thanked her, stifling the wish that Mr ter
Breukel had offered to take her, reminding herself

that he was a busy man and had wasted enough of his time on her anyway.

Her stepfather showed no pleasure at the sight of her, and, apprised of her plans, merely grunted. 'Do what you please, as long as you're back here to look after your mother when we go home. And that can't be soon enough.' He began a tirade against the nurses, the doctors, the food, and the fact that there was no private room available for him. Sarah, having heard it all before, listened patiently and assured him that he would be able to go home the moment he was allowed to, and then she slipped away. It seemed to her that the hospital staff would be only too glad to see the back of him.

Her mother was sitting in the Day Room, reading a magazine, and she greeted Sarah peevishly.

'Should you be reading?' asked Sarah.

'No, but the nurses don't come in here very often, and when they do I hide it under a cushion.' Mrs Holt allowed her mouth to droop. 'I have such a headache.'

'That's because you're reading.'

'Well, I'm bored. I want to go home…'

'I dare say it won't be much longer. Mother, I've got a job. Not paid, of course, but being a companion to an old lady while her usual companion goes home to look after her mother. I may stay there until we go back home.'

'Trust you to find a comfortable place to live while I have to stay in this dreary place.'

Sarah supposed that the concussion had made her mother so difficult. 'It's not so bad, Mother. I expect I'll be able to come and see you quite often.'

'When you do, bring me some nail varnish. Elizabeth Arden, pink—at least I can give myself a manicure.' Mrs Holt closed her eyes. 'I do have a headache…'

Sarah kissed her and left the hospital. On the way out she caught a glimpse of Mr ter Breukel, enormous even at a distance, surrounded by white-coated satellites. He didn't see her, but the sight of him cheered her up as she walked back to his house.

He had, in fact, turned his head in time to see her disappearing down one of the endless corridors. He would have liked to have taken her himself to his great-aunt's house, but to display too much interest might frighten her off…

Sarah got into Suzanne's car after they had had coffee and was driven into the centre of the city

to another old gabled house in a quiet street close
to the Grote Kerk. Suzanne didn't give Sarah time
to feel nervous. She urged her out of the car,
thumped the massive door-knocker and they were
admitted before Sarah could draw breath.

The old man who opened the door looked
shaky on his legs. He had white hair and pale blue
eyes in a wrinkled face. Suzanne threw her arms
around him and kissed his cheek, and said something to make him chuckle before she turned to
Sarah.

'Kaes has been with Great-Aunt for almost the
whole of his life. He's part of the house.' She
spoke to him again, and Sarah held out a hand
and smiled at the friendly old man. He studied
her for a moment and then led them down the hall
to double doors on one side of it, opened them,
said something to the room's occupant and trotted
off.

Suzanne gave Sarah a friendly shove, and Sarah
found herself crossing a vast expanse of carpet to
the very old lady sitting in a high-backed chair by
one of the tall windows.

Suzanne skipped to her side, kissed her and
spoke rapidly in Dutch, and then switched to
English.

'This is Sarah Beckwith, Tante, come to keep

you company until Juffrouw Telle gets back. She can't speak a word of Dutch, but that won't matter, will it? She will be able to read your English novels. You like being read to, don't you?'

The little old lady spoke. She had a soft voice, but now it had a slight edge to it. 'Suzanne, don't mumble. Where is this young woman who is to stay with me until Anna Telle returns? If she mumbles she will be of no use to me.'

Suzanne beckoned Sarah. 'She's here, Tante.'

Sarah stood quietly while she was studied through a pair of lorgnettes, and then took the small be-ringed hand and shook it gently. She said clearly, 'How do you do, *Mevrouw*? I hope I shall be of use to you until Juffrouw Telle returns. I am sorry I can't speak Dutch…'

'No matter, just as long as you speak your own language clearly. Suzanne, ring the bell, Reneke shall take Miss Beckwith to her room. We will have lunch together in half an hour.'

Which meant, reflected Sarah, that she was to go to her room and return in half an hour. She followed a stout, placid woman up the staircase at the end of the hall and into a room at the front of the house. It was large, and the furniture in it was solid. It was comfortable, too, and there were flowers in a little vase on the massive dressing table. There was a bathroom across the passage, as old-fashioned as the room, but equipped with modern comforts. The bath, thought Sarah, eyeing its size, in the middle of the room, balanced on its four iron feet, had been installed for a giant. Her thoughts wandered for a moment; Mr ter Breukel was a giant, and a very nice one...

She unpacked, tidied her person, examined her face in the oval mirror and wished for good looks, applied discreet lipstick and then went to look out of the window. It was tall and wide and gave her an excellent view of the street below and the buildings around it, with the Grote Kerk towering at its end. It was quiet there, but at the other end of the street she could see a busy thoroughfare and the glint of water. She would have to discover the best way to reach the hospital, but just for the moment the hospital, her mother, and all the adherent problems seemed blessedly far away.

She left the window. Like many old houses, this one was peaceful, and people had been happy living in it, just as she had felt at Mr ter Breukel's home.

She wandered round the room, looking at the few pictures on its wall, picking up ornaments and putting them down again. She hoped that she would see Mr ter Breukel again, for she liked him.

She examined a small porcelain figure on the bedside table, a charming trifle probably worth a
small fortune. She was thinking too much about
him and that wouldn't do. He had been kind, but
he was a man to be kind—to an old woman
crossing the street, or to a lost dog. Probably he
would forget all about her now that she was dealt
with—a problem solved...

The half-hour was up; she went back to the
room where the old lady and Suzanne were waiting.

'After lunch, when Suzanne has gone, I will
explain your duties to you,' said her hostess.
'They are, I believe, not onerous. You will be able
to visit your mother at St Bravo's. I am sure that
we shall get on well together.'

They had their lunch in a sombre room panelled
in some dark wood, sitting at a table which would
seat ten perfectly comfortably. It was a simple
meal, beautifully served, and Sarah, who had been
dreading it, found that she was enjoying herself.
Old Mevrouw ter Breukel might be getting on in
years, but there was nothing wrong with her brain.
She was as sharp as a needle: up to date with
politics, fashion and the latest books.

Presently wishing Suzanne goodbye, Sarah assured her that she was going to be happy in her

unexpected job. 'I'll do my best to please your aunt,' she said. 'You've been so kind, and so has Mr ter Breukel. Thank you both very much. I'll let you know when I'm going back to England.'

'Do, though I'll probably see you before then. I hope you won't find it too dull.'

Sarah thought of the uneventful life she led at home. 'It's the most exciting thing that's happened to me in years.'

Her duties were indeed light: she was to spend a good deal of the day with Mevrouw ter Breukel, reading, writing letters for her, fetching and carrying such odds and ends as the lady wanted, and making sure that she was comfortable and lacked for nothing. In the afternoon she was to have an hour or so free, and there would be plenty of time to go and see her mother.

Once her duties had been made known to her she was bidden to fetch a book and read aloud until the old lady had her afternoon nap.

The book took Sarah by surprise. It was the latest Ruth Rendell.

'Juffrouw Telle doesn't read English well, and it tires me to read. We will read as many books as possible while you are here,' said Mevrouw ter Breukel surprisingly. 'Litrik keeps me supplied with the books I enjoy—Jack Higgins, P.D.

James, Evelyn Anthony, Freeling. Sit there, child, I hear better on this side. I'm halfway through the book—there's a bookmark.'

Sarah found the place and started to read. She had a pleasant voice and the story was exciting; it kept them both absorbed until an elderly woman brought in the tea tray.

'No milk, no sugar,' commanded the old lady, 'and I'll have a biscuit.'

Sarah drank her tea from a paper-thin cup and answered the questions which Mevrouw ter Breukel fired at her in a soft voice. No, she didn't have a young man, nor had she any prospect of marrying one, and, no, she didn't have a job. Her life, outlined for the old lady's benefit, sounded dull in her ears.

They dined later, the two of them, in the dark grandeur of the dining room, and Sarah was glad that she had changed into the blue jersey, for Mevrouw ter Breukel was wearing black taffeta and diamonds.

Told, kindly enough, to go to bed soon after the *stoel* clock struck ten, Sarah went willingly. She wasn't tired, but the old lady had observed that occasionally, when she was unable to sleep, she expected someone to keep her company during the wakeful hours. But nothing happened to disturb Sarah's sleep.

She was up and dressed by eight o'clock and had gone, as she had been told, to Mevrouw ter Breukel's room, to find that old lady sitting up in a vast bed, a four-poster, doing a jigsaw puzzle.

They exchanged good mornings and Sarah spent five minutes picking up bits of the puzzle which had been flung aside before she was told to go and have her breakfast.

'And bring me my letters in half an hour or so. Then I shall not need you for a hour or more. Go to the hospital, if you wish, and enquire about your parents. Kaes will look after you and tell you how to get to St Bravo's.'

Dismissed, Sarah went downstairs and found Kaes waiting for her. Her breakfast had been laid with great elegance in a small room behind the dining room, and she enjoyed every morsel of it, keeping an eye on the clock. Half an hour later she went back with the post, and found Mevrouw ter Breukel still engrossed in her puzzle.

'Run along now, and be back here by half past ten.'

The hospital was ten minutes' walk away, and there were several ambulances parked by the Accident Room entrance. She went up to her mother's ward and met Sister coming out of the office.

'You have come to see your mother? She has slept well; she will be glad to see you. We are busy today. There has been a multiple car accident, and soon we shall have more patients here.'

Mrs Holt was sitting by a window. 'You must do some shopping for me,' she began, without preamble. 'I need some more mascara and another lipstick, and see if you can get me a decent magazine; I've nothing to read…'

'Don't they come round with books? I'm sure they'd find you something in English, Mother.'

'Oh, yes, but you know how quickly reading bores me.'

'TV?'

'In Dutch, my dear? You must be joking. I'm to see the consultant this morning. I shall ask to go home.'

'What about my stepfather?'

'Oh, they will arrange to send him home, too, of course. He must be able to travel by now.'

'Have you been to see him?'

'My dear Sarah, I'm not well; my nerves wouldn't stand it. Sister tells me from time to time how he is. You had better go and see him.'

Sarah went, unwillingly enough, but she saw it

as her duty. It was a waste of time, of course. Her stepfather did not wish to see her. Her visit was brief and she soon made her way back to the entrance, hoping that she might meet Mr ter Breukel; he would be too busy to stop and talk, but it would be nice just to say hello.

They met on a staircase. She was going down as he was going up, two steps at a time, followed by two younger men in long white coats. He didn't pause; she doubted if he had seen her.

He had, of course, but sudden emergencies took no account of personal feelings.

Sarah had the good sense to see that she had probably been invisible to him; he was so obviously involved in some dire situation. He had looked different, too, and she realised why. He had been wearing grey trousers and a high-necked pullover, and he hadn't shaved. Perhaps he had been up half the night.

The whole night, actually.

There was no time to shop for her mother, and she hurried back to Mevrouw ter Breukel, anxious not to be late.

The day went smoothly and pleasantly enough, and, to her surprise, quickly. She was kept busy, and when the old lady discovered that she could play chess, after a fashion, the evening hours were fully occupied. Sarah went to bed at length, feeling that the day had gone well. Only it would have been nice if Mr ter Breukel had called to see his aunt.

A wish, had she but known it, which he would have heartily endorsed.

But he came the next day. It was the quiet hour or so after tea, and Sarah was setting out the chess pieces, ready for a game after dinner, her neat head bent over the chessboard. He stood in the open doorway, watching her, studying her small person, wanting very much to go to her and gather her into his arms and tell her that he loved her. But not just yet, he warned himself, and went into the room.

His great-aunt was clearly taking a nap. Sarah turned round and saw him and smiled and put her finger to her lips. He smiled back, took her arm and led her to the far end of the room by the window. Only then did he say, 'Hello, Sarah.'

She beamed up at him. 'Hello. Mevrouw ter Breukel will wake presently. Do you want tea or anything?'

'Nothing, thank you. Have you settled down? Not too hard work?'

'I'm very happy, and it isn't like work at all. Your great-aunt is a darling old lady.' She spoke in a whisper, and, when he didn't answer, asked, 'Have you been busy? There were a lot of ambulances when I went to see Mother yesterday.'

'A day of emergencies.'

'I—I saw you yesterday—you didn't see me. It was on the stairs. You looked as though you have been up all night.'

'It was a night of emergencies, too. Sarah, before you return to England, I should like to show you something of Holland. I shall be free on Sunday, will you spend it with me?'

'With you? You mean all day?' The delight in her face changed to regret. 'But I can't; I'm here to be your aunt's companion.'

'But like all companions you are entitled to a free day each week. Besides, Suzanne is coming to spend the day here, and you won't be needed.'

When she would have protested, he added casually, 'I think we might enjoy each other's company.'

'Yes, well—but there must be other people—I mean friends you'd rather be with.'

'They are always here. You will go home shortly, and I think that you deserve at least a brief glimpse of Holland!'

'Well, thank you. I would like it very much.' And, Sarah being Sarah, she added, 'I'm afraid

I'm not a very interesting person to be with. I mean, I'm not clever or witty. You might get bored...'

Mr ter Breukel's expression of calm interest didn't alter. 'After the rush and hurry of St Bravo's I dare say I shall find your company restful. Shall we say nine o'clock on Sunday morning?'

'All right. But I must ask Mevrouw ter Breukel's permission.'

She was interrupted by that lady's voice demanding to know what they were talking about, and when she was told she observed that it suited her very well. 'For if Suzanne is to spend the day with me I'll not need Sarah here as well. Take her through the Veluwe, Litrik, and show her how lovely it is there.'

She offered a cheek for his kiss. 'Sarah, go for a walk, or amuse yourself for half an hour or so. We will have our game of chess after dinner.'

When Sarah had gone, and he had shut the door behind her, she said, 'Litrik, I may be an old woman but I still have my wits about me. You're in love with the girl, aren't you?'

He came and sat down opposite to her, speaking Dutch now. 'Yes, my dear. I knew that the moment I set eyes on her.'

'But she has no idea of that. Only she likes you very much indeed, I think.'

'Perhaps I am too old for her.'

'That's not going to stop you...'

Mr ter Breukel laughed. 'No, it's not!'

CHAPTER THREE

SARAH woke on Sunday to a fine spring morning. True, the sky was a very pale blue and held no warmth, but the tiled roofs of the houses around her sparkled and the air, when she leaned out of the window, was fresh.

At nine o'clock precisely she was borne away in the discreet luxury of Mr ter Breukel's Rolls, unaware of her companion's delight at her company since he had greeted her with casual friendliness and now began almost immediately to describe the various parts of Arnhem as he drove out of the city: the war memorial at the Rhine Bridge, the parks, the old houses which had survived the destruction of the War, the zoo.

Sarah craned her neck from side to side, anxious not to miss anything.

He drove north presently, through the High Veluwe national park, taking the narrow by-roads through the woods and stopping for coffee in Apeldoorn, where he walked her to the palace of Het Loo.

The park was open and they wandered to and

fro, explored the stable block, which was open to the public, and then got back into the car to drive on to Zwolle. Here they lunched at a small restaurant housed in an ancient house by the Stads Gracht, once a moat and now a canal, and were served *koffietafel*—a basket of various rolls and bread and slices of cheese on a vast platter, cold meat and sausage, hard-boiled eggs and a salad, accompanied by a pot of coffee.

Sarah eyed the table with pleasure; the morning's sightseeing and her pleasure in her companion's company had given her an appetite, moreover she felt happy. Somehow in Mr ter Breukel's placid company the future became vague and unthreatening.

They travelled on presently, through Meppel and into Friesland, to stop for tea in Sneek, and then had a brief glimpse of the lake before driving on to the coast. It was chilly here, and the North Sea looked grey and forbidding.

'Lovely in the summer,' Mr ter Breukel told her. 'Those islands you can see are popular with families. There are splendid beaches for children. You like children?'

Sarah was unaware of how wistful she looked. 'Oh, yes...'

Children, she thought, and dogs and cats and a

donkey, and an old house with a huge garden—
and a husband, of course. And what chance had
she of getting any of them? The future, so pleasantly vague, suddenly became only too real.

Mr ter Breukel took her arm and walked her
back to the car. In some way his hand on hers
dispelled her gloomy thoughts. The future didn't
matter, not for the moment at any rate.

He drove back over the Afsluitdijk, gave her a
glimpse of Alkmaar and raced south, bypassing
Amsterdam. 'You shall see that another time,' he
told her casually. 'There's rather a nice place
where we can have dinner just outside Utrecht.'

The 'nice place' was a seventeenth-century
mansion, very splendid, overlooking a pond and
tucked away in the centre of a small wood. Sarah,
led away to a well-equipped cloakroom, did her
hair and face, wishing for chestnut curls and a
pretty face as she did so, wishing too that she was
wearing a smart outfit worthy of her companion
and her surroundings. She told herself in her sensible way not to be silly, and joined Mr ter
Breukel in a large, rather old-fashioned lounge to
sip her sherry while they discussed what they
should eat.

Sarah, with gentle prompting from Mr ter
Breukel, chose tiny pancakes filled with goat's

cheese, sole served with a champagne sauce, and chocolate and almond pudding. She ate with a splendid appetite, her tongue nicely loosened by the white wine he had chosen, so that by seemingly casual questions he was made the recipient of a good deal of information concerning her life at Clapham Common. Not that she complained about it; it was what she *didn't* say that gave him an insight into its dullness. He was impatient to rescue her at once, but that, of course, was impossible. He must rely on a kindly Fate and his own plans.

Sarah looked up and caught his eye and smiled, and he schooled his features into a friendly glance and made a casual remark about their surroundings. He wondered what the surrounding diners would do if he were to swoop across the table and pick Sarah up and carry her off. Somewhere quiet, where he could kiss her at leisure. He smiled then, and Sarah said, 'Oh, it's lovely here. I shall remember it all when I get back home.'

'Good. You have only seen a small part of Holland, though.'

And all she was likely to see, thought Sarah. He hadn't suggested that he would take her out again, and she hadn't expected him to. But supposing he thought that she had hoped he *would*.

She had done her best to be good company, but probably he had found her rather dull, and after all he had been more than kind.

Suzanne was still at the house when they got back.

'I've helped Great-Aunt to bed,' she told them. 'We've had a lovely day, gossiping and playing backgammon. Did you two enjoy yourselves?'

Her brother said gravely that for his part he had had a most interesting day, which Sarah considered was neither one thing or the other.

'It was lovely,' she told Suzanne. 'I'll have so much to remember when I get back home.'

She bade them goodnight presently, before they drove away, and then went to her room and went to bed, remembering every minute of the day. Mr ter Breukel hadn't said anything about seeing her again, but of course they were bound to meet, even if it were only to make arrangements for her mother and stepfather's return to England. Besides, she reminded herself, he visited his great-aunt frequently.

But there was no sign of him. She had caught the occasional glimpse of him in the distance when she had visited her mother at the hospital, but he'd been so far away that only the size and height of him had made her sure that it was he. Certainly he didn't visit his great-aunt again, nor were there any messages concerning the transfer to England of her mother.

Mrs Holt, while still complaining bitterly, had settled down at last to the quiet routine of the hospital, and Sister had assured Sarah that she should be fit to return home very shortly. And her stepfather, although one of the worst patients the ward sister assured Sarah that she had ever had to nurse, was fit to travel.

'You will be told when arrangements have been made,' she said to Sarah kindly.

The best part of a week went by; there was no news of Juffrouw Telle's return, and when Sarah saw Suzanne, which was frequently, that young lady professed to know nothing.

It was on an early morning, when Sarah went down to her breakfast after peeping in to see if the old lady was still sleeping, that she found Mr ter Breukel sitting at the table in the small room where she took her meals when she was alone. Everything necessary for a good breakfast was arranged around him, and a folded newspaper was beside his plate.

Sarah paused in the doorway, delighted to see him but not sure if she was welcome. She said,

'Hello,' and then, more sedately, 'Good morning, Mr ter Breukel.'

He had got to his feet and pulled out a chair, and she saw that he was wearing a grey sweater and corduroy trousers. 'You've been up all night,' she observed, and indeed he looked tired; he had showered, but there were lines in his face which she hadn't seen before. 'I hope you will go straight to bed when you've had your breakfast.'

Mr ter Breukel, who had other plans, said that yes, he would, in a meek voice, and pushed the coffee pot towards her.

Sarah said in her practical way, 'Shouldn't you be at your own home?'

He had forgotten how tired he was; he looked into the future and saw with deep satisfaction homecomings in the small hours to Sarah's wifely concern.

'Indeed I should, but it seemed a good opportunity to see you about your mother and stepfather's transfer to England. It has been arranged for Tuesday—that gives you three days to carry out any plans you may have made. Your stepfather will need to travel by ambulance, and your mother can go with him. You will fly from Schiphol and an ambulance will collect you at Heathrow and get you home to Clapham. You will be travelling with them, of course. Someone will come for you on Tuesday morning at eight o'clock.'

Sarah didn't speak for a bit; she was battling with the sudden fright that she wasn't going to see him again. She choked it down and said gruffly, 'Thank you for making all the arrangements; we're very much in your debt. We're very grateful.' Well, *she* was; she wasn't sure about her mother and stepfather. 'I'll be ready, and if there's anything I should do, will someone let me know? And what about your great-aunt? I've loved being with her, and she does need someone, you know…'

Mr ter Breukel buttered a roll lavishly. 'It is amazing how things arrange themselves,' he observed blandly. 'Juffrouw Telle phoned last night to say that she would be returning on Monday evening.'

'Her mother's better? I'm glad, and how provi…'

'…dential,' finished Mr ter Breukel. 'Great-Aunt has enjoyed your company and you have been a great help to us. I'm only sorry you haven't had more time to see Holland.'

'I had a lovely day with you,' said Sarah. 'I shall remember it always.' She added hastily, in case he thought she meant him and his company, 'The country was delightful.'

He kept a straight face while he watched the colour wash over her cheeks. To have accompanied her to England would have been a delight, but he had decided against. First let her return to her own home; there was always the possibility that, viewed from the other side of the North Sea, their growing friendship might dwindle into a vague interlude. That was something he would have to discover later.

He smiled gently. 'Yes, it was a delightful day.' And five minutes later he was leaving, with the casual remark that he would see her before she left Arnhem.

'And go to bed—just for an hour or two,' said Sarah, in such a concerned voice that he was tempted to pick her up and kiss her. But he didn't, and bed, as far as he could see, was something to be deferred until he had dealt with his patients. So he smiled, patted her on a shoulder and was gone.

Sarah, visiting her mother later that day, found her in a state of excitement and with numerous requests to Sarah which she hadn't a hope of fulfilling. She pointed out that once they were home her mother could buy the things she declared she must have, that there was no need to be made up, have her hair done or send Sarah to buy the host of small unnecessary articles she required.

'Of course you *would* say that,' declared Mrs Holt crossly. 'The smallest thing I ask you to do for me and you have a reason for not doing it.'

She turned a shoulder to Sarah. 'You had better go and see your stepfather and see if he needs anything. And you're not to leave me on the journey. I feel ill at the very thought of it.'

Come to think of it, thought Sarah, I feel ill too...

Her stepfather did nothing to improve matters; he queried and argued about every arrangement made for his transfer, and grumbled that his car, which had been transported back to Clapham, was no doubt damaged beyond repair and that no one had seen fit to give him any information about it. He grumbled, too, at the expense of the ambulance, the special arrangements which had been made at the airports—indeed there was nothing about which he *didn't* grumble!

And Sarah made it worse by asking him for money to buy a thank-you gift for the nursing staff. She waited stoically while he vented his rage at the very idea, and then said, 'I should think about a hundred *gulden* would do—for a really handsome box of chocolates they can share around.'

There was no sign of Mr ter Breukel on Tuesday morning; her farewells said, Sarah was driven away to the hospital and found the ambulance already there. Her stepfather was already in it; she could hear his irate voice complaining bitterly about something—a useless exercise as everyone there was occupied with getting Mrs Holt into the ambulance in her turn. Now that she was actually leaving she had become a bundle of doubts, and it was only when Sarah arrived that she would consent to get into the ambulance.

Sarah went round the small group of nurses and the two ward sisters, uttering thanks and offering the chocolates. They must be glad to see the back of us, she reflected, dragging out her goodbyes for as long as possible, just in case Mr ter Breukel should come.

There was no reason why he should; Suzanne had wished her goodbye on the previous evening, and they had parted with mutual regret that their friendship would have to end. She would have liked to have said goodbye to Mr ter Breukel, too, although she didn't think that *he* would feel any regret...

She couldn't spin the time out any longer, and
went round to the front of the ambulance; she was
to sit with the driver so that the paramedic with
him could travel with her mother and stepfather.
She reached up to open the door, and Mr ter
Breukel's large hand lifted her hand away and
opened it for her.

'Have a safe journey,' he told her. 'Make sure
that you get all the documents before you board
the plane, the driver will let you have them at
Schiphol. I've written to your doctor, of course,
and sent the X-rays to him; if he needs to know
anything further he can reach me here.'

Sarah nodded. Now that she was actually seeing him for the last time she could think of nothing to say. If only she could think of something
which would remind him of her—she frowned
fiercely at the ridiculous idea and offered a hand.
She said, 'Thank you for all that you have done.
Everyone has been so kind and we must have
been a nuisance...'

He didn't deny that, but said, 'You have been
happy here, despite the circumstances?'

'Yes, oh, yes.'

He smiled then, still holding her hand, and then
gave it back to her and opened the door. Sarah
whispered, 'Goodbye,' and got in, because there

was nothing else that she could do. She could have got out again, of course, and refused to go, causing confusion and embarrassment to everyone there. For one wild moment she considered this, but only for a moment. She smiled and waved and was driven away, back to Clapham.

The journey went smoothly, despite untold hold-ups and complaints from the Holts, and they arrived in the late afternoon to find Mrs Twist, the housekeeper, waiting for them.

This was by far the hardest part of the journey for Sarah. She had coped well enough with documents, passports, various officials, her mother's endless demands and her stepfather's rantings, but now, once more in their own house, they both demanded instant attention.

Her mother wished to be put to bed immediately, and cosseted with a light meal, the male nurse who had been engaged to attend to Mr Holt hadn't arrived, and although Mr Holt was quite able to do a good deal for himself he also demanded assistance, and Mrs Twist, good soul though she was, found it all a bit too much and retired to the kitchen in tears.

It was long past midnight by the time the house was at last quiet and Sarah could take herself off

to bed. The nurse hadn't turned up. It was to be
hoped that he would arrive in the morning...

Dr Benson came first. Mrs Twist and Sarah had
just finished dealing with breakfast, and Sarah,
who had known him for some years, welcomed
him with open arms, handed over the various letters and papers she had been given and then went
to admit the nurse. He was a sober, middle-aged
man, who looked capable of dealing with her
stepfather's ill temper. He would come each day,
he told her, for a couple of hours in the morning
and again in the early evening.

Which left a good deal of the day during which
Mr Holt would expect attention. But now that her
mother was well again she could perhaps be persuaded to spend an hour or two with him each
afternoon, thought Sarah hopefully.

They settled down to an uneasy routine, for
Mrs Holt couldn't be relied upon to keep to any
routine, and was liable to go off for an afternoon's
shopping in a taxi without warning anyone, returning exhausted and demanding Sarah's instant
attention.

It was on Dr Benson's third visit that he
brought his partner with him: Robert Swift, a

young man with a cheerful face and a friendly way with him.

Over a cup of coffee, after visiting his patient, he told Sarah that he intended to stay in Clapham. 'I've got rooms here,' he told her, 'but I'm getting married next year and we've got our eyes on a rather nice flat close to the Common. We're both Londoners and Jennie likes it here. I'm jolly lucky to be taken on as Dr Benson's partner.'

Sarah liked him and listened, whenever he called, to his hopes for the future while he drank the coffee she always had ready for him.

They had been back a week when he suggested that she might like to go with him to see the flat he hoped to buy. 'I told Jennie about you,' he told her ingenuously. 'She's gone up to Yorkshire to nurse an aunt. You've lived here for a few years, haven't you, so you would know if it's in a decent part of Clapham. We want somewhere nice; I don't want Jennie to work when we're married.'

'I'd love to come. It would have to be when Kenneth's here—but the morning's no good for you, is it? He comes back each afternoon about five o'clock and stays for two hours.'

'Suits me! How about tomorrow? It's my half-day.' He gave her a friendly look. 'You don't get much time to yourself, do you?'

'Not just at the moment, but my stepfather is to have crutches very soon, and that will be a lot easier.'

A statement not to be believed for one moment. Mr Holt on crutches would be a menace, going round the house, interfering with all and sundry. Now, more or less chained to his bed, he had to be content to supervise his business by telephone, and an occasional visit from one of his underlings, but once up and about there would be no holding him. He wouldn't be able to drive the new car which had replaced the damaged one, which meant that Sarah would be expected to chauffeur him if he took a fancy to go to the office. And that would annoy her mother, who regarded her as an unpaid companion.

She must escape, but how?

Robert Swift arrived punctually the next day, and since Kenneth was already in the house Sarah went away to put on her outdoor things, find her mother and explain that she would be back within the hour. Robert was waiting in the hall and they went to the door together. It was a rather hideous door, with coloured glass panels and a loud bell. Somebody was ringing it now; she opened the door, laughing at something Robert had said as she did so.

Mr ter Breukel stood there.

'Oh, it's you,' cried Sarah. 'Oh, I never expected…!' Delight at the sight of him had taken her breath.

Mr ter Breukel said, in a calm voice which allowed none of his feelings to show, 'Hello, Sarah. I'm over here for a short while and thought I would look you up, but I see I've called at an awkward time. Don't let me keep you.'

'You're not—that is, we're only going to look at a flat. This is Dr Swift.' She looked at Robert. 'Mr ter Breukel is a consultant surgeon at the hospital where my stepfather and mother were…'

Mr ter Breukel offered a hand. 'They're doing well, I hope?'

'Yes—I'm only Dr Benson's junior partner, sir. Did you wish to see them? I'm sure Dr Benson…'

'No, no. I'll be phoning him before I go back to Holland. I'm sure they are in excellent hands.'

He smiled down at Sarah. 'I'm glad to see you looking so well and happy, Sarah. Suzanne sent her love.'

'She did? You'll come and see us before you go?'

He said smoothly, 'I doubt if I'll have the time.

And I mustn't keep you from viewing this flat.'
He looked at Robert. 'You intend to settle here?'

'Oh, yes. We both know this part of London
well, and it's a splendid practice.'

Mr ter Breukel offered a hand again. 'Then I
must wish you a happy future. And you too, of
course, Sarah.' He smiled. 'It didn't take you long
to discover that Clapham has its advantages over
Arnhem.'

His handshake was brief, and she was still gathering her woolly wits together when he turned,
walked down the short drive, got into his car and
drove away.

'He seems a nice chap,' said Robert. 'Not so
young, of course. But good at his job, I dare say.'

Sarah swallowed the tears which had kept her
silent. 'He's very nice, and he's quite young and
very clever. Shall we go? I mustn't be away for
too long.'

Robert was too full of his own plans to notice
her silence. She admired the flat, agreed that it
was in a good neighbourhood and would make a
perfect home for his Jennie, and presently he
drove her back.

'I won't ask you in,' she told him at the door.
'Mother expects me to see to her supper and help
get her ready for bed.'

'Of course. But surely Mrs Holt feels quite fit again?'

'Well, yes, Dr Benson says she's very well, but she—she suffers from her nerves and likes some-one to—to be with her...'

Robert gave her a thoughtful look. 'A compan-ion sounds the right answer to that. Wouldn't you like to be independent—find a job?'

'Very much, but it's not very easy at the mo-ment. Perhaps when my stepfather is quite recov-ered.' She added, in a bitter little voice, 'But, you see, I'm not trained for anything.'

'There are dozens of things you could do—a few months' training at whatever you choose and you're on your way.'

'You're right, Robert, and I'll see what I can do about it. You must think me a very spineless person.'

'No, you're a dutiful daughter tied by the leg.' He grinned suddenly. 'You have nice legs too. Goodbye, Sarah, I'll be in some time tomorrow.'

Sarah managed not to think too much about Mr ter Breukel that evening, but later, in bed, lying awake thinking about him, going over their brief meeting word for word, she was quite suddenly struck by an appalling thought, He had asked about Robert's flat, but Robert hadn't mentioned his Jennie, and then Mr ter Breukel had wished them both a happy future, and that would explain his remark about her liking Clapham better than Arnhem.

He thought that she and Robert were going to marry. What must he think of her after she had told him so plainly that she had no plans to marry, no boyfriend, and had let him see that she liked him?

And she had no idea where he was; she couldn't write and explain, let alone go and see him. He was in London, she supposed, but London was vast... She told herself to be sensible, and to think sensibly too. Presently she got out of bed and searched through her handbag. Sure enough, Suzanne had written down her phone number. 'So that we can give each other a ring from time to time,' she had said. And I will, decided Sarah, as soon as possible in the morning.

She got back into bed, and presently cried herself to sleep.

Breakfast dealt with, she went to her stepfather's study and dialled Suzanne's number. 'It's me,' she said in answer to a sleepy hello. 'Sarah. Mr ter...that is, your brother came to see us yesterday, only I was just going out and I—I wanted to see him but he went away and I don't know where he is. If I did I could go and see him or phone him…'

She wasn't being very sensible; Suzanne must think she was being silly.

Suzanne, who had known that Litrik was going to England, added two and two together and made five before Sarah could speak again.

'He's in London for several days. I'll give you his number and his address, and he'll be at two or three hospitals. Wait while I get my pocketbook.'

She read out the numbers, added addresses and advised Sarah to go and see him. 'You know how it is if you phone. Some dragon tells you he isn't there or he's engaged with a patient. That first address I gave you is the most likely—he'll be seeing private patients there in the mornings between nine o'clock and noon while he's in London. Nice to hear from you, Sarah.'

Her mother didn't take kindly to the idea of Sarah going off at a moment's notice that morning, but Sarah went all the same. She hadn't enough money for a taxi, and anyway her mother would want to know exactly why she needed to go somewhere in such a hurry, but the rush hour was over and a bus shouldn't take too long.

However, she had reckoned without an unkind Fate; an accident held up the traffic, buses were diverted... She reached the hospital at five minutes to twelve, and by the time she had asked her way to the wing used for consulting rooms it was five past the hour. And Mr ter Breukel, she was told, had been gone for five minutes.

'You don't know where?' asked Sarah of the receptionist.

The girl unwrapped a chocolate bar and took a bite. 'No idea. He won't be here in the hospital again today. You're not a patient?'

Sarah shook her head. 'No—I—it doesn't matter.'

So she went back home and, being a girl who liked to finish what she had started, studied the phone numbers and addresses Suzanne had given her. She decided against ringing him up—either one talked too much or too little on the phone— but there was a likely address. She looked it up on the street map in her stepfather's study and decided that it must be a private house, close to Harley Street. Either he would have rooms there or it was a service flat. If he was working he would hardly be at a hotel.

Her mind made up, she helped Mrs Twist with lunch, spent the afternoon with her mother, had

tea with her and took tea to her stepfather, then
went to the kitchen to help Mrs Twist with dinner.

The evening would be the best time to go and
see Mr ter Breukel, she had decided, and to strike
while the iron was hot seemed good sense.
Kenneth had arrived, and would be with her stepfather for a couple of hours, and friends had called
to see her mother.

'I'm going out,' she told Mrs Twist. 'I don't
expect I'll be very long. I'll tell Mother before I
go, but don't fuss if I'm not back in time for dinner.'

It was a chilly evening, but light, so she put on
a coat over her jersey dress, did her face and hair
carefully, told her mother that she would be back
presently and set out once more. It was quite a
long journey and she had ample time to rehearse
what she wanted to say. She wouldn't stay, of
course—after a day's work he would be tired—
but she had to explain…

The address she had been given was one of a
row of rather grand houses with steps leading up
to their important front doors. Not the kind of
house one would have expected to have been
turned into flats. The curtains were drawn across
the windows but there was a light showing
through the transom above the door. She glanced

at her watch; it was almost eight o'clock—later than she had thought, but it was too late to turn back now. She thumped the great brass knocker.

The door was opened by a severe-looking maid, very correctly dressed in a black dress with a white apron.

'Mr ter Breukel?' asked Sarah. 'He is staying here, I believe?'

'Yes, miss.' The girl wasn't unfriendly and Sarah took heart.

'Could I see him for a few minutes? If you would take my name…'

The girl stood aside and Sarah passed her into an elegant hall. 'Who shall I say, miss?'

'Sarah Beckwith—Miss.' She followed the girl across the hall and was close behind her when she opened one of the doors. The room, large, splendidly furnished and brilliantly lighted, was full of people dressed for the evening, drinks in their hands, and right at the end of it she could see Mr ter Breukel, elegant in black tie, talking to a group of equally elegant men and women.

The maid had left her, and Sarah, good sense flown out of her head, stood where she was, rooted to the spot. This was something she hadn't even imagined. She saw the maid speak to Mr ter Breukel and he looked up and saw her. He was a good way off, but near enough for her to see that he wasn't smiling. A belated idea to get out of the house as quickly as possible was nipped in the bud, because now he had spoken to a man nearby and was crossing the room.

'Oh, dear,' said Sarah and backed away. She would apologise for disturbing his evening and leave smartly...

His 'Good evening, Sarah,' was uttered in a voice which told her nothing, and after she asked the maid where they might go she followed him meekly across the hall and into a small room, cosily furnished and rather untidy. There was a large ginger cat curled up before the small fire, who took no notice of them as they went in.

'Do sit down,' said Mr ter Breukel. 'You wanted to see me urgently? Your parents?'

Sarah sat down on a small easy chair and the cat jumped onto her lap and was instantly asleep. She took one or two deep breaths, because she had read somewhere that that was the way to calm one's nerves.

'I'm sorry, I didn't know that you would be having a party. I tried to see you at the hospital this morning, but you had gone. There was a hold-up and the bus had to make a detour—the passengers got very annoyed, but really it wasn't the driver's fault...' She stopped, aware that she wasn't getting to the point, and Mr ter Breukel, watching her, fell in love with her all over again.

He said gently, 'You wanted to see me?'

She gave him a grateful glance. 'Yes, about yesterday. If I'd have known that you would be coming to see us, I would have told Robert not to come.'

'A wise decision...'

'Yes, well, you see, I could go and see the flat at any time—that is, when he's free—but you were unexpected, and anyway I didn't think fast enough. I should have told Robert to go away.'

'He seems a very pleasant young man. Only a little older than yourself?'

'He's thirty. I'm twenty-three. But you know that. What I wanted to make quite clear....' Her thoughts, darting here and there like mice in a trap, had taken on a life of their own. 'Do you live here? Suzanne gave me this address. It's a very nice house.'

Mr ter Breukel said with careful nonchalance, 'She phones you from time to time, I expect? She likes you.'

'I like her, too; she's so pretty. No, I phoned her. You see, I wanted to see you and make things clear.'

He crossed one leg over the other. Presumably his Sarah would soon come to the point. She was behaving as though she felt guilty about this Robert. He felt a dull despair at the thought of her marrying him, but if she was going to be happy then he would learn to live without her. He had allowed himself to daydream; he should have known better at his age. What girl would want to marry a man twelve years older than she?

Somewhere in the house a gong sounded, and Sarah said, 'Oh, dear, that's for dinner. You must go.'

'We haven't got very far, have we?' he said, and his voice was kind. 'You have been trying to tell me that you're going to marry Robert and for some reason you're scared to do so. I'm delighted for you, Sarah, and I'm sure you will be very happy.'

The door opened behind them and a young woman poked her head round it.

'Forgive me, but we're just going in to dinner. Perhaps your friend would like to stay?'

Sarah had got to her feet. 'No, no. I was just going. I'm sorry to have interrupted.'

She smiled at the young woman, who smiled back and disappeared down the hall. 'Come when you are ready, Litrik,' she called over a shoulder.

The maid was in the hall, waiting to open the door. Sarah made for it in a rush. To get out of the house and away from Mr ter Breukel was vital, for once out in the street she could cry as much as she wanted. She had made a fine mess of everything, but perhaps that was a good thing for he had said that he was delighted that she would be marrying Robert.

She put out a hand and had it shaken gently, muttered something, she had no idea what, and left the house very nearly at a run. If he had said anything to her she hadn't heard him, but really there was nothing more to say, was there? She began to walk very fast, letting the buses pass her. She had been a fool; all her carefully rehearsed speeches had been forgotten and she had talked a lot of rubbish—and anyway, what did it matter to him if she married someone else? Why had she been so anxious to explain his mistake in thinking that?

She gave a great gulping sob. She wasn't going to get married anyway. 'And I dare say I never shall,' she said, and a passer-by gave her a wary look.

She caught a bus presently, and went home to face Mrs Twist's anxious face, her mother's complaining voice and her stepfather roaring from his room.

'Not one of my best days,' said Sarah to herself later, gobbling her warmed-up dinner at the kitchen table. Mrs Twist had gone to bed, and presently she would set about settling her stepfather and her mother for the night.

She went to bed after that and, contrary to her expectations, slept at once. But she woke in the early hours, her mind very clear.

'It's funny I didn't think of it sooner. Of course I wanted to explain to him—because I'm in love with him.'

She felt a warm glow of happiness at the thought, but in the pale early-morning light common sense took over; the glow was still there but she must learn to keep it tucked away, out of sight and mind.

CHAPTER FOUR

FOR the next few days the hope that she would see Mr ter Breukel again coloured Sarah's dull daily round. She didn't sleep well, but each morning she got out of bed telling herself that surely he would phone her, or even come to say goodbye before he went back to Holland. And each night she went to bed and wept quietly. Not because she had hoped that they would meet again, but because he had seemed so pleased that she was, as he'd presumed, to marry Robert.

He would think nothing of her for keeping Robert up her sleeve, as it were, while accepting his friendship. And that was all it was, she reminded herself; she didn't expect anything warmer than that, but to have him as a friend would have been a wonderful thing.

Loving someone who didn't love you, reflected Sarah one night, mopping her eyes and blowing her small red nose, was very painful. She gave a great sniff and curled up in bed, wondering where he was and what he was doing. It was comforting, somehow, to know that somewhere out there, in the world she had so little chance of seeing much of, he would be working and eating and sleeping just as she was.

Which was exactly what he was doing. But, unlike her, he viewed the future in a different light. If Sarah was happy, if she wanted to marry this young doctor, then he would accept that, but first he had to be quite sure that this was so, and he *wasn't* sure…

Unlike Sarah, his days were full; he thrust her image to the back of his mind and dealt with consultations, clinics, patients and sessions in the operating theatre, as at home in the London hospitals as he was at Arnhem. He had been a consultant at both hospitals for some years now, and came to London several times a year. Nevertheless he did have opportunities to drive to Clapham Common and see Sarah, all of which he ignored.

If she were going to marry Robert then she would have little interest in another visit from him, and the thin thread of their friendship might snap. And he must still find out more about her and Robert; only when he knew with certainty that they were to marry would he abandon his hopes for the future.

Two weeks later, on the point of his return to

Arnhem, he telephoned Dr Benson, enquired as to
Mr Holt's progress and, after a brief discussion,
observed with just the right amount of interest that
he had met the doctor's young partner.

Dr Benson was enthusiastic about him. 'A good
doctor, and already well liked by my patients.
He's getting married shortly—his future wife,
Jennie, is a very nice girl, familiar with this area,
too. They're busy getting their flat ready. They
intended to marry next year, but since they've
found this place and he's settled in so well there's
no reason for them not to set up home sooner.
Some time in May, I believe. If you're over here
by any chance you must come to the wedding—
and take a look at Mr Holt at the same time. I
quite understand that your commitments pre-
vented you from seeing him this time, but I can
assure you that your good work will be continued
here.'

'I feel sure of that. And Mrs Holt and her
daughter?'

'Mrs Holt is quite herself again, a nervous and
delicate lady, as you no doubt know, depending
very much upon her daughter. And Sarah seems
none the worse for the accident. She is rather a
quiet girl, and seems even quieter now. She really
needs to be independent and leave home, but of

course she has no training, and Mrs Holt relies upon her for everything. She meets very few young people…'

All of which Mr ter Breukel thought about deeply as he took himself back to Arnhem. The overwhelming relief at discovering that it wasn't Sarah who was to marry Robert was overshadowed by concern for her happiness. His first impulse was to carry her off and marry her out of hand, but she might have other wishes as to her future. Probably she regarded him as a rather staid man to whom she owed gratitude.

She had told him something of her life, but very little about her own hopes for the future. For all he knew she might want to travel, become a career girl, go on the stage. He must, he told himself, on no account be impatient, and if possible think of some means whereby she might become independent and see something of the world, even if it were only another part of London. Only then would he find a way of resuming their friendship and finally marrying her.

He needed to think about it, but only after he had tackled the backlog of patients and operations waiting for him at St Bravo's.

That done, he set about his problem with calm logic. Suzanne first, for he wanted her opinion of the prospects of a job for a girl without any kind of training.

She said at once, 'Oh, you're thinking of Sarah. Why don't you marry her, Litrik? Then she won't need to get work.'

'That's an easy answer, my dear. But Sarah's never had a chance to spread her wings. Suppose she were to marry me and then discover that what she wanted was a career of some sort, a chance to meet people—men—of her own age? No, she must have a little time to discover what she really wants.'

Suzanne thought. 'Well, I'd look for a job where all that was needed was common sense and a willingness to do anything wanted.' She shrugged. 'Sounds hopeless, doesn't it?'

'No, it makes sense. It will have to be work where I can keep her under my eye.'

'What about the hospital—the London one?'

'I had thought of that, and that is a possibility, but I have to find a way to get her there…'

Suzanne gave him a sisterly peck on the cheek. 'And you will, Litrik. Let me know if I can help, won't you?'

Mr ter Breukel had many friends, some of them colleagues of long standing at the London hospital. He was on good terms with the hospital manager, too, and it was through him, by asking carefully casual questions, that he discovered that there was a shortage of unskilled labour in the kitchens, the house doctors' rooms and dining room, and in the staff canteen.

The kitchens wouldn't do at all, and nor would the house doctors' quarters; he wasn't so old that he couldn't remember that young housemen tended to relax like small boys when they had the chance... It would have to be the canteen.

Having settled that, his next problem was somewhat harder to solve. How to get her away from Clapham Common? He ignored her stepfather—the man was a bully, and lacking in any kind feeling towards her, but he wouldn't be able to stop Sarah leaving home. It was her mother who would do that if she could, playing upon Sarah's kind heart and her sense of duty. Mr ter Breukel sat at his desk night after night, with the faithful Max at his feet, and bent his powerful brain to the matter.

To good effect. The series of telephone calls he eventually made were entirely satisfactory, even though they were protracted and necessitated a good deal of discussion. The impossible, reflected Mr ter Breukel, is sometimes possible, provided one is determined enough. And he *was* determined.

Mr Holt's leg confining him to the house and depriving Mrs Holt of participating in their normal social life meant that she was unable to enjoy herself as she would wish. She had friends—but friends who were loath to invite her to dinner parties without her husband, unwilling for her to join in their usual social round on her own. She had to fall back on bridge afternoons and shopping and the occasional meeting for coffee while shopping. As a consequence her discontent grew, as did her peevishness, and since there was no one else she vented both on Sarah.

'It is a pity that you're not pretty and socially minded,' she complained, 'then at least there would be some young people about the house.'

To which Sarah said nothing, although she could have pointed out that young people had never been encouraged. She remembered with shame the few occasions when she had invited schoolfriends home and watched her mother with subtle charm eclipse her own efforts. Later on it had been worse, for such young men as she'd met had occasionally found her mother's pretty ways and gentle manner quite irresistible...

Now, as far as she could see, the faint hopes that she could persuade her mother to let her find work were fading. Sarah had brought the matter up already, on several occasions, and her mother had told her with a pitiful smile that she must please herself; no mother would prevent her child from doing what they wished, however selfish that child was.

The days seemed endless to Sarah, although she didn't allow her despondency to get the upper hand. She had plenty to do—shopping, helping with the ironing and cooking, giving Mrs Twist a hand around the house, paying dutiful visits to her stepfather, listening to her mother's complaining voice. Days in which she had very little time to herself.

And a good thing too, she told herself; if she had time on her hands she would waste it thinking about Mr ter Breukel, who, she assured herself a dozen times a day, meant nothing to her. She would, in time, be able to discard her love for him. She reflected that it was probably a flash in the pan, engendered by her lack of men-friends. Probably she would have fallen in love with the first man she met, given the circumstances...

It was April now, quite warm and sunny. Sarah was in the garden, casting an eye over the tubs

she had planted in the autumn, when Mrs Twist
called her indoors.

'Yer ma wants yer, Miss Sarah. Very excited
about something.'

Mrs Holt was in her bedroom, sitting at the
dressing table, making up her pretty face.
'Sarah—get my new grey dress for me. I've had
a phone call from Dr Benson. He's bringing some
important specialist to see your stepfather. For
heaven's sake, tidy yourself, and then go and get
coffee ready. They'll be here in half an hour.'

'Didn't you say they're coming to see my stepfather?'

'Yes. But they'll want to know how *I* am. I'm
sure I'll never be the same again after that horrible
accident.' She glanced at Sarah. 'Get the coffee
ready first, Sarah, then do something to your hair.
You won't need to see them, of course, but I suppose you'll bring in the coffee.'

Sarah paused at the door. 'Mother, if you don't
want me to be seen, you could fetch the coffee
from the kitchen yourself.'

'Sarah, what a dreadful way to speak to your
mother. You know how delicate my nerves are.'
Mrs Holt touched a handkerchief to a dry eye.
'Now I'm upset.'

Sarah went away and got the tray ready, with

the best china and a little dish of assorted biscuits. She popped two into her mouth and crossed the hall to the cloakroom. The breeze in the garden had ruffled her tidy hair, and she supposed that she had better run a comb through it. She was halfway across the hall when the doorbell was rung. She glanced at the long case clock by the stairs; it was far too soon for Dr Benson and this specialist—the postman, maybe, or someone trying to make a living selling dusters at the door? She opened the door and came face to face with Dr Benson.

'Oh, hello,' said Sarah. 'You're early. Mother said half an hour.' She smiled at him, for they were old friends, and then looked past him to the youngish man standing quietly behind him.

'This is Professor Smythe. I thought it a good idea if he were to cast an eye over your stepfather. And perhaps your mother would be glad of a word?'

Sarah held out a hand. 'I'm sure Mother and my stepfather will be glad to see you. Do come in.' She led the way to the drawing room. 'I'll fetch Mother. Would you like a cup of coffee?'

'Perhaps after we have seen Mr Holt?' Dr Benson looked at the professor, who nodded. 'Ah, here is your mother.'

Mrs Holt's voice could be heard through the half-open door, wanting to know who had rung the doorbell and why hadn't Sarah told her? She sounded cross, but as she came into the room and saw the two men she smiled charmingly. 'Dr Benson, how kind of you to come...' She turned to the professor and smiled even more charmingly. 'And this is the consultant you mentioned?'

'Professor Smythe, Mrs Holt. He will examine Mr Holt and give me any necessary advice.'

'I have been so anxious about him,' said Mrs Holt, offering a hand. 'I'm sure you're terribly clever. It was such a shock—the accident, you know. I feel that I shall never completely recover.'

The professor murmured. He would have a lovely bedside manner, thought Sarah, watching him from the door and then watching the three of them go upstairs to her stepfather's room. She didn't know if her mother had told Mr Holt of the impending visit, but whether he knew or not he would be annoyed by it.

They were upstairs for a long time. Sarah, keeping the coffee hot in the kitchen, ate two more biscuits, and when they finally came downstairs, she carried the tray into the drawing room. The professor took it from her with a smile, and sat down opposite Mrs Holt, while Sarah passed round cups and the biscuits.

'Sarah, run along, dear. I'm sure you don't want to be bored with our talk. Besides, I want a little chat with these two kind men. I've made light of my troubles, but I do feel that I need professional help.'

Sarah didn't say anything, but the professor put his cup and saucer down and went to open the door for her. She looked at him as she went past. He had a kind face and was smiling.

She shared a pot of tea with Mrs Twist and, since she had nothing else to do, sat at the kitchen table chopping up vegetables for the casserole which Mrs Twist was intending to cook.

They were a long time, she thought uneasily, then looked up as the door opened and Professor Smythe came in.

Sarah jumped up. 'Have you lost your way? The drawing room's on the other side of the house—down the passage and across the hall.'

'No. No, I wish to talk to you.' He glanced at Mrs Twist and smiled, and that lady put down the knife with which she had been cutting up the meat.

'You'd best stay here,' she said. 'I've plenty to get on with upstairs.'

He opened the door for her and thanked her with another smile, and then pulled out a chair and sat down opposite Sarah.

'You really shouldn't be here in the kitchen,' said Sarah. 'I mean, you're a professor...'

'I like kitchens.' He had a pleasant voice, very quiet. 'We always have breakfast in our kitchen; it's so much easier with two small children.'

'Boys or girls?'

'One of each, soon to be joined by a third.'

'How nice... I mustn't waste your time. Did you want to tell me something? Is Mother ill?' she asked worriedly.

'Your mother is in the best of health, but I have suggested certain changes which might improve her physically and mentally.'

When Sarah gave him a questioning look he said, 'Your mother is bored; she needs a complete change in her lifestyle. Dr Benson and I have had a chat and he fully endorses my suggestion that your mother and stepfather should close the house for a period and spend time at a hotel, somewhere where your mother can enjoy something of a social life. Your stepfather can be given all the attention he wants—massage, daily visits from a nurse—for a gradual return to the full use of his leg. I suggested Bournemouth—good hotels, shops, entertainment, access to private nursing facilities. I understand that there will be no financial problems…'

Sarah opened her mouth, closed it, and shook her head. She didn't speak but her eyes looked a question.

'Your mother agrees with me that a fresh environment and new faces would be ideal, and I suggested that she would benefit greatly from meeting people about whom she knew nothing and who knew nothing of her and your stepfather. I think that it would be wise if you do not go with them, and your mother has been persuaded that this is the right thing to do.'

'I don't have to go, too? I can stay here with Mrs Twist?' Sarah beamed at him. 'For how long? You're sure Mother won't change her mind and I'd have to go, too?'

'Quite sure, and we've suggested a period of two to three months.'

He watched her face light up. A plain girl, but nice eyes, and when she smiled she looked almost beautiful. No wonder Litrik was interested in her. The things one does for one's old friends, reflected Professor Smythe.

'Dr Benson has made a most sensible suggestion,' he went on smoothly. 'Why not get a job while you are here with the housekeeper? It will fill your days, and you will meet people and earn some money.'

'I'd like that very much, but you see I'm not trained for anything. When I left school Mother wasn't very well, and she gets very upset if I suggest leaving home.'

'Then why not take this opportunity to try your hand at something? There are jobs which require little or no training, you know. I'm sure Dr Benson can advise you.'

Sarah sat up straight in her chair. 'Oh, my goodness, wouldn't it be absolutely marvellous?' She sounded like a schoolgirl, he thought, and looked like one too in her skirt and sweater. He had noticed that Mrs Holt was dressed fashionably. Either her daughter had no dress sense, or no money with which to buy pretty clothes. He had formed a low opinion of her stepfather—not a man to open a generous purse.

'Then shall we go and tell your mother that you agree with us that a short period in new surroundings will be beneficial to her health?'

Sarah said yes; he sounded exactly as a professor should sound, very sure of himself.

Her mother was talking animatedly to Dr Benson, but broke off to exclaim, 'Sarah, is this not a splendid idea of these two kind gentlemen? And your stepfather has agreed. You won't blame your poor little mother for leaving you alone for a few weeks? You will have Mrs Twist. I know that we shall return completely cured and able to resume our normal lives again.'

Sarah eyed her mother with patient tolerance. 'It's a splendid idea, Mother. I shall be quite all right here with Mrs Twist.'

'That's what I thought, dear. There must be many things you want to do, and now you will have the time.'

Sarah agreed pleasantly, and tried not to look too pleased.

The two men left presently, and her mother went to discuss their plans with her husband. So Sarah went to the kitchen and gave Mrs Twist an account of the doctor's visit, leaving out the news that she intended to go to work. Mrs Twist was a dear soul, and her staunch friend, but there was just a chance that she might inadvertently let the cat out of the bag.

Now that the decision had been taken, Mrs Holt lost no time. Hotel brochures were scanned, dates were decided upon, and a good deal of shopping was done—for a new environment needed new clothes. It was left to Sarah to search out a nursing agency who would send a nurse and a masseuse each day to the hotel, and it was she who booked rooms at a splendid hotel on the seafront. When it came to his own comfort, her stepfather spent lavishly, and just as lavishly but rather less willingly on his wife.

He was less concerned for Sarah. He arranged for expenses for the household to be paid weekly, together with Mrs Twist's wages, and in a sudden display of generosity told Sarah that if she needed money for any other reason she could ask him for it.

'As long as it's a reasonable amount,' he cautioned her. 'This is an expensive undertaking. If anyone at the office should need me urgently, refer them to me.'

Mr ter Breukel, kept up to date by his friend Professor Smythe, was satisfied. The next step would be taken by Dr Benson, primed by him after another satisfactory phone call to the hospital manager in London.

Mr ter Breukel possessed his soul in patience and waited for the next move in his scheme.

The removal to Bournemouth was almost as big an undertaking as the journey back from Holland had been. Mr Holt had a new car now, and a hired chauffeur, and between them he and Mrs Holt had a vast quantity of luggage. And the business of getting him comfortable with a leg still in a small plaster took time and the efforts of several persons. But at last he pronounced himself satisfied, Sarah's mother got in beside him, the chauffeur got behind the wheel and drove away. Sarah and Mrs Twist waved, but went unnoticed.

The pair of them went back to the kitchen, and over a pot of tea Sarah told her plans. 'Of course I have to find a job,' she explained, 'and that might take a few days. You won't mind? I'll find work where I can come home each evening. Oh, Mrs Twist, it's the chance I've always hoped for and never thought I'd get—not without running away in the middle of the night. But that wouldn't have been very practical…'

Mrs Twist pronounced the scheme a good one. 'High time a young lady like you got out and about a bit—never a moment to yourself. What'll yer do?'

'I've no idea…' But she was soon to find out.

It was two days later when Dr Benson called. Sarah was in the kitchen, working her way through the 'Jobs Vacant' columns of several newspapers. She had already searched the adverts in *The Lady* magazine, and marked several likely posts, but most of them were out of London. The local paper might be more fruitful. She looked up as Mrs Twist ushered the doctor into the kitchen and got to her feet.

'Dr Benson—is something wrong? Mother? My stepfather?'

'No, no, Sarah, my visit concerns yourself. You do remember we talked about you finding a job?' His eye fell on the pile of newspapers. 'You're looking for something? Well, unless you've arranged anything, I've heard of something you might care to try. Perhaps not quite your touch, but it would give you a start if you really want to strike out on your own.'

'Oh, I do. I'll do anything—well, not computers or typing or anything clever, and I don't think I'd be much good in a shop...'

'No skill needed for this job. Just patience and a friendly manner and an ability to stay on your feet for hours.' At her questioning look he added, 'The canteen at one of the hospitals is desperately short of staff. Serving meals, clearing away, fetching and carrying. Long hours, and shift work—twelve o'clock until eight in the evening, five days a week—but you wouldn't have to work on Saturday or Sunday. It's not much, I know, but

you would meet people, Sarah, and it seems to
me that that is something you have never had the
chance of doing, other than your mother's bridge
partners and your stepfather's business acquaintances.' He added, 'The pay's not much...'

When he told her she said, 'Not much? And I
can spend it on myself, clothes and things?'

'Of course. Look, I'll give you the phone number and you can ask for an interview. Here's the
number. Use my name as a reference and don't
go looking too smart.'

Sarah said matter-of-factly, 'I haven't any
smart clothes. And thank you very much; I shall
phone this morning.' She laughed suddenly. 'It's
the first step towards my marvellous future.'

Dr Benson agreed. He hoped that Mr ter
Breukel's schemes wouldn't go awry. He was
pushing his luck, giving her the opportunity to
savour an independent life. Would it not have
been better to have snapped her up at once and
carried her off to Holland? On second thoughts,
Dr Benson felt not. Sarah, for all her unassuming
ways, had always refused to be led, and her stepfather's dislike of her hadn't helped.

Sarah believed in striking while the iron was
hot; she phoned the moment Dr Benson had left

the house, and was given an appointment for the next morning.

It wasn't until she had entered the rather gloomy portals of the hospital that doubts assailed her. She was to be interviewed by someone called the Domestic Supervisor. She might be disliked on sight; her references might not be sufficient to please this personage. By the time Sarah had reached the door to which she had been directed, the Domestic Supervisor had become the female equivalent of an ogre!

The voice which bade her enter was small and high-pitched, and to her relief Sarah saw that her imagined ogre was a very small, very round woman, with salt and pepper hair screwed into a bun and a nice smile.

'Come in, dearie. Miss Beckwith, isn't it? Sit down while we have a little chat.'

Fifteen minutes later Sarah rose from the chair. The job was hers. She was to start on the following day at noon.

'You may find it a bit of a rush for a day or two, but the girls will help you. You'll get your dinner at two o'clock, tea at five. The canteen closes down then, until first suppers at seven o'clock, but you'll be kept busy getting them ready. Second supper is at eight o'clock, and that's when the night shift take over. Hard work, my dear, but we'll see how you get on, shall we? A week's notice on either side.'

Sarah went back to Clapham Common and told Mrs Twist all about it. They arranged their days to suit them both. 'And if by any chance my mother should ring up, would you just tell her I'm out? But I don't expect her to telephone during the day.'

'Wear comfortable shoes,' advised Mrs Twist. 'Your feet are going to kill you.'

They didn't kill her, but by the end of her shift they ached so much she thought that she would never be able to go to work the next morning. But that was in a weak moment; lying in a hot bath, after supper with Mrs Twist, she knew that of course she would go to work in the morning. What was more, she would continue to do so until she found better work.

She had enjoyed her day, she reflected, adding more hot water. Dressed in a striped cotton dress, a white pinny and a white cap, she had presented herself to the Head Counter Assistant, admitted cheerfully that she had very little idea as to what she had to do, and had been borne away by two middle-aged women who'd called her 'ducks', showed her where everything was and, when the food arrived, stood her in front of a great container of chips. 'Dole 'em out, and no need to be mean about it. A couple of spoons and a bit over. Give us a shout if yer in a fix.'

She had managed very well; it seemed that everyone ate chips, and some of the housemen on duty, unable to get to their own dining room, had had two helpings. And everyone had been so friendly, asking her name, making little jokes. Though it had shaken her a bit when she had been dishing out chips to a bunch of nurses, standing there with their plates and discussing an accident case which had been admitted that morning. Sarah had tried not to hear the details. Nurses, she'd thought, must be wonderful people—able to take the sight of broken bones and blood everywhere, and still pile their plates with a wholesome dinner....

The only part of her day which she hadn't enjoyed was coming home. It was quite a long journey to and from the hospital, and although the April evenings were light, by the time she'd got off the bus evening had closed in, and the five-minute walk to her home was through more or less deserted streets. But that was something to which she would become accustomed; she had never had the chance to be out on her own in the evenings, only in her mother's company, or going with her and her stepfather to some function when he considered it good for his public image to be seen as a kindly stepfather and devoted husband.

By the end of the week her feet had accustomed themselves to standing for long periods, she had learnt her way around the canteen, made friends with the other girls and was on nodding terms with the hungry hordes who came to eat. They were always in a hurry, either on duty, or off duty and hurrying to get away. She exchanged rather guarded chat with anyone who lingered to talk for a moment, and took care to note which of the ward sisters liked a salad instead of vegetables.

She was always famished by two o'clock, but none of them wasted much time over their meal; there was tea to get ready, the first of the staff would start trickling in at about half past three, and after a brief pause there would be a second round of tea...and then a rush to get suppers on the counter.

But she had enjoyed it. She had met more people in a week than she had in all the years since she left school, and she had a pay packet in her pocket. What mattered most was that she had been so busy that she had been able to banish Mr ter Breukel from her thoughts for minutes at a time…

She took Mrs Twist out to supper on Saturday evening, to a small restaurant in the High Street, and Mrs Twist, in a hat suitable to the occasion, ate her way through the three-course meal and pronounced it as well cooked as she herself could have done. 'A real treat,' she declared, 'eating something I haven't 'ad to cook meself.'

On Sunday Mrs Twist went to spend the day with her sister; Sarah washed her hair and her smalls, did her nails, read the Sunday papers from end to end and thought about Mr ter Breukel. Mrs Twist safely back, they had their supper and went to bed.

'I shall never see him again,' said Sarah, looking at the moon through a sudden rush of tears. She wiped them away at once, told herself not to be a sentimental fool and got into bed.

It was halfway through her second week, as she was on the point of going down to the basement to start another day's work, that the lift door beside the staircase opened and Mr ter Breukel got out.

He had seen her, of course. 'Ah, Sarah, how nice to see you again.'

Her heart was beating so loudly he must surely

be able to hear it. She had gone very red, and then pale, and hadn't said a word.

She found her breath. 'I shall be late,' she told him, and flew down the stairs.

He stood watching her race away, smiling to himself. She reminded him of the White Rabbit in *Alice in Wonderland*. He glanced at his watch; she would be off duty at eight o'clock. He had a clinic that afternoon, and post-operative patients to see later, but he would be free by then.

Everyone in the canteen acknowledged that Sarah was a good worker, willing to help out and not afraid of hard work, but today she surpassed herself: she served the meals, cleaned the tables and laid them again, swabbed the floor where someone had upset a bottle of tomato sauce, even offered to stay on for an extra hour or two as they were short-handed that day. An offer which wasn't accepted.

'You've worked yourself to death,' it was pointed out to her. 'You'll go off at eight sharp and no nonsense.'

All the same she was held up at the last minute by one of the staff coming in for sandwiches for the operating theatre staff, so that when she got to the changing room everyone else had gone.

She'd had some half-formed idea that if she

went out of the hospital in a bunch with the other girls and saw Mr ter Breukel there would be no need to speak to him. Indeed, she could pretend not to see him... Now she would have to hope that he would be gone or, better still, in Theatre, operating.

She changed rapidly and climbed the stairs to the ground floor, taking the last few steps with all the wariness of a rabbit coming out of its burrow. The corridor was empty; she skimmed down it and saw that there was no one in the entrance hall. It was a relief not to meet him, although she ached with disappointment. Just that one glimpse of him coming out of the lift had been enough to undo all her sternly suppressed feelings since she had last seen him.

She called goodnight to the porter and pushed open the heavy doors. April had turned contrary; it was cold and windy and heavy clouds threatened rain. She paused to button her coat collar, and found herself face to face with Mr ter Breukel.

For the second time that day she lost her tongue, staring up at his face, trying to think of something suitable to say. Hello was a bit too familiar; good evening sounded all wrong. 'It's not a very nice evening,' said Sarah.

'Very unpleasant,' he agreed cheerfully. 'Shall we have a meal out, or go to your place?'

'But they're not there—Mother and my stepfather. They're in Bournemouth recuperating.'

'Indeed? Then let us find a restaurant.'

'No, no, I can't. I mean, it's very kind of you to ask me, but Mrs Twist's waiting for me with supper. She'll wonder where I am.'

'Then let us go to Clapham Common and perhaps you will invite me to supper?'

Sarah, mindful of her manners, invited him, then added, 'Why are you here?'

He popped her into the car and got in beside her. 'I come here to work fairly frequently. You're working at the hospital?'

'Yes. Dr Benson and a Professor Smythe came to see my stepfather, and they thought it would do him and mother good to go away for a while. So they're in Bournemouth, and since I'm at home with Mrs Twist Dr Benson suggested that I got a job.' She added defiantly, 'I serve the meals at the canteen.'

'You enjoy that? Meeting new faces, making friends? You must have missed that, Sarah?'

'Yes. When Mother and my stepfather come back I shall move out—find a room, get a better job if I can, train for something.'

She glanced at his hands on the wheel and looked away quickly. They were large, beautifully kept, and they reminded her how very much she loved him.

He parked the car outside the house and went in with her. Mrs Twist, coming into the hall, gave him a shrewd look as Sarah introduced them.

'Pleased ter meet yer, I'm sure,' she told him, and took the hand that he held out. 'Staying for supper? It's steak and kidney pie and apple turnovers. Miss Sarah, you go into the drawing room and have a drink while I lay the table.'

Sarah frowned. 'Mrs Twist—it's all ready in the kitchen, isn't it?'

'I like kitchens,' said Mr ter Breukel, and smiled at Mrs Twist.

'Well, then, if you say so, sir.'

'I'll get the sherry,' said Sarah, and went to the drawing room.

Mr ter Breukel followed her, took the bottle from her, dropped a kiss on her cheek and said quietly, 'We must find time to talk, but not just yet.'

He smiled down at her. 'The pie smells delicious. Come and tell me about your job while we eat.'

CHAPTER FIVE

MRS TWIST was at first reluctant to eat her supper with Sarah and Mr ter Breukel. 'I know me place,' she had said sharply, but then under his kindly eye she had changed her mind.

'Well, if that's what you want, sir. I should've thought you'd want ter be on yer own, like, with Miss Sarah.'

'Ah, but you see Sarah and I have all the time in the world to be together.'

A remark which caused Sarah to give him a surprised look, which he met with a bland smile. He was putting Mrs Twist at her ease, she reflected.

The meal was a success; Mrs Twist was a great talker, and Mr ter Breukel was adept at maintaining a conversation, and if Sarah was rather silent no one noticed. They didn't hurry over it, and when it was eaten Mr ter Breukel accepted Mrs Twist's offer of a cup of tea with every appearance of pleasure, drinking the powerful brew with evident appreciation before helping to clear the table and then making his departure, saying all the right things to Mrs Twist, bidding Sarah a friendly goodnight, and driving away without fuss.

While Mrs Twist washed up Sarah set the table for breakfast.

'Now there's a man for you,' said Mrs Twist. 'A real gent, even if 'e is a bit of a la-di-da. Fancy me eating me supper with the likes of 'im. Whatever would your ma say?'

'Well, she won't know,' said Sarah. 'I shan't tell, and you won't either.'

'Lor' bless you, no. Known 'im long?'

'Well, I don't really know him very well. He looked after my stepfather at the Arnhem hospital; he's a Consultant there too, as well as over here.'

'A bit lonely over here on his own?' Mrs Twist was dying of curiosity.

'I don't suppose so. He's well known at the hospital, I think, and he must have lots of friends.'

'Well, I dare say you'll see a bit more of 'im while 'e's 'ere.'

'I doubt it,' said Sarah. 'The senior staff don't come to the canteen.'

But they were in the same building, she reflected, and if she took the long way round to the canteen she might see him.

During the next few days, though, there wasn't so much as a glimpse of him. You wouldn't think, thought Sarah, that such a large man could become so invisible. And he *was* in the hospital; dishing dinners to a group of staff nurses, she couldn't help but overhear their gossip. Mr ter Breukel, it seemed, had won the hearts of all the nurses who had had the good fortune to encounter him.

Sarah swallowed a sharp pang of jealousy and told herself not to be a fool. The sooner he went back to Holland the better, she decided. Life would never be the same again without him, but at least she could make a new life for herself now that she had work. She wasn't sure what would be the next step, but she was determined that it would be up, taking her away from Clapham Common. A month or two more working in the canteen, and then she would apply for the night shift; the pay was better. Several of the girls had rooms close to the hospital; she would do the same, save what money she could, and look for a better job.

She told herself that she was happy and content, that the future was exciting; she would become a successful career woman. She had no idea how this was to be achieved, but the thought of it made her days bearable as each successive one went by without a sight of Mr ter Breukel.

And when at last she saw him again it was disastrous. It was the end of her shift, and, last as
usual, she climbed the stairs with one of the
housemen who had been to the canteen to gobble
a hasty supper. He was a nice lad, and lonely, and
so was she. They dawdled up the staircase, making the most of a few moments of idle conversation, not really interested in each other, only
glad to talk to someone.

They lingered on the top step, reluctant to go
their separate ways, and Mr ter Breukel, intent on
whisking Sarah out for a meal, came to an abrupt
silent halt. Sarah was laughing and the young doctor laughed too, enjoying the small interlude, and
instead of going straight to the wards he turned
to walk to the entrance with her, still talking.

It was then that Sarah saw Mr ter Breukel,
walking towards them, and she paused in mid-
sentence, smiling her delight at the sight of him.

A pity he didn't know that; he went past them
with a brief, unsmiling nod and turned into the
consultants' room, shutting the door firmly behind
him.

Sarah parted with her companion in the entrance hall, hardly aware of how she had got
there. Mr ter Breukel could have smiled, even
wished her good evening. Perhaps he didn't care

to be on speaking terms with a member of the domestic staff. She dismissed that thought as unworthy of him, left the hospital and walked to the bus stop.

There was no reason, she told herself, why he *should* speak to her. He was doubtless a busy man; moreover, he must have many friends in London. Taking her home the other evening had been an impulsive gesture which he clearly didn't intend to repeat.

Mr ter Breukel closed the door gently, quelling a desire to slam it or wrench it open again and pluck Sarah away from the cheerful young man with her. He would like to shake her until her teeth rattled. Better still, he would like to wrap his arms round her and kiss her.

He did none of these things, but went and sat down in one of the leather chairs arranged round the sombre room. He had no reason to be angry; he had planned this deliberately so that Sarah would have a chance to be independent and meet people. Well, his plan was working. It was early days, though, he reminded himself. He must have patience still, leave her free to choose her friends, plan her future. He was deeply in love with her, but he wanted her to be happy even at the cost of his own happiness.

So the best part of another week went by; he would be returning to Holland soon now...

As for Sarah, she felt herself to be a seasoned worker now, with little time to brood. Only at the weekends, alone in the house while Mrs Twist visited friends or family, did she admit to herself that life wasn't very satisfactory. It would be better, of course, once she could forget Mr ter Breukel...

One Friday evening, her pay packet in her pocket, she left the hospital rather later than usual. There had been no one in the cloakroom to tell her that there was a rowdy demonstration over something or other making its way towards the streets around the hospital, and the porter, deep in his evening paper, hadn't seen her slip out of the doors. The other canteen staff had left in a bunch, so he had warned them, thinking that they were all there. It was only as the doors swung back that he looked up and caught a glimpse of Sarah, hurrying away. Too late to go after her, he decided, and someone would have told her to avoid the main roads.

Mr ter Breukel, on the point of departure, having done a ward round and taken a look at his operation cases for that day, spoke to the ward sister, wishing her good evening and a pleasant weekend. She remarked, 'I expect you've heard that there's some kind of demonstration coming this way, sir? Most of it is peaceful enough, but there are the usual rowdies roaming around, making trouble. The staff going off duty have been warned to avoid them.'

Mr ter Breukel glanced at the clock. Ten minutes past eight. Sarah would have left or be on the point of leaving. He bade Sister a courteous goodnight and went down to the entrance hall.

The porter put his paper down and stood up. Mr ter Breukel had that effect upon people, although he was unconscious of it.

'The canteen staff?' he asked. 'Have they left?'

'Yes, a minute or two after eight o'clock. I passed on the warning that they should keep clear of any disturbances.'

'And no one has left since?'

'Well, now you mention it, sir, someone slipped out while I had my back turned. She was halfway across the forecourt before I heard the door close.'

'You have no idea who it was?'

'No, sorry, sir, only she wasn't very big and she had a red umbrella.' He added unnecessarily, 'It's raining, sir.'

Mr ter Breukel thanked him politely and went out into the drizzle, walking fast. He knew which bus stop Sarah used, and he had seen the red umbrella before. He searched the queue there. There was no sign of her; she was already on her way home, then. He turned away and saw a red umbrella a long way ahead of him, and at the same time several groups of noisy youths marching arm-in-arm on the pavement, pushing aside all the people.

He lengthened his stride, ignoring the catcalls, pushing and shoving. The pavement was almost empty of other people, who were prudently taking cover in doorways and shops. Sarah was in plain sight, and why she was ignoring the fracas around her was something he couldn't understand—until he saw that she was with someone, another woman, and that they were both burdened with shopping bags.

There were some side roads lined by small brick houses, their doors opening onto the pavement. He saw Sarah turn into one such road and reached the corner of it only a few yards behind her. The road was empty save for three youths running from its other end, swooping down on her and her companion, yelling and shouting. The woman dropped her shopping bags and struggled to open the door of a house, but she dropped the key from a shaking hand as the three youths rushed at them.

Sarah furled her umbrella and poked the nearest boy in the ribs, then she thumped his companion and would have done the same for the third, but he caught it and tore it from her hand, waved it wildly and swung it down...

It didn't reach its mark; Mr ter Breukel swept Sarah aside with one arm, lifted the youth by his coat collar and set him down in a sprawling heap on the pavement, then sent the other two tumbling after him.

They stared up at him; he might look like a gentleman, but he was certainly a giant, and for all they knew a prizefighter in his best suit out for a stroll. They edged themselves backwards, scrambled to their feet and rushed away.

Mr ter Breukel hadn't said a word; he wasn't breathing fast either. He stooped, picked up the key and handed it to the woman, and then, since she was still all of a tremble, took it from her, opened the door and stood aside for her to go in. He handed in her shopping bags too, assuring her that she was now quite safe, then brushed aside her thanks, waiting patiently while she thanked Sarah at some length and at last closed her door.

Only then did he turn to Sarah, standing rather quiet and pale beside him.

'Much as I commend your bravery, Sarah, I must beg you never to risk your safety again—I cannot keep an eye on you all the time...'

'Keep an eye on me?' Her voice was rather shrill, what with indignation and delayed fright. 'I haven't seen you for days.'

Mr ter Breukel sighed. 'No, and for several good reasons. The answer is for us to get married.'

'Well, you may if you wish,' snapped Sarah. 'I'll have to wait until someone asks me.'

'If you would just listen, you silly girl. I *am* asking you.'

She looked at him as though he had lost his wits; the drizzle had ceased, there was even a patch or two of blue sky, but the wind was cold and she shivered, as much with the chilliness as the shock of his words.

'You're asking me?'

He was leaning against the door; now he drew her to stand beside him and put an arm around her shoulders.

'Yes, I am, but let me explain.' He paused, before going on carefully, 'It had occurred to me that we would be happy together as man and wife, but I felt—still do feel—that you should first have the opportunity of finding your feet away from home. You have had no chance to do so, have you? You would have continued to live at home, tied to your mother's every wish and whim, disliked by and disliking your stepfather, gradually losing heart and becoming resigned. You see, Sarah, other girls might run away, but you have too tender a heart. But now you have discovered independence, and perhaps you want to spread your wings?'

She found her voice. 'You want to marry me? But you don't know anything about me, do you? And—and you don't love me...'

'Have I not said that I believe we could be happy together? And if you wished to have a career of some sort I wouldn't stand in your way; you would be free to follow your own interests.'

She stared into his calm face. He sounded so kind and so reasonable, as though getting married was a simple act, shorn of all doubts. And his argument made sense too. But it wouldn't be simple at all, she reflected. She loved him, but he hadn't said that he loved her, and if she married him she had no wish to be anything other than his wife, behaving like other wives: being at home when he got home, seeing that he had nourishing meals and spotless linen, listening with a sympathetic ear to him after a hard day's work. And children—she wanted children—and she wanted him to love her...

She said slowly, 'I've never been asked to marry anyone before, so I'm not sure what to say.'

He smiled then. 'Then don't say anything. We will go back to the hospital and I'll drive you home. I shan't stay. Think about it as much as you wish, and when you're ready we'll talk again.'

He stopped himself just in time from kissing her, which was a pity, for it would have put an end to their misunderstanding. Instead he took her arm and walked her back through the almost quiet streets. There were a few people standing about, shopkeepers sweeping up broken glass, car owners examining damaged cars, the odd scuffle as police collected up the remnants of the street gangs.

Sarah was far too busy with her thoughts to notice any of these things. She got into the car and sat without speaking until they reached her home.

Mr ter Breukel got out, opened her door and stood beside her on the pavement.

'You said that you haven't seen me, Sarah. But do remember that I am always there.' He rang the doorbell, waited until Mrs Twist opened the door, and then went back to his car.

Sarah watched him drive away. She longed to marry him, but she wouldn't. He had said that they would be happy together, but supposing that he met a woman he loved? What then?

She followed Mrs Twist into the kitchen, and over supper gave her a watered-down version of the evening.

'A blessing that dear man went after you,' said Mrs Twist. 'A pity 'e couldn't stay for 'is supper.'

Sarah remembered then that she hadn't even offered him a cup of coffee. He had said that he couldn't stay, but she could at least have offered something.

She went to bed presently, and lay awake a long time, imagining life as his wife, until she went to sleep, only to wake in the morning knowing that she was going to refuse him.

She must think up some really good reason—a career in something or other—computers. She had been told that once one had mastered them, there were unending opportunities—super jobs, marvellous salaries, meeting important people. She would find out as much as possible about them so that she would sound convincing. And he would be secretly relieved, she felt sure.

She rehearsed several suitable speeches on her way to work on Monday; she must be ready to give him his answer when next they met—perhaps not that day, but certainly before the week was out. Satisfied that she couldn't improve upon them, she worked even harder than usual in her canteen, outwardly cheerful but with a heart grieving for what might have been.

She didn't see Mr ter Breukel that day, nor the next, and when she did see him again her carefully worded speeches went unspoken.

The letter which had come by that morning's post from her mother had for the moment driven all other thoughts out of her head. She had sat down to read it after breakfast, while Mrs Twist went to the shops. She had read it, and then read it again, not quite believing it.

The letter wasn't long, and a good deal of it was taken up with instructions. Mrs Holt wrote to say that they had decided to move to Bournemouth; they liked the town, they had made many friends, and they had seen a delightful house close to the sea. Her stepfather, went on Mrs Holt, intended to more or less retire, so he would need to go to London only very infrequently. The house at Clapham Common was to be sold, and Sarah and Mrs Twist were to remain in it until a buyer had been found, after which they could travel to Bournemouth. There would be no need for Mrs Holt to return for the moment. Sarah could deal with the estate agents and any prospective buyers, and she and Mrs Twist could start to pack away any silver and china not in use, together with her and Mr Holt's clothes.

Sarah, reading the letter yet again, had looked in vain for some comment as to how she and Mrs Twist might feel about it; her mother had taken it for granted that they would be happy to fall in with her plans. And Sarah was to tell Mrs Twist...

She'd decided to wait and tell the housekeeper when she got home that evening; they could discuss it at their leisure. Perhaps Mrs Twist would choose to go to Bournemouth, after all. But her relations and friends were scattered in and around London, so she might not want to. As for herself, Sarah knew that she would never go to Bournemouth.

But perhaps here was the solution to her problem; she could tell Mr ter Breukel that her mother and stepfather were moving from the Clapham Common house and wished her to join them. She would be able to find a job there, she would tell him, and meet any number of people. She wouldn't be telling a lie, she assured herself, just altering the truth a little, and as soon as he had gone back to Holland she would find other work.

It shouldn't be too hard; she would get a reference from the hospital, and she had been saving her wages. Not to marry him would break her heart, but even worse was the thought of marrying a man who didn't love her. Oh, he liked her, they were friends, and he had been unfailingly kind each time they had met, but that was no foundation for a marriage.

She rehearsed a number of now suitable speeches, and then, when they did meet, forgot them all.

They came face to face in the entrance hall, she on her way home, he on the way to check on his patients from his morning list in Theatre. It was no place in which to have a lengthy talk but he stopped in front of her, blocking her path with his bulk.

'Are you going home?' he asked without preamble. 'Because if you are may I come and see you later?'

Sarah said quickly, 'Can you spare five minutes now? I'll be very quick. I've had a letter from my mother. They're selling the house at Clapham Common and have bought one in Bournemouth. They want me to go and live with them there. It's a bit of a surprise, but it's like an answer, isn't it? I mean, I'll be able to start afresh, get a job, meet people.'

Mr ter Breukel's face showed none of his feelings; he said in a level voice, 'That is what you want, Sarah? You believe that this is really your chance to change your life, become independent? You would be happy?'

'Oh, yes,' said Sarah, and prayed for forgiveness for such a whopping lie. 'So you see there's no need for you to marry me.' She swallowed the lump in her throat. 'Thank you very much for asking me.'

He smiled. It was a bitter smile, but his voice was friendly enough. 'I must be glad that your future has become so promising. I'm sure you will make a success of whatever you choose to do.'

Sarah said, 'Yes, so there's no need for you to come this evening.' She looked up into his expressionless face. 'I wouldn't have liked you to have come all the way to Clapham just to hear that I'd decided to change my mind.'

He agreed gravely. So she *had* intended to marry him, had she? And now she had changed her mind. He wondered why. Something he would find out.

They parted in a friendly fashion, going their separate ways, he to his patients, thrusting all thoughts of her from his mind for the moment, she to stand in a long queue for a bus, longing to get home so that she could go somewhere quiet and cry until she had no tears left.

She saw him two days later, passing him on her way to the basement stairs. He stopped, wished her a friendly good afternoon, and told her that he would be returning to Holland on the following day.

Sarah put out a hand and managed a smile. 'I hope you have a good journey. Will you be in Holland for a long time?'

'Three weeks—a month. Then back here very briefly. You will probably be gone by then.'

'Yes, I suppose so. Please give my love to Suzanne. And thank you for all your kindness.'

There was really nothing more to say. 'I'll be late,' she said, and raced down the stairs. Well, that's over, she told herself, I must get away from here before he comes back. Brave words, drowned in unshed tears.

Mrs Twist, informed of her employers' plans, had refused to go to Bournemouth; her family and friends were scattered around London and that was where she belonged. She'd agreed to stay at home until it was sold.

Mrs Holt had written Sarah another long letter demanding that she went to Bournemouth as quickly as possible so that she might accompany her mother on the shopping expeditions necessary for the new house. She was to pack up the ornaments and silver, and their clothes, and oversee the removal of a good deal of the furniture.

'Two weeks should be ample time for you to see to this,' the letter had said. 'We shall expect you no later than that.'

Mr ter Breukel had gone; Sarah gave in her notice and wrote and told her mother that she would see to the packing up of the things she wished for, and arrange for the furniture to be collected, but that she herself would be staying in London. 'I have a good job and somewhere to live,' she wrote recklessly, 'and I intend to become independent. I am sure that you and my stepfather will be very happy in your new home, but please understand that I would like to lead a life of my own…'

Naturally enough, this letter caused a flood of telephone calls and indignant letters, to which Sarah replied firmly. 'It isn't that I don't love you, Mother, as you suggest, but I do wish for my own life, and you must agree with me that my step-father will be glad not to have me in the house. Once you are settled in, with a good housekeeper and everything to your liking, I'm sure that you will see the good sense of this. Later on, when I get my holidays, I will come and visit you.'

Mrs Twist, shocked at first at Sarah's decision, agreed that it was a chance which might never occur again. 'Just as long as yer get a good job…'

'Oh, I shall,' said Sarah airily. 'I'll stay here until I do. It may take a week or two until I find something I would like to do.'

Mrs Twist studied her face. 'Let's hope so. You look peaked, Miss Sarah, and you've got thin. That job at the hospital was too hard work.'

It had certainly been that, agreed Sarah silently, but Litrik had been there too. She thought about him constantly, and now she would never see him again she called him Litrik. It didn't matter any more; he had really gone out of her life, and now she had left the canteen there were no more snatches of gossip to be gleaned about him.

She began looking for work, setting about it in a dogged fashion, answering anything which sounded suitable for her meagre talents. But she had no luck; her letters were ignored, or she was told the job had been filled, and the few interviews she went to were unsuccessful. She had so few skills, and serving in a canteen, however good her reference was, wasn't enough.

Finally she found work, filling shelves at a supermarket. It was part-time, from half past seven in the morning until noon, and it was work she could do without needing anything other than an ability to work hard and quickly and to be honest. It was only a short bus ride from her home too, and although the wages weren't much she was able to save almost all of her pay packet since she was still living at home.

But there was a prospective buyer for the house, and she would need to earn more money if she had to find a bedsitter. She became a little thinner, and a little paler, and muddled in with her worries was the constant image of Litrik.

Sarah had been working at the supermarket for a week when Mr ter Breukel returned to London.

And, being a man very much in love despite the hopelessness of the situation, he went straight to the hospital; he wanted to be sure that she was still intent on going to Bournemouth. He had no intention of giving up until she actually left London; indeed he had no intention of giving up even then.

He found his way to the Domestic Supervisor's office, exchanged civilities, and enquired if Sarah Beckwith was still working on the same shift.

The supervisor managed not to look surprised. Whatever next? A senior consultant seeking the whereabouts of one of the girls in the canteen? All the same, she answered him readily enough.

'Sarah? She left us, let me see, about three weeks ago. A good worker, too; I was sorry to see her go, sir.'

He thanked her pleasantly and went back to his car, then made the slow journey through the rush-hour traffic to Clapham Common. It was still early morning; if Sarah was at home he would have no compunction in getting her out of her bed. For all he knew she might be on the point of leaving.

The house, when he reached it, looked forlorn, and as he waited for someone to answer his knock he noticed that the downstairs windows lacked curtains. But someone was there; he heard footsteps in the hall and a moment later Mrs Twist opened the door.

'Lor' bless me, sir, and here was me thinking I'd never see you again.'

She stood aside for him to go in and he saw that the hall carpet had been taken up and that there were pale squares on the walls where the pictures had hung.

'Sarah has gone to Bournemouth, Mrs Twist?'

'No, sir, and never meant to. 'Ad a bit of a do with her ma, told 'er she'd got a good job here and meant to stay.' Mrs Twist snorted. 'Good job—she's working part-time at the supermarket in the High Street, filling shelves. Goes in the morning early and finishes at midday. And what she'll do in a week's time when the new owners move in, I don't know.'

Mr ter Breukel frowned. 'She told me she was going to live with her mother and stepfather... Where is this supermarket?'

'Go left at the end of the road and then take the second turning on the right; that'll bring you to it. There's a car park.'

He smiled suddenly. 'We shall be back shortly, Mrs Twist...'

Mrs Twist's nose twitched at the scent of romance. '*We*, sir?'

'Yes, Mrs Twist.'

The supermarket was crowded with shoppers. Mr ter Breukel found an assistant and asked to be taken to the Manager. Presently he found himself in a small crowded office with a harassed-looking man at the desk.

'If I might have a word,' began Mr ter Breukel, assuming what could only be described as his best bedside manner. Ten minutes later they left the office together, threading their way to the back of the place where the manager opened a door and invited him to go in.

'Will you need to see Miss Beckwith again?' asked Mr ter Breukel.

'No, there's no need. This is all very unusual, but in the circumstances...'

They shook hands, and Mr ter Breukel went in and shut the door behind him. Sarah was unpacking tomato soup, stacking the tins on a small trolley. She didn't turn round when she heard the door close.

'This is the last lot, when you're ready.'

She turned round then, and saw him. It was as though someone had lighted her pale face with a soft glow, and he allowed himself a huge sigh of relief.

'Oh,' said Sarah, 'how did you get here? Who told you? Why are you here anyway?'

He said with commendable calm, 'Hello, Sarah. I came in my car. Mrs Twist told me where to find you, and I've come to take you home.'

She said in a shaky voice, 'Well, I can't come yet. It's only half past ten.'

'You've resigned. I have seen the manager; you're free to leave now.'

Her mouth fell open. 'Resigned? But I've only been here a week, and I need a job.'

'No, you don't. But let us not stand here arguing. If you will get your coat I'll drive you back, then we can talk.'

'What about?'

'Us.'

She could see that there would be no arguing about it. Meekly she took off her overall, found her coat and went with him to his car. They drove the short distance without saying a word. Sarah felt as though she had been hit on the head and had become delirious, while he was perfectly calm and relaxed.

Mrs Twist made coffee and they sat in the kitchen, the only room in the house that still held any comfort. Mr ter Breukel ate all the biscuits, since he had missed his breakfast, and listened sympathetically to Mrs Twist's problems until Sarah, unable to sit there any longer wondering what was to happen next, murmured something about packing the china. All nonsense, of course, but it got her out of the room.

Mr ter Breukel paused long enough to thank Mrs Twist for his coffee and went after her, to find her in the dining room at the back of the house, which was now quite empty, smelling slightly of damp and emptiness. He shut the door after him and crossed the bare boards, and turned her round to face him.

'Before we say anything else, let us get one thing quite clear. I love you, Sarah, and I want to marry you. And if you would just throw your odd notions out of the window and learn to love me a little, I believe that we will be extremely happy together.'

He put his arms around her and pulled her close. 'I fell in love with you when I saw you first. I've told you that, but I'll tell you again…'

'You didn't tell me that you loved me.'

'No, I wanted you to be free to choose.' He kissed the top of her head. 'You told me that you were going to Bournemouth, and I thought you had chosen.'

'I didn't know you loved me, did I? Oh, Litrik, I love you too, only I've been so silly.'

'My darling girl, never that. At cross purposes, perhaps.' He wrapped her even closer and began to kiss her…

Presently, Sarah asked, 'How long will you be here in London?'

'A week only. You can stay here? No, that's unthinkable.' He thought for a moment, then kissed her once more. 'I have it. I have a little house in a village in Somerset; you shall go there, and Mrs Twist shall go with you if she would like that. We can be married there—the church is small and beautiful. I'll ask Suzanne to come over and keep you company. I'll have to go back to Arnhem for a couple of days, but I'll get a special licence and we'll marry the moment I come back.'

Sarah said, 'I haven't anything to wear.'

'That's easily dealt with. Am I going too fast for you, my dearest?'

'Yes, but I rather like it.' She stretched up to kiss him, to lend weight to her words. 'Of course there are all kinds of problems. Mother…?'

'We'll drive down and tell her. I'm free on Sunday.'

'She'll be angry.'

'I'll be with you, darling.'

They went out to lunch then, taking Mrs Twist with them, who was thrilled to bits at the idea of the wedding and equally delighted to go with Sarah to Somerset.

By the end of the meal Litrik had everything arranged. He would take her and Mrs Twist straight from Bournemouth to his country home, they would see the rector, and there would be no need for Sarah to return to London. And as for Mrs Twist, she had no doubt that she could get a nephew to mind the house while she was away. He left after lunch, and Sarah went back to the house with Mrs Twist and sat in the kitchen, wrapped in dreams.

It all went exactly as planned. Her mother had been angry, and then peevish, and Sarah, with Litrik beside her, had listened a little sadly, for it was apparent that her mother regarded her as an unpaid companion who would have to be replaced. Whatever Litrik had had to say to her stepfather had been brief. He'd refused to come to their wedding, but when Litrik had suggested that he would send a car to take her mother to ceremony, she'd agreed to go. 'I hope it's a decent affair,' she'd said, 'and not some hole-and-corner ceremony.'

They had left then, and driven up to Somerset to the small village where Litrik had his house. A nice, solid old house, not too large, with a lovely garden and open country at its back. He had a housekeeper there, a widow lady who lived in the village. She had opened the door to them with a warm smile, and a moment later a door had opened and Suzanne had rushed to meet them.

'I'm here until the wedding. It's Litrik's idea; I hope you're glad. We're going shopping...'

Litrik had left them then, and driven back to London. That evening he'd made a number of phone calls. After all, what were old friends for? Everything had gone according to plan. The rector had been helpful, the business of getting the licence was well in hand.

Litrik slept the sleep of a contented man, emptied his head of everything but his work each day, and only each evening did he phone Sarah.

Sarah got up early on her wedding day, and went to look out of the window. It was going to be good weather: blue sky and warm sunshine. And Litrik would be coming. The week had been restful and pleasant, for Suzanne was a good com-

panion. They had shopped, and Suzanne had insisted on buying a white dress and a little veil. It
was a very simple dress, but it suited her, and
presently she went to her room to put it on. She
was still in her dressing gown when Litrik
knocked and came in.

He caught her close and kissed her. 'Mrs Twist
is shocked. I'm not supposed to see you until we
meet at church.' He took two cases from a pocket.
'There has been no time. We'll have to be engaged for an hour or so.' He slipped a sapphire
and diamond ring on her finger and then opened
the other case, saying, 'Pearls for my bride.'

He saw the tears in her eyes. 'My darling, don't
cry.'

'I'm not. I'm just so happy.' She smiled then.
'Litrik, I don't know anything—will someone
give me away? And where are we going afterwards, or may we stay here? And will the church
be empty?'

He stooped to kiss her once more. 'Dr Benson
is giving you away.'

He had gone again before she could ask any
more questions. 'It's all topsy-turvy,' she told her
reflection in the mirror as she arranged her veil
just so. 'The bride's mother usually does everything and the bridegroom just turns up.'

Presently she found herself in the church porch, a bouquet of white roses in her hand and Dr Benson beside her. When they entered the church it wasn't empty at all. There was her mother, in a magnificent hat, there was Mrs Twist and Litrik's housekeeper, and there was Suzanne and the nice Professor Smythe. There were others too, friends of Litrik, she supposed, and people from the village.

She was suddenly so happy that she wanted to sing and dance, only of course she couldn't, not in this beautiful little church, with the organ playing softly and the rector waiting to marry them. And Litrik, dear Litrik, turning to look at her as she reached his side, a look so full of love that she caught her breath.

The rector began, 'Dearly beloved…' And Sarah thought, Oh, how exactly right, and slipped her hand into Litrik's. She felt his firm clasp, knowing that his hand would always be there when she needed it. She looked at the rector then, and he saw that she, whom he had thought of as a rather plain girl, was beautiful.

THE MAN SHE'LL MARRY
by
Carole Mortimer

Carole Mortimer has a long-standing reputation as one of the most popular Mills & Boon® authors. Readers love her likeable heroines and strong, charismatic heroes, so it's not surprising that over 40 million copies of her books have been distributed internationally. She says, 'I was born in England, the youngest of three children—I have two older brothers. I started writing in 1978, and have now written 100 books for Mills & Boon. I have four sons, Matthew, Joshua, Timothy and Peter, and a bearded collie dog called Merlyn. I'm in a very happy relationship with Peter senior; we're best friends as well as lovers, which is probably the best recipe for a successful relationship. We live on the Isle of Man.'

Recent titles by Carole Mortimer:

To Be a Bridegroom, March 1999
To Be a Husband, February 1999
To Woo a Wife, January 1999

CHAPTER ONE

'Is YOUR mother at home?'

Merry stared at the man who stood on the door-step. She knew she was being rude; her 'mother' had taught her all the necessary social niceties. But, looking the way this man did, he had to be used to women staring at him. Dani would have described him as 'drop-dead gorgeous', and for the first time Merry understood exactly what she meant by that phrase; this man had to set female hearts pounding, pulses racing, wherever he went!

'Is Dani anything like you?'

The second question was fired at her before she'd even had chance to formulate an answer to the first one. It had been a long day, and she had only got in a short time ago, though long enough to have quickly changed into an old pair of black denims Dani had outgrown some years before, and a sloppy green jumper that hung loosely down to mid-thigh. Not exactly the height of fashion, but she was comfortable.

At least she had been, until faced with the elegance of her visitor. This man, well over six feet

159

in height, with his 'drop-dead gorgeous' good
looks—slightly overlong blond hair, a face that
looked hewn from granite, eyes a deep blue, nose
long and arrogant, mouth sensual above a
squarely challenging jaw—wore his own designer-label clothes with a complete disregard for
those labels, or for how well his blue jacket and
pale blue shirt emphasised the width of his shoulders and the narrowness of his waist, his blue
jeans simply adding to his rugged handsomeness.
Dani's cast-offs, which were slightly too big at
that, did not do the same for her own appearance!

He frowned at her now, although the laughter
lines beside his eyes and mouth said he wasn't
always this serious. '*Is* your mother at home?' he
persisted.

'No,' she answered him honestly, intrigued in
spite of herself. Oh, not by his looks; good looks
alone had never impressed her. Well, only the
once. And she had learnt bitterly from the experience. No, what intrigued her about this particular man was that he obviously knew of Dani but
he had no idea what Dani actually looked like…!

Because Dani was nothing like Merry. Her own
long hair was dark, almost black, whereas Dani's
was a riot of blonde curls, and Dani's eyes were
brown, whereas her own were green, and Dani, at

eighteen, was much taller than her own five foot nothing. So who was this man? He knew *of* Dani, but nothing else about her—except her address…

He gave an impatient sigh. 'I don't suppose your sister is here, either? No.' He answered his own question. 'David said they were going to some coffee shop or other this evening. Damn,' he muttered, looking thoughtful. 'I don't suppose I could come in and wait, could I?' His imperious tone of voice totally belied the request that his words should have been.

A man used to getting his own way, Merry surmised ruefully. Probably in his late thirties, and with no ring on his left hand to say whether or not he was married. The fact that he wasn't wearing a ring said he would do as he damn well pleased, not that he wasn't actually *married*. Everything about this man quietly cried self-assurance and determination.

'No, I don't suppose you could,' she answered dryly.

Blond brows rose over those deep blue eyes, his mouth quirking wryly. 'Well, at least one of the family seems to have some sense!' he allowed.

She remembered again that it had been a long day and she had only been home from work for a short time; what she really wanted right now was to sit down with a glass of cooled white wine and simply unwind before thinking about preparing dinner. Her unexpected guest did not fit in with those plans at all. Besides, exactly what did he want to come in and wait *for*?

'One of the family?' she echoed smoothly, the mildness of her tone totally masking her impatience.

He nodded. 'You and Dani. You are obviously the elder—'

'Obviously,' she acknowledged crisply. Why state the *obvious*?

He gave her a sharp look, visibly making an effort to relax. 'I didn't mean to sound insulting, Miss Baker—'

'You may not have meant to, Mr...?' She paused pointedly; he knew her name while she had absolutely no idea what his might be.

'Kingston,' he supplied. 'Zack Kingston.'

Merry frowned. Kingston? The name *did* sound familiar. Dani had mentioned someone at university by that name. David Kingston... 'David would be your son—'

'Nephew,' Zack Kingston corrected. 'Dani has obviously talked to you about him!'

Merry didn't like the accusation in his tone. Any more than she liked standing on the doorstep having this conversation with him. 'Mr Kingston, I was just about to have a glass of wine. Would you like to join me?' Green eyes steadily met blue.

How much 'sense' did he think she had now? The trouble with Mr Zack Kingston was that he formed snap judgements, and had taken one look at her and decided she was small and defenceless. It was only one of several wrong assumptions he had made!

That direct blue gaze was reassessing now, moving slowly from her bare feet, over the faded black denims, the too-large jumper, to the wild cascade of her long dark hair, the small gamine face dominated by challenging eyes.

To Merry's amusement, she could see he was none the wiser for his review of her. She obviously didn't look to him what she actually was. There was something to be said for a man-free—and therefore problem-free—life, after all!

'Make your mind up, Mr Kingston,' she advised mockingly. 'I don't intend standing here all evening waiting for your answer!'

Anger flared briefly in his deep blue eyes before he quickly brought it under control. Here was a man used to calling the shots, Merry guessed again, not the other way around. Well, this was her home, and her time, and if he wanted to continue this conversation he could do it inside, where she could relax. She had absolutely no idea what he was doing here, what it had to do with Dani—if anything—and she had no intention of discussing it any further standing on the doorstep!

'You'll be quite safe, Mr Kingston,' she added derisively. 'I make it a rule never to attack defenceless men on—what is it today?—on a Tuesday evening,' she teased as she turned and walked back inside the house, sure he would follow her; he had come here this evening with something to say, and unless she was mistaken he hadn't said it yet!

'I can assure you, Miss Baker, I am far from defenceless!'

She was right; he *had* followed her! And as she looked up from pouring two glasses of wine she tried hard not to notice how his large frame dominated the bright but compact kitchen. 'You are?' she returned as she handed him his glass.

'I are— I mean— Oh, hell.' He scowled. 'Tell me, Miss Baker—'

'Merry,' she put in lightly, sitting up on one of the bar stools. 'Short for Meredith,' she tacked on, to save him the bother of asking; he was the sort of man who would want to know!

He nodded. 'Tell me, Merry,' he murmured softly as he sat on the second bar stool, his bent knee only inches away from her own. 'What happens to ''defenceless men'' on the other evenings of the week?'

Different approach. Anger hadn't worked, so now he was going to try cajoling, revealing some of that humour she had guessed at when she first saw him.

Merry quirked dark brows at him over the top of her wine glass. 'Why don't you come back tomorrow and find out?' she replied.

For a moment he looked perplexed. And then he smiled, and laughed.

Whew! Merry continued sipping her wine, mainly as a way of hiding the way her breath had caught in her throat. 'Drop-dead gorgeous'! That laugh only made him more so. A young Robert Redford, she decided admiringly.

He sobered, shaking his head as he still smiled. 'If Dani is anything like you, then I think I understand David's dilemma,' he said.

'David has a dilemma?' she prompted softly.

The laughter had all gone now; Zack Kingston's expression one of grim disapproval. '*I* consider it a dilemma, but I doubt that he does!'

Merry didn't understand how his nephew's dilemma could have anything to do with Dani. Dani had begun her studies at university at the end of September, and, being gregarious by nature, she had quickly made friends. David Kingston was only one of several Dani had mentioned during the last couple of months. Merry certainly couldn't think of any reason for the boy's uncle to come here in search of Dani...

'When do you expect your mother home?' Zack Kingston continued restlessly, putting down his glass of barely touched white wine.

Which wasn't altogether fair on the wine. Merry didn't consider herself a connoisseur by any means, but her taste was discerning, and the wine was a delicious Chablis, perfectly chilled.

'I don't,' she told him consideringly. 'David's dilemma has something to do with Dani?' An uneasy fluttering sensation was beginning in the pit of her stomach.

Dani wasn't only gregarious, she was absolutely beautiful. And there was no bias involved in that observation; Dani had been bowling men off their feet since she was in her cradle!

'Tell me,' Merry said slowly, 'is David anything like you?'

'What the hell does that have to do—?' Zack Kingston broke off, shaking his head impatiently.

'David was the son of my older brother and his wife. Unfortunately they were both killed in a car accident ten years ago, which is when I took over his guardianship.'

Very commendable, considering the demands a child could make on you—even more so when he wasn't actually your own...

'That doesn't actually answer my question, Mr Kingston,' Merry persisted.

'I don't see what it has to do with anything—'

'It has a great deal to do with it,' she said tersely; a twenty-ish version of this man could be devastating to a girl like Dani. 'David is tall, blond, and gorgeous, right?'

Now he was the one to look mockingly at her. 'Like me?' he returned.

Merry glared at him. 'You're too old to be playing these sort of games, Mr Kingston—'

'The name is Zack—Merry,' he cut in. 'And I don't consider myself "too old" for anything!'

The chill in his tone would have frozen a lesser woman into silence, but Merry didn't consider herself a 'lesser' anything! And she never would!

'So David *is* like you?' she said irritably. Oh, Dani, sweet Dani, what have you done?

Zack shrugged. 'There's a certain similarity, yes. But—'

'It's enough,' Merry waved a dismissive hand. 'Dani told me she was meeting friends for coffee this evening. Am I to take it David is that friend?' Singular, not plural. But not exactly a lie, either. Not that she had thought for a moment that it would be; she and Dani had never lied to each other.

Those blue eyes were narrowed now. 'That's what he told me before he left this morning to attend classes, yes,' Zack agreed. 'Amongst other things,' he added. 'I called here earlier in the day in the hope I could talk to Dani's mother without—'

'I work, Mr Kingston,' Merry told him caustically. Unlike some people, obviously… The cut of his clothes, and that air of arrogance, spoke of wealth, and a nature that didn't suffer fools gladly. Well, she certainly didn't have the former, but she didn't suffer fools, either; and this man was taking an awful long time to get to his point!

He was staring at her now, seemingly speechless—not something that happened often, Merry was sure!

She had realised a few minutes ago that he assumed she was Dani's sister.

'I suggest we dispense with any misconceptions you may have formed when you arrived, Mr

Kingston,' she told him briskly. 'Dani doesn't *have* a sister, older or otherwise. In fact, Dani is an only child.' She met his eyes steadily.

Zack Kingston blinked, and then blinked again, his head tilted to one side as he reassessed the situation a second time. Finally he shook his head. 'You aren't old enough to be Dani's mother! Unless—' His gaze sharpened in dismay. 'Exactly how old is Dani?'

Merry was unabashed. 'Daniella—Dani—is eighteen.'

He looked relieved to hear that, but his puzzled vision returned to Merry once again, raking over her appearance once more, from the top of her head down to her bare toes, returning to her face—a face full of good humour, her green eyes clear and bright, her nose small and pert, her mouth wide and inclined to turn up at the corners, giving her a happy look even when she didn't feel much like smiling.

As she didn't now. This man, she had come to realise over the last few minutes, had come here to tell her something important about his nephew and her daughter. And in view of the way Dani had made her own way into life, Merry couldn't help the feelings of foreboding that were seething over her. She no longer found this man's mistake over her identity a cause for amusement, merely questioned the urgency of his need to talk to Dani's mother.

Zack drew in a controlling breath. 'Miss Baker—Er, Mrs—'

'*Miss* Baker,' Merry corrected stiltedly. What was that saying about 'the sins of the father'…? Did it also apply to 'the mistakes of the mother'? 'I've never been a Mrs Anything, Mr Kingston,' she informed him flatly, pointed chin raised defiantly.

He nodded abruptly. 'Well, Miss Baker, it appears you're about to have a wedding in the family now! My nephew David informed me this morning that he intends marrying your daughter!'

Merry swallowed hard, feeling the colour drain from her cheeks. Dani. Eighteen-year-old Dani. Beautiful Dani, who had her whole life before her. Dani, who had only been at university for two months. It couldn't be happening all over again!

Was the mistake of the mother being repeated by the daughter…?

CHAPTER TWO

'HERE, drink this,'

Merry looked up at Zack. 'This' turned out to be what was left of the wine in his glass. There could only be one reason—in the present circumstances!—why Zack Kingston was encouraging her to drink it.

She pushed the glass away, glaring at him. 'I am not in need of restorative alcohol, thank you,' she told him frostily. 'Did you say you have been David's guardian for the last ten years?'

'Almost ten and a half, to be exact,' he confirmed, frowning at the question.

Merry couldn't see what difference that six months made! 'Oh, let's, by all means, be exact,' she snapped caustically, looking him up and down, once again noticing the expensive cut of his clothes, his only jewellery a signet ring on the little finger of his right hand. 'Are you married, Mr Kingston?' she demanded in clipped tones.

His mouth twisted. 'Fortunately not.'

She had thought not; he didn't give the impression of a man in a hurry to get back to his home. Or a wife. 'You do have some intelligence, then,' she replied dismissively. 'In that case—'

'You consider it intelligent not to be married, Miss—Merry?' he interrupted.

She looked at him pityingly. She could well understand his amazement at finding a woman who wasn't interested in marriage; considering the way he looked, his apparent wealth and his bachelor status, she could imagine he had met far too many women desperate to get married—to him!

'As I've already pointed out to you, marriage is an unknown quantity to me personally.' She shrugged. 'And it seems to me, from the amount of separation and divorce, that marriage has become an overrated state to be in!'

'You—'

'However, that does not mean I advocate single motherhood, either,' she continued firmly. 'I know from experience how hard that can be. For the mother left on her own to bring up the child, not the father,' she added heatedly. 'He usually walks away without any responsibilities!'

That deep blue gaze watched her consideringly. 'Is that what happened to you?'

She bristled defensively. 'We weren't talking about me!' Merry snapped back.

Zack shook his head dazedly. 'Then I would like to know who we are talking about?'

'Dani, of course!' Despite her refusal of his wine a few minutes ago, she now took a grateful sip from her own glass. 'You are the boy's guardian. Didn't you teach him any of the facts of life?' She shook her head with angry disgust. 'Or are you one of those men who believe it's the woman's responsibility to take care of the precautions?' That seemed all too often to be the case nowadays; woman's demand for equality, and therefore independence, had rebounded on them in the case of sexual relationships!

'Dani suffers from a similar problem to me, in that she is medically unable to take the pill,' she told Zack coldly.

'I'll file that information away for future reference,' he said, sounding amused.

Merry could feel the heat in her cheeks. This man was making fun of her! 'I'm glad you find this situation funny, Mr Kingston—'

'"Funny" is far from the right word to describe how I feel about what's happened,' he bit out, suddenly looking at her with an arctic chill in his eyes. 'You are obviously under some misapprehension concerning Dani and David's relation-

ship. Contrary to the conclusion you seem to have
jumped to, your daughter is not pregnant!'

Merry stared at him uncomprehending. Not...?
When Zack Kingston informed her of his
nephew's determination to marry Dani, it had
seemed to her there could be only one reason for
such impetuosity. Distressing as that conclusion
might have been. But he was saying Dani *wasn't*
pregnant!

'I don't understand.' She shook her head.

'I *didn't*,' he rasped. 'But, having now met you,
I'm beginning to!'

Merry looked at him blankly. What was that
supposed to mean? What could she possibly have
to do with his nephew's announcement that he
intended marrying Dani; she had never even met
the young man!

'Perhaps you would care to explain that remark?' she invited coolly, green eyes sparkling.

He gave an abrupt laugh. 'I most certainly
would,' he rasped. 'You obviously have an attitude towards pre-marital sex—'

'I have an attitude towards marriage too!' she
jumped in. How dared this man come into her
home and make snap judgements about her? He
didn't even know her! He was an arrogant swine,
and if he thought she was going to let her daugh-

ter have anything to do with a relative of his, then he was sadly—

'We'll get to that in a minute,' he dismissed, with that arrogance she had just mentally attributed to him. 'I was about to say that, in the circumstances, your attitude towards pre-marital relationships is perfectly understandable.'

'Exactly what "circumstances" would you be referring to, Mr Kingston?' Merry prompted fiercely, raising herself to her full height of five feet and half an inch—and making absolutely no impression on him, judging by the way he looked down his arrogant nose at her!

As she had expected, he looked unperturbed. 'Obviously the circumstances of Dani's birth—'

'Which you know absolutely nothing about!' she returned furiously. He raised his blond brows questioningly. Well, he could question all he liked; it was none of his business what those 'circumstances' might have been! Besides, he seemed to have already drawn his own conclusions.

The silence stretched between them, as green eyes warred with blue. But Merry had no intention of being the one to back down.

'Which I know absolutely nothing about,' Zack was finally the one to slowly admit. 'But I believe it has everything to do with Dani's own feelings towards relationships.'

'You already said that,' Merry retorted.

His mouth tightened. 'Having now thought about this, it's my belief—though I won't be able to confirm this until I've spoken to David again— that he and Dani are in love, and that, like all young people in love, they wish to consummate their physical attraction towards each other, but that Dani would rather wait until after they are married.'

'I can't see anything wrong with that,' Merry scorned.

'There is if their only solution to the problem is for them to marry immediately!' Zack returned exasperatedly.

Dani had watched Merry's struggles over the years to cope with working and being a mother, and she knew exactly how difficult it had been for Merry to acquire a career at all when she had become pregnant during her first term at university. *Had* that coloured Dani's own views on marriage and lovemaking? If it had, was that really such a bad thing? Dani was so young still, not much more than a child, really, not old enough for the responsibility of either marriage or a family.

Thinking of Dani dissipated Merry's anger and distress, cleared the initial panic from her mind. She and Dani were close, and she didn't believe, now that she could think straight, that Dani would agree to marry someone and then not tell her own mother about it. Admittedly, Dani seemed to have kept the intensity of this particular relationship with David Kingston to herself, not seeming to have mentioned him any more than the other new friends she had made in the last couple of months. But a marriage proposal, and its acceptance, was something else entirely...

Merry looked up at Zack Kingston with a new confidence. 'I don't believe they *have* decided to marry, immediately or otherwise,' she told him calmly. 'I think you may have been a little premature in coming here today, Mr Kingston—'

'For God's sake call me Zack!' he exploded. 'And no matter what you may think, Merry, I did not imagine David's announcement to me this morning—it totally destroyed my appetite for breakfast!'

Merry felt her mouth twitching with humour, had to bite her lip to stop herself from smiling. She could picture Zack now, seated at the end of a long dining table, newspaper spread out in front of him, while some meticulous, silent servant served him bacon and eggs—the latter would be scrambled, of course, no messy egg-yolks for this man to deal with! And then, just as he was about to take his first mouthful of the mouthwatering food, David dropping his bombshell!

'I trust you managed to eat lunch, Zack?' she said soothingly. 'It really isn't good for the blood sugar for you to go without food for too long. It impairs your judgement, and—'

'My judgement is not impaired, Merry,' he bit out. 'David told me—'

'I'm not disputing what he told you,' she assured him evenly. 'I'm merely questioning the validity of the news that *Dani* intends marrying *him*. I must admit I was thrown for a few minutes after your initial announcement, but I've had time to collect my thoughts now. I know Dani, the two of us are friends, as well as mother and daughter, and if she were serious about your nephew then I believe she would have told me about him.' Merry's confidence increased even as she spoke the words. She *did* know Dani, and what this man was suggesting didn't sound at all like her daughter. 'I don't disbelieve that David told you how he felt towards Dani—'

'Thank you for that, at least!' Zack snapped with sarcastic impatience.

She couldn't exactly blame him for feeling this way; he had obviously had a tough day since David's intentions had destroyed his breakfast. They had certainly dispelled her own earlier tiredness too!

'I don't mean to sound patronising, Zack,' she assured him. She might not have meant to, but in retrospect that was exactly what she had sounded! 'I'm just doubtful of Dani's part in all of this.' She absently poured them both another glassful of wine, wordlessly handing his over. 'Dani and I have never had secrets. There's never been any reason for us to,' she revealed, thinking of her own years without romantic involvement.

When Dani had been very young there just hadn't been the time, between studying and caring for a young child, and there had only been the occasional date in the years following. Most men of a similar age to herself were either already married, running away from an unhappy relationship, or had no interest in a woman with a young child. None of them had appealed to Merry either. In fact, there had been no relationships that she couldn't happily talk to Dani about because there had been none that were serious!

'If Dani were in love,' she told Zack assuredly,

'then I believe she would have told me about it. And about him!'

'I—' Zack broke off as the sound of the front door opening and closing could clearly be heard.

'That will be Dani now,' Merry warned him softly, putting a lightly restraining hand on his arm. 'Let me handle this, please,' she advised gently as she heard Dani walking down the hall-way.

'Mum, I'm home—' Dani broke off her cheer-ful greeting as she entered the kitchen and saw that her mother wasn't alone, her glance resting interestedly on the man who stood there.

Merry looked at her daughter with pride; she would never cease to be amazed that this glori-ously beautiful creature was her own daughter. Almost six feet in height, Dani towered over her. Her hair was a long riot of honey-blonde curls that reached down the length of her spine, and her face as beautiful as any model's, with eyes of deep honey-brown.

Merry glanced sideways at Zack Kingston to see what his reaction was to this vision of love-liness that was her daughter. He looked stunned! But then so did every other man who looked at Dani. Including Zack's nephew, it seemed...

But, seeing Dani now, Merry was even more

assured that her surmise concerning that situation was correct; Dani looked as carefree and open as she always did, and if she were hiding something as serious as a secret engagement then she wouldn't have done. Dani had never been any good at keeping secrets!

'Hello, darling.' Merry moved to hug her daughter. 'Had a good day?'

'Pretty good,' Dani responded vaguely, obviously fascinated by the man standing watching them from across the room—which wasn't surprising, considering what conclusion she must have come to concerning Zack's presence here; it was over a year since Merry's last date, and she certainly hadn't brought him home!

'This is Zack,' Merry introduced. 'He just called in for a chat,' she added meaningfully—for his benefit!

'Zack,' Dani greeted, politely shaking the hand he offered before turning to her mother. 'I'll just go and freshen up, and then I'll help you with dinner. Will you be eating with us, Zack?' she added mischievously, obviously intrigued by this male friend of her mother's who had just dropped by for 'a chat'.

Zack looked briefly at Merry. 'Er—no,' he answered huskily. 'As your mother said, I only called in briefly.'

'Oh, well.' Dani shrugged lightly. 'Perhaps I'll see you again some time.' She left the kitchen, her movements unconsciously graceful, taking her boundless energy and effervescence with her, her footsteps soft on the stairs.

Merry gave Zack another glance from beneath lowered lashes. If he had looked stunned before, he now looked speechless!

He swallowed hard.

'She takes after her father,' Merry told him.

'Tall, blond, and gorgeous,' he acknowledged heavily.

Jeff had been all of those things. He had also been a lot of other things Dani wasn't...

'Yes,' Merry confirmed quickly. 'But the important thing is that Dani doesn't look to me like a young girl in the emotional throes of a secret love affair.'

'Or to me either,' Zack rejoined, obviously deeply annoyed now at the embarrassing situation he found himself in.

Which wasn't surprising, really. Zack Kingston gave every impression of being totally self-assured, in control of any situation he should happen to find himself in; Merry could only imagine the inner squirming he was going through at this moment!

'I think I'll take your advice and talk to David again,' he said grimly, putting down his empty wine glass. 'One of us has obviously got his wires crossed.'

As it wasn't Merry or Dani who were at fault, then the blame had to be on his side. Merry felt almost sorry for him. Almost… Except he had put her through some of the most traumatic moments of her life such a short time ago!

CHAPTER THREE

'YOU really should take more care, Merry,' drawled a familiar voice. 'I could have walked off with your handbag just now,' Zack pointed out.

Him again!

And she could see what he meant; her handbag was sitting on the bonnet of the car while she loaded her shopping into the boot.

She straightened. 'I doubt it, Zack,' she told him dryly. 'Mr Patel is a good friend of mine.' She nodded in the direction of the convenience store where she had just done her shopping; the sunny-faced proprietor was undoubtedly watching their exchange through the window. 'And if he failed to stop you, there's five pounds of potatoes in this bag.' She held up a plastic carrier before putting it into the boot with the rest of her bags. 'I would simply have hit you around the head with it!'

Zack's mouth twisted. 'And asked questions later!'

Merry nodded. 'When you regained consciousness, yes.'

He looked at her for several seconds, and then he chuckled, seemingly more relaxed today. 'You would, too!'

'Of course I would; I have all my money in there.' She slammed the boot shut, taking her handbag from his unresisting fingers and placing it inside the car on the passenger seat. 'Wonderful as it is to see you again, Zack,' she said with no sincerity at all, as he made no effort to move away from the driver's door to allow her to get into her car, 'I do have to get on.' She looked up at him challengingly.

To her dismay, he looked just as gorgeous today as he had yesterday, the blue jumper that he wore so casually a perfect match in colour for those 'come-to-bed' eyes of his and he was slim and powerful in black denims.

After he had left her house the previous evening she had convinced herself that he couldn't possibly be as heart-stoppingly handsome as she had thought he was, but, looking at him now, in the rapidly fading daylight, she knew that he was even more so. In fact, he shouldn't be allowed out, was likely to cause traffic accidents. All to women, of course. Because instead of looking at the road they would be unable to take their eyes off Zack Kingston!

She had lain awake in her bed last night thinking about him. And then she'd been furious with herself. To lose sleep at all was bad enough, but to lose it over a man she hardly knew was unforgivable!

'I was just driving over to see you when I saw you come out of the shop,' Zack said, still leaning against the side of her car.

Merry stiffened. 'Why were you coming to see me?' she demanded warily.

'It seems I owe you an apology—'

'Accepted,' she said quickly, knowing exactly what he was apologising for. Casual conversation with Dani over dinner the evening before had assured her that Zack Kingston had definitely made a mistake where Dani and David were concerned.

David Kingston had only come into the conversation briefly, but it had been enough to tell Merry that her daughter had no more interest in him than she did in any of her other new friends at university. Dani certainly didn't know David well enough to realise he had *had* an Uncle Zack, let alone that she was expected to marry into his family!

'If I could just get into my car?' Merry asked pointedly; she was going to physically push him out of the way if he didn't move soon!

Zack gave her a quizzical look. 'Are you usually this rude?'

'With men that accost me in car parks? Yes!'

'So it was true, what you said about the other days of the week!'

She knew exactly what he was referring to. 'You aren't defenceless, Zack—on any day of the week!'

'True,' he responded. 'I would, however, like to make my apology properly—'

'The ground is too wet for you to get down on your knees,' she broke in disparagingly; it had been raining most of the day, adding to the misery of the cold November weather.

He shook his head, his eyes glowing with laughter. 'I had dinner more in mind than grovelling in front of you on my knees!'

Dinner? With this man? He had to be joking! She might as well stand in front of a double-decker bus and simply let it run her down. That was how dangerous she knew this man to be! And she had no intention of standing in front of that bus—or having dinner with Zack Kingston!

'For one thing, Zack,' she sighed, 'I have already accepted your apology—'

'I haven't made it yet,' he put in softly.

'For another—' she glared at him for the interruption '—I have just been into the shop and purchased the makings of dinner for Dani and myself.'

'That's fine,' he said. 'Dani wasn't included in the invitation anyway.'

'And for yet another,' she added with firm determination, 'I have no wish to go out to dinner with you!'

He folded his arms in front of his chest, leaning back against the door she wanted to open so she could get inside the car. 'Tell me,' he prompted lightly, 'have there been many men in your life since Dani's father?'

The question might have been casually put, but the audacity of it made Merry gasp. What on earth did it have to do with him? 'Mind your own damned business!' she responded indignantly.

'Hmm, I thought not,' he answered consideringly. 'Well, I'm thirty-nine years of age, and have never been engaged or married. Although I have no aversion to either state, I just didn't meet the right woman. I own a publishing house, have a home here in London and a villa in the south of France. I like children and dogs, and not necessarily in that order,' he added with a smile. 'Cats tend to make me sneeze, but if you happen to already have a cat, I'm sure I could learn to live with the sneezing. I—'

'Why are you telling me all these things?' Merry finally managed to break in. This man had been an irritation in her life since—was it only yesterday they had met for the first time? It seemed like much longer! Now he wasn't just an irritation to her; he was fast becoming a nuisance!

He shrugged. 'Character reference. I realise all of this is usually covered in the first date, but as you refuse to even *have* that initial ceremony, I thought I should tell you a little about myself.'

'You missed out the bad points,' she taunted. First date, indeed!

He looked sceptical. 'I didn't know I had any,' he mocked.

Her eyes flashed deeply green. 'That arrogance is just one of them! You're also opinionated, judgemental, and—and you're so tall I get a crick in my neck just looking up at you!' she concluded irritably—and then felt irritated with herself. He was too tall…! What on earth was she talking—babbling—about?

It didn't help that Zack's grin widened at her remark. 'If we were seated at a dinner table that wouldn't happen,' he pointed out. 'It also wouldn't apply if we were lying—'

'You're so damned presumptuous!' she cut in huskily, her face fiery red. God, he had her blushing like a schoolgirl! But, considering she had met this man only about twenty-four hours ago, he was being damned familiar!

'On a beach somewhere warm,' he finished smoothly, blue eyes gleaming with laughter—at her expense. 'Don't you find the English winters cold and damp?' he continued, both of them knowing exactly what she had thought he was going to say.

'I love the cold and the damp of England.' She suppressed the shiver that just talking about it gave her. 'I can imagine nothing worse than spending Christmas on a hot beach somewhere.' She shook her head. 'Now, if you don't mind, my peas are defrosting and my chicken needs cooking!'

''I love roast chicken,' Zack told her hopefully.

'I'm deep-frying it.' She had just decided—stubbornly.

He shrugged. 'I can live with that.'

Merry stared at him exasperatedly. She didn't want to invite him to dinner. But as she looked up into his face, the arrogant set of his jaw, the unrelenting steel of his gaze, she had a feeling it wasn't going to be her decision.

Which was ridiculous. She was thirty-seven years old, totally independent; she didn't have to do anything she didn't want to do. And spending any more time in this man's company was not only stupid, it could be downright dangerous!

'Okay, but you're peeling the potatoes,' she heard herself say—her mouth functioning in total opposition to her brain—and then she found herself wondering if he knew *how* to peel potatoes. After all, a man who owned a publishing company, a house in London, *and* a villa in France, was also sure to have that army of servants, like the one she had envisaged serving him breakfast yesterday morning. The breakfast he hadn't been able to eat. Obviously there was nothing wrong with his appetite today! 'On second thoughts, you can lay the table,' she decided—if she had really decided anything at all...!

She had *decided* yesterday that she didn't ever want to talk to this man again. And yet now she appeared to be doing just that...

She also had no interest in having dinner with him, either. And yet now it appeared she was going to... Even if it would be in her own home, and he was going to help her cook it!

Which was precisely what they were doing an hour later, when Dani came into the house. This time her daughter didn't just look surprised to see a man in their kitchen—the same man as yesterday evening!—she looked pleased too!

'Hi, Zack,' she greeted familiarly, bending to kiss Merry lightly on the cheek before helping herself to an apple from the fruit bowl, biting into it hungrily as she sat down on one of the kitchen stools.

'You'll ruin your appetite for dinner,' Merry chided indulgently; she knew from experience that nothing dampened her daughter's love of food, and yet she maintained a model-slim body. Dani could probably eat six apples and manage to eat a full meal afterwards!

Her daughter grinned dismissively. 'This is just to tide me over until my pizza later.'

Pizza? But Dani *had* mentioned something this morning about going out with some friends for a pizza this evening...

Merry had forgotten the conversation during the rush of the day, but it came flooding back to her now. And Zack Kingston had invited himself to dinner. A dinner, it now appeared, they were going to enjoy alone. Enjoy...? It was the last word she should have used to describe the next few hours she was going to have to spend in his company!

'I believe you know my nephew,'' Zack put in conversationally, looking enquiringly at Dani. 'David. David Kingston,' he explained at Dani's blank look.

Dani's eyes widened. 'You're David's uncle?' she looked surprised—but nothing more than that, Merry noted with satisfaction. 'I would never have guessed.' Dani shook her head, grinning widely now. 'You look nothing alike, do you?'

Merry turned accusingly to Zack. When she had asked him yesterday he had told her that he and David had 'a certain similarity'. And she, she remembered now with an inward wince, had said, 'tall, blond, and gorgeous'!

'To look at, no,' Zack replied. 'But in temperament we're very similar,' he amended, with a mocking sideways glance at Merry.

Arrogant, opinionated, and judgemental! Thank goodness Dani *wasn't* heavily involved with the younger Kingston!

'How incredible!' Dani jumped lightly to the floor, almost as tall as Zack in her heeled boots. 'David's coming out for a pizza with us; I can't wait to tell him you're here having dinner with my mother!' She looked pleased at the thought.

'Dani!' Merry panicked at the thought of her daughter leaving her alone here with Zack.

'I'm only going upstairs to change, Mum,' Dani assured her lightly. 'I'll come back in and say goodbye before I leave.'

'I hope you all have a good time,' Zack put in agreeably, moving so that he stood beside Merry, his arm curving about her shoulders. 'And don't feel you have to hurry back,' he tacked on laughingly.

Merry looked up at him sharply, just in time to see him give Dani a conspiratorial wink. Really! The man had come here yesterday, breathing fire and accusations about her daughter, and now he was giving Dani the impression that the two of them, that he and she, were— There was no 'he and she'!

'Gotcha,' Dani shot back at him before Merry could say anything. 'I'll be down again in about ten minutes,' she warned teasingly, before leaving them alone in the kitchen.

Merry moved pointedly out of the curve of Zack's arm, turning to face him accusingly. 'Exactly what do you think you're doing?' she demanded, green eyes bright with annoyance. 'Dani now thinks— She now has the impression—' Merry could hardly speak!

'Would you rather Dani knows I came here on a wild-goose chase yesterday?' Zack asked. 'That she be made aware of the fact that David made a declaration concerning her of which she has no knowledge? I spoke to David last night,' he added at Merry's questioning look, 'and learnt that he's never so much as taken her out on her own, let alone kissed her or told her he's in love with her! What he was actually saying to me yesterday morning was that he's *seen* the girl he wants to marry, not that he has actually asked her and has been accepted!' he explained.

That was more or less the conclusion Merry had come to—once she'd been able to think at all! And, no, she didn't want to humiliate David Kingston by telling Dani what had happened yesterday. That would only be embarrassing for everyone involved.

Besides, she had done things, made statements herself, at the same age, that hadn't always been tactful or well thought out...

'You told me that David looks like you!' she attacked, not willing to let this man off the hook quite that easily. After all, he was the one who had overreacted...

'No, I didn't,' Zack denied easily. 'I said there was "a certain similarity". And I wasn't referring to the way we look. David is several inches shorter than me, with the dark colouring of his mother. But he's very like I was at his age, over-serious and hard-working—that was the reason I made the jump in assuming his relationship with Dani was an actual thing; David doesn't make light-hearted statements.' He looked rueful. 'He still hasn't. We talked a little about Dani last night, and although the relationship hasn't gone anywhere so far, I can assure you he does intend marrying her!'

'Dani is too young to marry anyone just yet,' Merry insisted stubbornly. 'No matter how, serious and hard-working your nephew might be!'

Zack seemed unfazed. 'I would say that's for the two of them to sort out, in their own time. Hopefully, not for several more years yet.' His mouth quirked. 'That's definitely one aspect of mine and David's personalities that differs. Or maybe it's just that I'm older and so there doesn't seem to be so much time; David has immense patience, whereas I—I don't have any patience at all. But then neither of us are children, are we, Merry?' he finished with satisfaction.

She gave him a startled look. *'We..?'*

He nodded. 'David may have taken one look at Dani and decided he wants to marry her, but yesterday I did the same thing where her mother was concerned. That's why, when you asked me, I counted it fortunate that I wasn't already married. You see, there *is* going to be a wedding in the family after all, Merry—ours!'

She had felt this way when she was a child, riding on the merry-go-round, slightly dizzy, slightly disorientated—and very definitely speechless!

CHAPTER FOUR

THE feeling didn't last very long—thank goodness!

'You didn't tell me that insanity ran rife in your family!' she burst out, moving a suitable distance away from him. As much as the confines of her kitchen would allow!

He and his nephew were prime candidates for treatment as far as she was concerned. Dipsticks. Fruit loops. One slice short of a loaf.

However it was put, Zack Kingston was definitely deranged!

He smiled at her now, that slow, lazy smile that only made him appear more handsome. What a pity he was also insane!

'It doesn't,' he answered her easily.

'Then it's just you and David who are afflicted,' she accepted. A day ago she had been quietly living her life, completely unaware of the existence of Zack and David Kingston. And she would like to go back to that unawareness!

Zack shook his head, perfectly relaxed as he leant back against one of the kitchen units, smil-

ing unconcernedly, appearing completely unabashed by the fact that he had just announced his
intention of marrying her.

'David and I both have an IQ of over one hundred and fifty,' he drawled mockingly.

'Which just goes to prove the point of that saying ''there's a very fine line between genius and
insanity''!' Merry cried. 'David appears to be
pretty close, but you are obviously way over the
edge!'

Zack chuckled softly. 'One of the things I like
about you is your sense of humour.'

She shook her head pityingly. 'I wasn't joking.'

'I know that,' he sobered. 'But I wasn't joking
either,' he told her seriously.

Completely off his trolley, Merry decided.
Thank goodness Dani hadn't gone out yet; she
might need some help getting Zack out of the
house.

'Mr Kingston—Zack,' she amended soothingly
as he raised his brows at the formality; no point
in disturbing him unnecessarily! 'How many
women have you invited to marry you this week?'
she prompted conversationally, willing Dani to
finish changing and come back down the stairs.
She needed her assistance!

He met her gaze unblinkingly, although there

was laughter in the depths of his clear blue eyes. 'I can say with all honesty—'

'Honesty is good,' Merry encouraged, still eyeing him warily.

He gave an inclination of his head. 'I think so too. Dishonesty engenders mistrust, and a relationship cannot be built on either of those things.' He straightened. 'As I told you yesterday, I am thirty-nine years old, and in all that time I have suggested marriage to only one woman. You,' he added, so that there could be no misunderstanding on her part.

Her… Why her? What had she done to deserve being singled out in this way? Or perhaps that was it; she had made no secret of her feelings towards men and marriage, and maybe Zack Kingston was one of those men who couldn't resist a challenge? Well, he was going to find her a lot more than a challenge!

'I'm sure it's a great honour, Zack,' she told him with heavy sarcasm. 'But my answer has to be no.'

His mouth twisted. 'I haven't asked you yet,' he reminded her.

No, he hadn't asked, but he had told! 'I'm advising you to save your breath,' she bit out impatiently.

'Oh, I don't intend asking you until I'm sure you'll say yes,' he assured her.

'Indeed? Has someone given you prior knowledge of hell freezing over?' she said pleasantly.

Zack chuckled again. 'See what I mean? Great sense of humour.'

'I wasn't joking,' she snapped. 'I'm sure you're a great marital catch, Zack.' If one overlooked the insanity! 'Passably good-looking.' Gorgeous! 'Rich.' The Jaguar XJS that he had driven while he followed her home was testament to that! 'It's just that I've reached the age of thirty-seven without marrying anyone—and I have no immediate plans to change my status!' Dani, where are you? she mentally pleaded with her absent daughter. 'And, in the circumstances, I don't think it would be a good idea for you to stay to dinner,' she finished reasoningly.

'That's a bit unfair—since I helped to cook it,' he protested lightly.

Peeling four potatoes, and two of them for himself, did not constitute helping her cook dinner as far as she was concerned! Although she accepted it was probably the first time Zack had ever peeled even *one* potato—judging by the amount of potato he had cut off with the peel, his hundred and fifty-something IQ obviously served him no useful purpose when it came to practicalities!

'Besides,' he went on persuasively, 'you need someone to help you eat all that food now that Dani is going out.'

Merry's mouth set. 'I don't wish to seem rude, Zack—'

'Of course you do,' he laughed. 'It's another part of your charm.'

Being rude was charming? This man certainly had a warped sense of what he found attractive in a woman. Or perhaps it was just that he was surrounded by yes-men—and women—most of the time...?

'Thank you,' she dismissed. 'I think I'm beginning to understand now why it is you've never married before; you only want to marry women who have no interest in you!' Although, his insanity aside, she didn't think there could be too many of those—besides herself!

He laughed once more, not at all perturbed by her insult. 'That's quite an interesting theory, Merry.' He moved to pour some of the wine from the half-bottle that had been left from the evening before, handing her one of the glasses. 'Completely untrue, of course. But interesting.' He sipped his wine thoughtfully. 'I would just like to repeat that I had never asked *any* woman to marry me before I met you.'

'Then why change the habit of a lifetime?' Merry prompted desperately, taking a thirsty gulp of her wine—a wine, moreover, that was supposed to be sipped and enjoyed, not thrown down the throat like its cheaper imitators. But this man, with his determination, was starting to grate on her nerves.

'You see,' he grinned. 'Life with you will never be boring!'

'I can be boring—if that's what it takes to get rid of you!' she assured him.

Zack folded his arms. 'I'm not going anywhere.' And, as if to prove his point further, he made himself comfortable on one of the kitchen stools.

'I'm thirty-seven—'

'You don't look it,' he assured her admiringly.

'A single mother—'

'We can have more children, if you would like them,' he confirmed softly.

Merry glared at him. He had deliberately misunderstood the statement. 'I spend my days working—'

'Wonderful,' he agreed.

She drew in a breath. 'My nights—'

'We'll get to your *nights* in a moment,' he butted in. 'I'm interested in what sort of work you do.'

'It's completely unnecessary for you to know what work I do—considering we are never going to meet again after tonight!' Merry glared at him.

Zack remained unruffled. 'Humour me,' he encouraged.

She had been humouring him for the last ten minutes; in any other circumstances she would have got as far away from him as possible. But as it was her home he was the one who had to leave. Something he didn't seem inclined to do!

She turned off the heat beneath the potatoes, having no interest in eating them now; a proposal of marriage was sure to rob her of her appetite! 'I teach,' she told him abruptly.

'Subject?'

She sighed. 'Art,' she told him, tensing as she waited for his scorn.

She had heard all the criticism about teaching art, mostly that it was a waste of time—her own and her pupils'. She didn't happen to agree with those critics, felt there was so much more to individuals than their academic capabilities, that there was an artist of some sort inside everyone.

'I should have guessed,' he murmured softly.

'There's a certain style to the way you look and dress,' he explained at her frowning look.

Merry looked down at her long floral skirt and the skimpy black top she wore with it. 'Today's "style" is a charity shop,' she told him dryly. 'And yesterday's was post-Dani; I don't have a lot of spare cash to spend on stylish clothes for myself.' She gave a pointed look at his own expensively tailored clothes.

'I acknowledge the put-down, Merry,' he accepted. 'But I certainly wasn't being patronising—as you thought I was,' he guessed correctly. 'Some people have a style of their own, so much so that they look good in whatever they wear— you are one of those people.'

There wasn't a lot she could say to a remark like that. Fashionable clothes had never been something she was too interested in—just as well, in the circumstances. But over the years she had developed a certain style she considered her own, one that suited the slenderness of her figure and the dark wildness of her long hair. What surprised her was that Zack Kingston had recognised it as such…

Now who was being patronising? Wasn't she giving in to a little reverse snobbery here? Which was totally unlike her. She liked her life the way it was, loved her job, being mother to Dani, and never minded that most people had more money than she did. Even if she had money herself, there was nothing about her life she would want to change. Well... Perhaps one thing. But that was only a dream of hers...

'Thank you,' she accepted huskily.

'Don't be too quick to thank me, Merry,' he replied, blue eyes alight with wicked humour. 'I've also spent a considerable amount of the last twenty-four hours imagining what you would look like *without* the clothes!'

She drew in a shaky breath, colour burning her cheeks as she stared at him wide-eyed. 'You—'

'I'm off now, Mum.' Dani bounced back into the room, lovelier than ever in a brown fitted top and brown jeans that hugged the perfection of her statuesque figure. 'Enjoy your evening.' She grinned at both of them.

'Are you sure you wouldn't like to join us for dinner before you go out?' Merry pressed. 'We—I've cooked plenty,' she amended, annoyed with herself for even verbally coupling herself with Zack Kingston. For goodness' sake, he had been fantasising about her *naked*!

Dani looked puzzled. 'I thought I explained; we're all having pizza.' She gave a hurried glance at her watch. 'I really do have to go now, or I'll be late.'

'Dani?' Zack called to her as she was leaving the room. 'Have you ever been a bridesmaid?' She turned back to him questioningly.

'A bridesmaid?' she repeated. 'No, I—' Her eyes widened as she looked at the two of them, Zack so quietly self-assured, her mother now ashen-faced.

Merry had eyes for no one but Zack, her whole body tense with fury. 'You are taking this joke too damned far!' she bit out forcefully, hands clenched tightly at her sides.

Ordinarily a woman who abhorred violence, she was in danger of hitting him! He had walked into their lives—invaded them!—but he certainly wasn't staying!

'Go ahead and enjoy your evening, Dani.' She spoke as calmly as she could to her daughter, even managing to smile a little. 'Mr Kingston's idea of a joke seems to be vastly different from ours,' she added scornfully.

Dani glanced at him, and then she turned back to Merry—as if she very much doubted he would joke about something like that. 'Sure, Mum,' she said, taking her leave this time without any hindrance.

The silence she left behind her was so heavy with tension it could have been cut with a knife…!

CHAPTER FIVE

'YOU may have helped me prepare the dinner, Zack,' Merry told him flatly. 'But this last fifteen minutes in your company has completely robbed me of any desire to eat!' She turned off the oven—having decided to roast the chicken pieces, after all!

'Love,' he informed her unconcernedly. 'They tell me it does that to you,' he explained at her enquiring look.

Her brow cleared, her exasperation rising. 'Zack, I am not in love. With you or anyone else!' she pronounced firmly. 'I don't even know you. And what I do know I don't particularly like!'

'You've already said that,' he replied. 'For "arrogance" I think you should read self-assurance. For "opinionated" probably straightforward.' He began to tick off the list of her earlier accusations concerning his nature. '"Judgemental"? No—I don't think so. As for the being tall part, I could just as easily make the observation you're a little on the short side.' He looked at her, a smile playing around his lips.

As well it might. There was certainly nothing wrong with his memory! Even down to that last babbling comment she had made about his height...! Except that it *had* been complete babbling; his height, that air of self-assurance, all combined to make her feel small and feminine. She had battled so hard for years not to feel that way, not to need anyone, to rise and fall on her own merits. And, even if she said so herself, she hadn't done too bad a job of it.

But Zack Kingston, with his smooth self-confidence, made her feel vulnerable, while at the same time his admiration of her independent nature gave her a confidence in that vulnerability. Dangerous territory, indeed...

She couldn't actually be feeling attracted to this man! Could she...?

She glanced across at him, only to find he was staring right back at her. As he saw the confusion in her expression he stood up, moving slowly across the kitchen towards her.

He was going to kiss her, she decided in the split second before he gathered her into his arms and did exactly that!

Insane or not, Zack certainly knew how to kiss, his mouth insistent, and yet at the same time infinitely tender. And then his kiss deepened, pas-

sion flaring between them as Zack's arms tightened and his lips became more demanding on
hers.

She responded. She would have been lying if
she'd tried to claim that she didn't. Her arms up
about his neck as she stood on tiptoe to meet him,
the curves of her body somehow seeming to fit
perfectly into his. Which was odd, given the difference in their heights...

'Mum, could I—? Oops!' gasped a surprised
Dani.

Merry broke quickly away from the strength of
Zack's arms, though he was reluctant to release
her. She moved several feet away from him, turning to look at Dani as she stood wide-eyed in the
doorway. Which wasn't surprising; Merry
couldn't remember the last date she had been on,
let alone when she had last been kissed. And her
daughter certainly hadn't been a witness to it!

Merry took a deep breath, her cheeks fiery red.
'Yes, Dani?' Her voice sounded slightly huskier
than usual, but at least she had managed to speak!

Flustered as she felt, she hadn't been sure she
would be able to speak at all. She still trembled
from the intensity of the passion that had risen so
quickly between Zack and herself.

Dani looked slightly embarrassed at having in-

terrupted so intimate a situation. 'I forgot earlier.
We thought we might all go back to Jane's after
our pizza and listen to music. I wondered if I
could borrow some of your CDs?' She grimaced
her regret at having burst in on them.

'Er—yes, of course you can.' Merry still felt
flustered, while Zack, damn him, appeared completely unruffled. Appeared... Because a closer
look showed her that his hands, which he was
thrusting into his trouser pockets, were shaking a
little. Not so unconcerned, after all. 'They're in
the lounge,' she told Dani. 'Help yourself.'

'Thanks.' Dani looked relieved at being allowed a quick getaway. Although she paused at
the door. 'I promise I won't be back again for
hours,' she said mischievously.

'Tactful young lady,' Zack murmured once he
and Merry were alone again, the front door closing firmly behind Dani as she left—'for hours'!
'So you like music, too?' he continued, before
Merry could make the sharp reply she wanted to.
'David plays music all the time when he's at
home,' he explained at her questioning look.
'Consequently I find that my music tastes don't
match those of my peers'. He shrugged. 'I suppose that's what happens when you have a teenager constantly about the house.' He certainly

wasn't complaining about it, merely making an observation.

Merry hadn't quite looked at it in this way before, but, even though their circumstances were vastly different, Zack was, in effect, a single parent too...

'Not so different, after all, are we?' Zack drawled as he watched the candid emotions flickering across her face.

Her defences were certainly slipping where he was concerned—and it simply wouldn't do!

'Oh, but we are,' she dismissed scathingly. 'No doubt you were able to hire a nanny for David when he was younger—' She broke off as Zack shook his head.

'I felt David had already suffered enough heartache losing his parents at such a young age, and it didn't seem fair that I farmed the responsibility of him out to someone else. So during school terms I fitted my work in around his hours, and during the holidays I worked mainly from home.'

'The benefit of being your own boss?' Merry derided, not letting him off that easily.

'Possibly, Merry,' he accepted harshly. 'Although ten years ago Thorndyke Brooks was a struggling publishing house, and a lot of work was involved in making it viable again.'

Her eyes widened. 'It's Thorndyke Books that you own?'

Now one of the top publishing houses, ten years ago it had been on the brink of bankruptcy. Zack Kingston was the entrepreneur who had stepped in and turned the company around? Very successfully, if she remembered correctly. They had a dozen international top authors working for them now, and their non-fiction books were of a very high standard indeed—several Thorndyke textbooks were used at the school where Merry worked.

'You're *that* Kingston?' His business successes had been reported in the newspapers for years, but somehow she had always imagined—if she had thought of it at all!—that he would be older. Much older...

'It is. And I am,' Zack confirmed. 'And you're changing the subject, Merry,' he added with gentle reproof. 'I was endeavouring to point out the things we do have in common, not the things we don't.'

She knew what he had been doing—which was precisely the reason she had tried—and apparently not succeeded!—in putting him on the defensive for a change. She didn't want to have things in common with Zack; it was so much easier to believe their lives—and consequently the two of them!—were completely incompatible.

'You can't do that, Zack,' she denied, smiling wryly. 'The one doesn't outweigh the other.'

'It would be extremely boring if we were exactly the same, Merry,' he returned dryly. 'It's the differences that add the spark. For instance, I like not knowing what you are going to do or say next.'

She pulled a face. 'I'm going to say something I've already said several times this evening—dinner is off!'

His blue eyes glittered teasingly. 'It's a terrible waste of food, and you don't strike me as a woman who approves of waste,' he responded softly. 'Besides, it's my cook's night off, so you'll be condemning me to a takeaway if you make me leave now.'

'You could always join Dani and David for a pizza,' Merry suggested mockingly.

Zack grimaced. 'The pizza would be fine; it's all those over-intense students I'd find hard to stomach. I can't believe we were ever like that, can you?'

He was doing it again, and it wasn't going to work this time. 'I'm not sure I like being a stand-in for your cook!' She took the plates out of the warmer and began to dish up the food that was rapidly spoiling.

'If you could see Mrs Jenkins you would realise exactly how untrue that remark is!' He grinned, straining water from the peas without being asked. 'I'm quite self-sufficient, Merry,' he stated as she watched his efficient movements. 'I only employed a cook once David came to live with me. Bachelor fare isn't suitable for a growing child.'

She laughed, able to imagine what sort of food he had eaten when he was on his own. 'I'm sure David wouldn't have minded!'

'Maybe not,' Zack accepted. 'But I take my duties as his guardian rather seriously.'

Merry gave him a humorous glance. 'So I noticed yesterday,' she came back.

He grinned again that boyish, heart-stopping grin that was so hard to resist. 'I don't regret yesterday. Oh, I wish I hadn't walked in here with all guns firing and made such an idiot of myself,' he admitted. 'But at the same time, if I hadn't, then I wouldn't have met you.'

There was no answer to that, so Merry didn't make one. 'Would you like to eat here or in the dining room?' The food was served onto the plates now, and needed to be eaten before it got cold.

'Here will be just fine,' he assured her. 'I have a bottle of wine for us in the car. I'll just go and get it.'

A bottle of—? He had intended having dinner with her this evening no matter what!

'Close your mouth, Merry.' He bent and kissed her. 'Find me a corkscrew to open it with, would you?' he instructed, before striding outside to his car.

He couldn't just walk in here and take over! He couldn't— He already had…! She wasn't used to this, had been on her own too long to meekly accept—

Her outraged thoughts came to an abrupt halt as Zack returned to the kitchen and she saw the bottle of wine in his hand. It was exactly the same vintage and from the same region as the one she had given him last night—her favourite wine, a small luxury she allowed herself from time to time. She didn't believe for a moment that it was a coincidence—or indeed a shared taste—that had prompted Zack to choose it; he had clearly made a mental note of it the evening before, and deliberately brought a bottle for them to drink together this evening…

'It's quite chilled from being outside in the

car,' Zack told her as he took the corkscrew from her unresisting fingers.

Merry was glad of his concentration on removing the cork from the bottle so that she had time to blink back the tears that were threatening to fall. It had been so long since anyone had cared enough to have noticed such a small detail as the wine she liked to drink. If anyone ever had! Oh, Dani was wonderful, and took a lot of care over birthday and Christmas presents, but Merry doubted that even her daughter had taken the trouble to note what wine she favoured.

But Zack had. And he had noticed her individual style of dressing too...

He was far too observant for comfort. Too much time spent in the company of someone so attentive and she might even start to—No! She was not going to fall in love with Zack Kingston. He wasn't right for her at all. He wasn't just attentive, he took over! He—

'To us.' Zack held out one of the glasses of wine to her, challenge in every muscle of his body as he waited for her to return the toast.

'To Christmas,' she returned dryly, refusing to return such an intimate toast. There wasn't an 'us', and there never would be!

'Just as good,' he nodded his satisfaction. 'Excuse the pun,' he went on, 'but I have the feeling it's going to be a very *Merry* Christmas now that I've met you!'

Merry was quite happy to excuse his pun, it was the quiet determination in his voice that bothered her!

CHAPTER SIX

'TALKING of Christmas—'

'You were; I wasn't,' Merry quipped. The two of them, having enjoyed their meal—and the wine!—were now seated in the sitting room in front of the roaring fire Zack had insisted he build for them in the grate. Merry's reluctance to have him light the fire hadn't stemmed from a need to be independent, but from the fact that she knew it was all too cosy and comfortable with the flames glowing!

Zack looked unconcerned by her interruption. 'I have a pre-Christmas cocktail party I have to attend tomorrow evening. I wondered if you would like to come with me?'

Merry just stared back at him. A cocktail party. Did she look like the type who went to *cocktail parties*?—where dozens of bored people, who usually didn't know each other very well, stood around with drinks in their hands, nibbling away at unrecognisable canapé that did absolutely nothing to satisfy one's hunger. She might have a tiny build, but she had a healthy appetite—as this eve-

ning's meal should have told him!—and the
thought of spending hours at this man's side, trying to look decorous, did not appeal to her one
little bit. Besides—

'I'll take your silence as acceptance—'

'I shouldn't if I were you,' Merry calmly
stopped him. 'Cocktail parties aren't my scene.'

'If you're worried about being fed, I promise
I'll take you out to dinner later in the evening,'
Zack assured her dryly.

She gave him a glare, more because he *had*
realised she appreciated her food than anything
else. 'You're jumping two steps ahead, Zack,
when I've already turned down the original request!'

'Oh, come on,' he cajoled. 'What harm can it
do you to come along with me? You'll stop me
being bored out of my mind!'

It couldn't do her any harm; she was more than
capable of looking after herself! That wasn't the
point of her refusal at all. She was an adult, and
for the most part she could pick and choose what
she did. Accompanying this man to a cocktail
party was not high on her list of priorities.

But, a little voice inside her head reasoned,
Zack *had* helped her unpack her shopping earlier,
had helped her to cook dinner, *and* he'd produced

a bottle of her favourite wine for them to drink with it. He—

None of those things changed the fact that he had also announced his intention of marrying her!'

In that case, she asked herself almost a day later, as she studied her reflection in the mirror, what on earth was she doing all dressed up as she waited for Zack to arrive before driving them both to the cocktail party?

Merry shook her head dazedly; the man was like a steamroller, knocking down any obstacles—including the word 'no'!—that got in his way.

She looked at her appearance critically. Not bad, she decided. Not bad at all. The black fitted knee-length pencil-slim dress was almost twenty years old, but it was back in fashion, and considering the amount of times she had found to wear it during those years—nil!—it was in pristine condition. Her figure had returned to its natural slenderness after she had given birth to Dani. Her hair she had left loose in dark curls down her spine, adding a little make-up to her normally peachy complexion and a peach gloss to her lips. Yes, she didn't look bad at all for a thirty-seven-year-old mother…!

She gave a rueful smile as she turned away from the mirror. She didn't look bad, but a thirty-seven-year-old woman, with an eighteen-year-old daughter, was *exactly* what she was—and the sooner Zack realised it the better!

But Dani's comment, when Merry walked down the stairs a few minutes later, did nothing to reassure her she would convince him of that this evening.

'You look gorgeous, Mum!' Dani announced admiringly. 'I don't think I've seen you in that dress before.'

Merry smiled. 'If you had, no doubt you would have borrowed it before now!' Dani was a lot taller than her, but both of them had size ten figures.

Dani touched the silkily soft material. 'It's beautiful, Mom. It must have cost—' She broke off as the doorbell rang.

'That will be Zack,' Merry said gratefully—she had never thought she would be relieved at his arrival, but on this occasion she most certainly was.

She did not want to get into a discussion with Dani about her dress... Maybe she shouldn't have worn it, but quite honestly she just didn't have anything else suitable to wear. Cinderella in reverse. She did have something to wear to the ball—but that something had already provoked her daughter's curiosity...

Other than telling her she looked beautiful, Zack made no comment on the dress. But Merry somehow doubted its designer-label style had missed his eagle-eyed attention.

She shouldn't have worn it, did not want to pique Zack's interest in her any more than it already was piqued. But the temptation not to look like the poor relation had been too much for her. Vanity. Ridiculous, in the circumstances...

'David and Dani are going to the cinema together this evening,' Zack announced as he drove them to the party.

'I know,' she replied. 'And until a few days ago—' until Zack himself had come into their lives! '—Dani was barely aware of your nephew's existence.' Any more than she had been aware of Zack's! 'Obviously optimism runs in the family!'

Zack grinned unabashedly. 'I told you, David is a lot like me.'

And what David hadn't been able to achieve on his own—Dani noticing him as more than just one of the crowd!—his uncle had done for him. Dani was now intrigued by the Kingston family. David, she had informed Merry earlier, was a very intel-

ligent young man. Dani had never been attracted
to overtly good-looking young men, was more interested in the brain behind the looks. Remembering Dani's father, and the way she herself had
stupidly fallen for his golden good looks, it was
a trait Merry had encouraged in her daughter.
David Kingston, Dani had decided, had an 'intelligent' mind…

'I know, I know,' Zack said as he saw Merry's
expression. 'I was mad as hell two days ago at
the thought of David wanting to marry anyone.
But, having now met Dani…'' He paused. 'She's
too much like you to be pushed into anything she
doesn't want to do.'

'Remember that,' Merry returned quickly, trying to salvage at least some control over what was
happening in her own life. This man was a bull-
dozer, and at the moment she didn't seem to be
holding her ground at all. As evidenced by this
evening! 'Exactly where is this party?' She
changed the subject as she straightened her colourful shawl, its long length covering the dress
totally.

'A hotel in the city,' Zack returned economi-
cally.

There was something to be said for being

driven in the luxury of the XJS, the smell of doe-leather, the warmth of the interior.

The close proximity of Zack in the confines of the sports car...

He looked, and smelt, gorgeous, the black dinner suit and snowy white shirt doing nothing to hide the power of the body beneath, his hair newly washed and gleaming golden, his after-shave elusively male. No doubt heads would turn—female, of course!—when they reached the party.

Although she was unprepared for the absolute silence that greeted their entry into the crowded private room where the party was being held, or the spontaneous applause that quickly followed that silence.

Merry turned to look behind her, expecting to see someone famous entering behind them. But only Zack and herself stood in the doorway. And as they couldn't be clapping her...

She turned frowningly to Zack as the tiny band at the other end of the room began to play 'For He's a Jolly Good Fellow'. Exactly what sort of party was this? And why was Zack being welcomed in such a fashion?

An elegantly dressed woman in her fifties moved forward out of the crowd to kiss him warmly on the cheek. 'Wonderful party, Zack,' she congratulated throatily.

Merry knew this woman, recognised her instantly. It would be difficult not to; Diana Melbrook was the author of several number one bestselling books, her last having been turned into a television mini-series. The authoress had appeared on several chat shows in the weeks preceding its broadcast.

As Merry glanced around the room she saw several other well-known people: top authors, several actors, a number of television personalities too.

This wasn't just any old cocktail party Zack had brought her to, this was a Thorndyke Books cocktail party—and Zack, as the owner of the publishing house, was also the host!

What did that make her…?

CHAPTER SEVEN

'YOU'VE stopped smiling,' Zack murmured softly against her ear as the conversation began to flow around them once again and they were no longer the centre of attention.

Stopped smiling? That was the least of her worries! She felt frozen to the spot by what she had just realised, wasn't sure she was going to be able to move when the time came for them to mingle with the other guests.

She had imagined a large, impersonal party, a short time spent in inane conversation with complete strangers, and then the two of them could quietly leave. As the host of this party, Zack could hardly leave until the last guest had gone. Which could be in several hours' time!

She turned to him accusingly. 'You could have warned me!'

He spoke unconcernedly. 'If I had, you wouldn't have come.'

'Of course I wouldn't—' She broke off, breathing deeply to steady her nerves. 'What am

I supposed to do now?' Her glittering green gaze told him of her tension.

'Enjoy yourself?'

Enjoy herself…? She didn't know anyone else here, except Zack. No doubt that was what he meant!

She smiled up at him, aware that people were eyeing them curiously. 'I intend getting out of here the first opportunity I get—'

'Merry? Merry Baker? It is you, isn't it?'

Merry froze once more. Not only did someone else at this party know her, and her name, but she knew them too, recognised that voice! It had been about nineteen years since she had last heard it, but it was a voice she would never forget.

'I thought so,' Karen Jacobs drawled derisively as Merry turned slowly to face her. 'You haven't changed a bit.' Her gaze swept over Merry's appearance. 'Same hairstyle. Same dress,' she added pointedly.

Karen obviously hadn't changed, either, she had always been a first-class bitch. Albeit a beautiful one, with an eye for style—which was probably why she'd recognised the dress! It was a talent that had made her editor of one of the top fashion magazines. A tall, willowy blonde, the other woman was as slender as she had always been. Although years ago her hair had been long, now it was cut short, framing the perfect beauty of her face, her eyes deeply blue, and fringed by long, dark lashes.

Merry's eyes turned to the man standing awkwardly at Karen's side; he was tall and dark, almost too good-looking, and there was a weakness about his mouth and in his deep brown eyes that couldn't quite meet Merry's. Here was one person, at least, who would rather not have renewed the acquaintance!

Zack merely looked puzzled by the couple, frowning as he stood slightly on the outside of the group, watching them with narrowed eyes. Like a spectator at a play. Except Merry didn't intend letting him remain that way; he was the one who had brought her here in the first place!

'Darling.' She curved her arm intimately through the crook of his, pulling him gently, but firmly, to her side. 'I would like to introduce you to Karen and Roger Jacobs.'

'Zack and I already know each other,' Karen told her coolly.

Merry nodded. 'But I doubt he realises that you are the younger sister of my sister-in-law,' she said lightly, shooting Zack a warning look as he looked stunned by this information.

As well he might. Karen and Roger Jacobs were as different in lifestyle to Merry as chalk was to cheese; the other couple, with their fine clothes and rich jewellery, were obviously far wealthier than schoolmistress Merry. It hadn't had to be that way, of course, but the price for remaining a part of her family had been far too high for her to pay.

'How *are* Glenda and Stephen?' she prompted Roger, trying to draw him into the conversation; he and Karen hadn't been married when she'd known them all those years ago, but Merry hadn't missed the diamond-studded wedding ring on Karen's left hand. 'And my mother and father, of course,' she added tonelessly.

She couldn't mention Glenda and Stephen without bringing her parents into the picture too. A dutiful son, Stephen, her older brother, had married the woman of their mother's choice. Merry had no reason to doubt that Stephen had since continued to do exactly as he was told. The two of them had been close when they were children, but their differences had become glaring when they were older. 'Dutiful' was not a word that could ever be applied to Merry—or to anything that she did!

Roger didn't look at all happy with this situation. 'They are well,' he answered abruptly, obviously uncomfortable with the whole conversation.

Merry couldn't claim to be exactly thrilled about it herself. As for Zack, he wasn't saying anything, but stood taking in everything that was being discussed. And formulating some questions of his own, no doubt!

'How is your—what did you have, by the way?' Karen raised supercilious brows as she looked at Merry. 'You'll have to excuse us, Zack,' she told him throatily, resting her hand briefly on his arm in a gesture of intimacy. 'As a family, we're always shamelessly lax about keeping in touch with one another.' She gave a tinkling laugh.

Merry returned the other woman's gaze coldly. She hadn't considered this woman part of her family nineteen years ago, and she certainly didn't do so now. Dani was her family now, her only family…

'I have a daughter,' she told the other couple flatly. 'How about you? Do you have children?'

'Certainly not,' Karen dismissed disgustedly. 'I can't imagine anything worse than a screaming little brat hanging onto my ankles. And pregnancy seems to play havoc with a woman's figure,' she concluded bitchily, the fitted red dress she wore showing not an ounce of superfluous flesh on her body.

Zack moved at last, putting his arm possessively about Merry's waist as he drew her closer to his side. 'Let me be the first to assure you that pregnancy did absolutely nothing negative to Merry's body,' he stated, his own eyes challenging now as he looked at Karen. 'She's perfect exactly as she is.'

While she was grateful for his support, at the same time Merry really didn't need the bitchy Karen to get any bitchier—and Zack's remark was sure to make her so!

'Do Glenda and Stephen have children now?' Merry put in quickly.

'No,' the other woman rejoined abruptly. 'Glenda is as averse to pregnancy as I am.'

Merry somehow doubted that; an heir for the Baker family had been paramount in her mother's plans. But it seemed there wasn't one...

'What did happen to that ghastly man you were involved with?' Karen was being deliberately provocative. 'And his equally ghastly wife?' she went on, before Merry could make any reply.

Merry felt herself pale. She hadn't known Jeff was married when she'd fallen so recklessly in love with him. Not that the fact changed anything; he *had* been married, and it had been a marriage he'd had no intention of leaving. Certainly not for a pregnant eighteen-year-old!

She opened her mouth to reply to the insult— only to find Zack had got there first.

'Family reminiscences can be so amusing, can't they?' he put in lightly, the strength of his arm about Merry not light at all! 'We must remember to invite you all to the wedding.'

'Wedding?' Karen echoed sharply, eyes narrowed maliciously as she looked at the two of them suspiciously.

'Yes—our wedding,' Merry heard herself confirm—and then almost gasped out loud as she realised what she had said.

'Well, well, well,' Karen drawled speculatively. 'Could it be that we hear the patter of tiny feet once again?' she asked, looking Merry up and down.

Merry had moved instinctively to slap the other woman for the deliberate jibe; Karen's implication was unmistakable: Merry would only be able to catch a husband like Zack by becoming pregnant! But again Zack was quicker than her, his hand tightly grasping her arm before it could swing upwards and her hand could make contact with the other woman's mocking, smiling face.

The pleasant expression on Zack's face didn't so much as waver, although only a fool could have missed the steely glint in his eyes. 'Funny you should mention that—' his voice was silkily soft—though that silk barely covered the steel beneath, '—we were talking only yesterday about the possibility of getting ourselves a dog once we're married!'

Karen looked startled, momentarily disconcerted. 'A dog?'

'A dog,' Merry concurred, recovering quickly from the other woman's insults; she was no longer an immature teenager, she was a mother, with a responsible job. She had made a success of her life, she realised, despite her family. 'Cats make Zack sneeze,' she continued conversationally, shooting him a grateful look from beneath lowered lashes; the worst thing she could do would be to reduce herself to Karen's level.

'They most certainly—*atishoo*!' Right on cue, Zack sneezed. 'Please excuse me,' he apologised blandly. 'I—*atishoo*!' He sneezed again. 'It seems it's not only the furry kind that have that effect on me,' he added, his expression one of complete innocence.

Roger shot Karen an apprehensive glance as her face tightened furiously. 'I think we should go and circulate, darling.' He took a firm hold of his wife's arm. 'I'm sure we've monopolised enough of Zack's attention for one evening.'

Karen visibly forced herself to relax, her mouth curving into a fixed smile, although her eyes remained glacially hard. 'It was wonderful to see you again,' she said insincerely. 'Your parents will be pleased to know you've done so well for yourself,' she told Merry haughtily.

Merry replied with stony silence. Her parents, her mother, at least, had shown no interest in her over the last nineteen years, and she had no reason to suppose this chance meeting tonight would change any of that. In fact, she didn't want it to— could imagine nothing worse than having to deal with her mother once again!

'Nice to see you again, Roger.' She moved to kiss him lightly on the cheek, smiling at him reassuringly as he gave her an appeasing look. Roger always had been the nicer of this couple! Although weak, very weak...

'You really are looking wonderful, Merry,' he braved his wife's wrath to tell her warmly.

Not so weak after all, Merry acknowledged lightly, returning his smile.

'I always did like you in that dress,' Karen added as her own parting comment.

Merry gave a rueful shake of her head as she watched the other couple walk away. The rich and the beautiful. How sad they really were.

'Meow,' Zack murmured laughingly in her ear.

Zack!

What on earth must he be thinking of her now? Not only were her family awful, but she was a single mother whose lover had been a married man!

Merry had been so young, not much older than Dani was now. Although she had always loved her father, it had been her mother who'd made the decisions, her mother who had decided on the schools her two children would attend, on the universities they eventually went to. She had even chosen Stephen's wife for him. While Merry's father had been a good man, a kind, loving man, he had always meekly acquiesced to his wife's decisions, aware that she was the one who held the pursestrings.

Merry hadn't realised it at the time—although she had had plenty of time in the years that followed!—but at eighteen she had been looking for a man who was strong and dependable, a man who knew who he was, and where he was going.

Jeff had seemed all of those things to Merry's inexperienced eye—but ultimately he had proved he was weaker than her father and brother, a man who used his marriage like a shield while he indulged in numerous affairs that could never go anywhere because he already had a wife! Merry had only learnt the full truth of that when she'd found herself pregnant with his child…

But Zack didn't know any of that, had merely been told by the bitchy Karen that the father of her baby had been a married man. A man who obviously hadn't stood by her when she needed him.

What must Zack be thinking?

He moved to stand in front of her, his hands moving to tenderly cup either side of her face as he tilted it up to his. 'You do realise,' he told her huskily, 'that I intend keeping you to the statement?'

Which statement? There had been so many in the last ten minutes—and none of them complimentary to her!

'The wedding,' Zack explained teasingly as she looked blank. 'I could sue you for breach of contract if you try to back out of marrying me now!'

He could sue her? What did *she* possibly possess that he could sue her for?

Nothing, came the immediate answer. But Zack was telling her, more succinctly than ever, that what he had heard in the last ten minutes hadn't changed how he felt about her at all...!

Merry laughed, a light, relieved laugh. Of course she had no intention of marrying him, but at the same time she didn't want him to think badly of her either. And he didn't...

'That's better.' He spoke his satisfaction at her laugh, his hands leaving her cheeks as he reached down and placed one of her own hands firmly in his. 'And now I believe it's time to get ourselves a drink and circulate.'

'Circulate' meant accompanying Zack as he spoke briefly with every person in the room, Zack charming and assured as he did so. It quickly became obvious that not only did his guests like him, they trusted and respected him too.

Zack Kingston, Merry realised dazedly, *was* a strong, dependable man, a man who knew who he was and where he was going...

Oh, help!

CHAPTER EIGHT

'I WAS eighteen when I met Jeff,' Merry told Zack a couple of hours later, when the two of them were sitting in a quiet restaurant together enjoying a late supper. Although Merry's appetite deserted her the moment she began to talk about that disastrous relationship nineteen years ago. A relationship that had ultimately changed the whole of her life…

She had been eighteen, the daughter of a wealthy family, beginning her art degree. The whole world had been at her feet, her future choices unlimited. Then she'd met Jeff.

'You really don't have to tell me any of this, you know,' Zack assured her. 'I think I know enough about human nature by now to realise that Karen Jacobs is not a nice woman.' He paused. 'That her version of events is coloured by her own unhappiness.'

Merry's eyes widened. 'What makes you say that?' Karen had struck her as a woman comfortable with her own success.

Zack sipped at his wine, his first alcoholic drink

of the evening. He had stuck to drinking orange juice throughout the cocktail party, explaining quietly to Merry that it was work and not pleasure. Most of the guest list had been made up of Thorndyke authors, the rest of them television, newspaper, and magazine personalities—hence Karen's invitation at all. Despite the impression Karen had tried to give of a greater intimacy between herself and Zack, Merry knew which version she believed!

'Merry, you have so much more than Karen does. Oh, yes, you do,' he confirmed as she tried to protest. 'Bullies rarely pick on people they actually consider inferior to them, even though it might seem that they do. It's invariably someone who really possesses something they wish they had.'

'I can assure you,' Merry snorted, 'I have nothing Karen could possibly want!'

'How about independence? You obviously broke away from family ties. And personal success—you couldn't look and behave the way you do if you weren't perfectly satisfied with your life exactly as it is— What is it?' he pounced sharply as she pondered this last comment.

'Nothing.' She forced a brightness into her smile. 'None of us can claim to have everything we want.' She excused her brief moment of regret. She had everything she *needed*...

'That's true,' Zack acknowledged slowly. 'I thought my life was running along quite nicely—until I met you and realised it had a damned great hole in it!'

'Zack,' she warned reprovingly.

'Okay, don't believe me,' he said. 'But David is about as close as I've ever had to someone I could sit down and talk to the way I do with you. And as we both know, that isn't the same thing at all!'

She did know. Close as she and Dani were, friends as well as mother and daughter, that latter relationship precluded her from talking to Dani about some things. Besides, there was a generation gap that wasn't there between Zack and herself.

Help again!

'You're a successful woman in your own right, Merry, through your own endeavours and not through a family connection,' Zack continued determinedly. 'You also have something else that Karen and her sister, your sister-in-law do not have.'

Now Merry was very puzzled. What could she

possibly have—Zack? He surely didn't mean himself?

Had that intimate hand on his arm meant something, after all? There was no doubting that Karen was a beautiful woman, and—

'I have no idea what you're thinking now.' Zack cut in on her racing thoughts. 'From the expression on your face, I don't think I want to know, either! I was talking about Dani, Merry,' he explained as she looked at him uncomprehendingly once again. 'You have a child.'

'But—'

'I was watching Roger's face during that part of the conversation.' Zack shook his head. 'Karen may have chosen not to have children; I accept that part of it. But I have a feeling it's something else completely with your sister-in-law. Roger looked taken aback when Karen claimed her sister didn't want children either, which leads me to believe that she probably can't have any... Does that sound feasible to you?' he asked thoughtfully.

Merry remembered her mother's glee when Stephen had married Glenda; her wish had been that the young couple provided her with grandchildren as quickly as possible. And Merry's brother had always been so dutiful...

'How sad,' Merry sighed—and sincerely meant

it. Glenda was too much like Karen for her and Merry ever to have been friends, but even so she couldn't help feeling for the other woman, if what Zack suggested was true. It *did* sound feasible.

Her own life would have been so much bleaker without Dani in it. Less complicated too, she accepted that, but she wouldn't change her life for Karen's or Glenda's. Which was exactly what Zack had been talking about all the time...

'Will you see any of your family again?' Zack prompted gently as he watched the emotions flickering across her face.

Merry gave him a startled look. 'Why on earth should I? One chance meeting with the sister of my sister-in-law—the first in nineteen years, I might add—' she told him hurriedly—one step into *his* life and she had been thrown into the company of people she hadn't seen since she was a teenager, whom she'd had no wish to see during that time, either! '—gives me no interest in seeing again the family who totally rejected me and my unborn child!' The last came out slightly bitterly, although it came as a surprise to Merry that she should still feel that way.

She didn't know what reaction she had expected from her parents on learning of her pregnancy, but it certainly hadn't been the one she had got. Of course, her brother, Stephen, weak as usual, hadn't questioned their decision.

'That's what happened, isn't it?' Zack said understandingly. 'You broke the acceptable code, and so they threw you out.' His mouth tightened grimly at the thought.

'Oh, I could have stayed,' Merry informed him with barely concealed distaste. 'All I had to do to remain part of the Baker family was destroy my own child before it was born! It's ironic, really,' she went on. 'That unwanted grandchild is now the only one they have.'

'Their only heir,' he confirmed. 'You didn't tell me you were *that* Baker,' he tacked on playfully, reminding her of her comment when she'd realised he was the Kingston who owned Thorndyke Books.

But she knew exactly what he meant by his remark; the Baker family were old money—owned property all over the world, had shares in numerous companies. Her father had even been the one to change *his* surname when he'd married her mother; as the only Baker heir of her generation, her mother had had no intention of relinquishing hers.

But the name, and all that went with it, had

meant nothing to Merry, and she didn't want the
family inheritance for Dani either...

'You didn't ask,' she replied. 'And Dani may
be the only heir,' she added tightly, 'but she has
nothing to do with the family!'

Zack persisted. 'She may not feel that way.
And Karen strikes me as a troublemaker...'

He was right, of course; Karen had always liked
to stir things up and then sit back and watch the
situation develop! To mention this evening's ac-
cidental meeting with Merry to her family would
benefit no one. Which was exactly why Karen
would do such a thing, of course!

'What a mess,' Merry muttered irritably.

'And all my fault,' Zack put in ruefully.

She looked at him sharply, feeling the colour
in her cheeks. 'I didn't say that.'

'You didn't have to,' he responded, reaching
across the table to take one of her hands in his.
'I can tell exactly what you're thinking. Merry,
I'm really sorry this has happened, but at the same
time I suggest you let Dani make her own mind
up about this if—or when—the time comes. She's
your daughter; she'll know the right thing to do.'

Dani *was* her daughter, and she hoped that she
had been a good mother to her, that she had in-
stilled all the right values in her. It was just that

the Baker family could be so powerful if they chose to be.

Not with her daughter, they couldn't! Dani might only be eighteen, but she had her own code of moral values, a sense of what was right and what was wrong—though a few days ago Merry *had* made the erroneous assumption that Dani was pregnant with David Kingston's child…!

No! Dani was a sensible young lady, would never do anything to hurt someone else, would never be taken in by the lavish lifestyle the Baker family had to offer. Dani simply wasn't impetuous.

Merry wasn't quite so sure about that when they arrived back at the house a short time later and Dani dreamily greeted her at the front door with the words, 'Mum, I've met the man I'm going to marry!'

Not another one! What was *wrong* with everyone all of a sudden?

This was just too much!

CHAPTER NINE

'I *WAS* mistaken.' Zack's voice came from behind Merry. 'David *is* as impatient as I am!'

Merry wasn't in the mood for levity. This whole situation was becoming ridiculous. 'Dani.' She spoke firmly to her daughter. 'I suggest we talk about this once Zack has left.'

'Oh, hi, Zack.' Dani looked at him as he stood in the shadows behind her mother. 'I didn't see you there.' She looked a little embarrassed at having been quite so open in his presence. 'I'll leave the two of you to finish your evening,' she apologised. 'I just wanted to... Night, Mum.' She bent to kiss Merry on the cheek. 'Zack.' She ran up the stairs, not dwelling on her outspokenness.

Merry didn't move. What was wrong with everybody. Had they put something in the water? What, for goodness' sake? Because suddenly everyone around her wanted to get married!

Zack strolled past her into the house, turning back when Merry still didn't move. 'It *was* David she was talking about, wasn't it?' he queried.

Merry shot him an impatient glance. 'Unless

247

she met someone else before or after the film—of course it was David!' She marched determinedly into the house after slamming the door behind her. 'What is it with your family?' she demanded accusingly. 'You have to leave, Zack. You and your nephew. You're turning our lives upside down. We were fine as we were. We don't need—*I* don't need—' Where had these tears come from, cascading hotly down her cheeks, making speech impossible, and her whole body tremble with reaction?

'Merry!' Zack enveloped her in warm, comforting arms, holding her against his chest.

This was exactly what she didn't want! But she was too upset, too tired, too emotionally fraught to fight against it at this moment. She had been fighting too long, alone against so many obstacles. Right now she simply didn't have the strength to fight against the protection Zack's arms gave her against those obstacles. It was all too easy just to give herself up to being the one who was looked after for a change, rather than the one who did the looking after.

She could barely see Zack as she looked up at him through her tears, had no idea how vulnerable she looked. But she did feel the gentle pressure of Zack's lips against hers, the way her body melted into his as she returned his kiss, and not gently at all.

She needed—oh, God, at this moment she needed Zack! To be kissed by him. Not to have to think, if only for a brief time. Bliss!

She had never been kissed like this in her life before!

Zack's lips wreaked havoc on the softness of hers, his arms like steel bands as he moulded her body to the hard contours of his. Once again Merry was amazed at how well their bodies fitted together, even if he was too tall...

She was babbling again—but in her head this time!

Her neck arched as Zack's lips trailed a fiery path to the creamy hollows the black dress left bare, one of his hands lightly caressing the full upthrust of her breast, her nipple pulsating with pleasure beneath the silky material.

'Oh, Zack...!' she groaned weakly, knowing that if this continued much longer she was going to be completely lost. Dani was upstairs—

Dear Lord, Dani! She couldn't behave in this wanton fashion with her daughter only feet away, albeit up the stairs and in her own bedroom with the door firmly closed. Dreaming about David, no doubt!

Zack released Merry reluctantly as she pulled away. 'Don't look so upset, Merry,' he chided. 'It was only a kiss.'

Only a kiss? She didn't think so! The truth of the matter was, she was falling in love with this man. If she wasn't already in love with him! And *that* terrified the life out of her...!

'That isn't what I'm upset about.' She retreated into anger. 'You came here the other day, insisting that my daughter couldn't marry your nephew; now I suggest you go home and tell him the same thing.'

As she warmed to the subject, she really did feel angry. Zack had made things worse by coming here two days ago; until that time Dani hadn't so much as given David a second glance—now it appeared she was in love with him!

'They are both far too young to think about getting married,' she snapped. 'And Dani wouldn't even have thought about taking David seriously if you hadn't piqued her interest,' she accused, eyes brightly green.

'Merry—'

'Don't you "Merry" me in that patronising tone!'

'Another fault to add to the long list?' Zack

arched blond brows, his hair falling endearingly onto his forehead.

But Merry only felt more irritated as she noticed his tousled hair—it had been her fingers running through it that had caused the disarray! 'Just the truth,' she bit out coldly. 'You have only complicated my life—'

'Isn't that better than just emotionally skimming along the surface?' he suggested softly.

She became very still. 'Exactly what do you mean by that remark?' But she knew; she *knew*!

Zack drew in a deep breath, slowly releasing it again. 'Merry, I know what you're trying to do—and I'm not going to fight you,' he added quickly as she went to speak. 'I care about you very much, Merry, and I know I've been bulldozing you the last few days. I also accept that it isn't working, that I'm only succeeding in upsetting you. It's my way. See what I want—and go for it. It probably has something to do with that arrogance you once accused me of,' he admitted.

He was trying to lighten up now, and in a way he was succeeding. Because it was his previous remark that had hit her with the force of a sledgehammer. Emotionally skimming on the surface of life... Was that what she had been doing the last nineteen years...?

The first few years after Dani's birth had been hard, looking after a small child, working hard on her degree course, living on a small allowance. By the time Dani began school herself, Merry had been ready to begin her teaching career. Since then, the years had simply flown by, filled with Dani and her job, and her personal life put almost on permanent hold; even the few dates she had accepted had always been with men with whom she had a mutual interest, but whom she hadn't found particular attractive. Emotionally skimming, Zack had called it...

''Merry, you know that I want you in my life.' Zack lightly gripped the tops of her arms. 'But I want you there permanently, as my wife, and I won't accept anything less.'

He was so different from Jeff it was difficult to take in. The last thing Jeff had wanted was to marry her; Zack wouldn't accept anything less...

'I want a white wedding,' he continued with assurance. 'The walking down the aisle and the ''till death us do part'' bits. I would like us to have a child together. But you have to want all those things too. And until you do, perhaps it's better if I stay out of your way,' he concluded heavily. 'I can love and cherish you, but until you love me in return you're only going to view my actions with suspicion—and great caution. I don't want that. I don't want to go on causing you distress, either.'

He was leaving her life! As quickly as he had come into it, he was leaving!

'I'll have a chat with David,' he promised, releasing her, stepping back, the happiness gone from his face now, his expression as grim as the first day he had knocked on her door. 'See what plans he and Dani have. If any,' he added self-disgustedly. 'I won't jump to any conclusions this time!'

And neither would Merry! She had totally misjudged the whole situation last time, although common sense—and her knowledge of Dani— had thankfully kicked into action.

But that was for later, once Zack had gone. Because he *was* leaving. And he wasn't coming back. There was nothing she could do or say that would stop him—because she couldn't say the words he wanted to hear! Maybe it was emotionally skimming, but at least this way no one had been able to hurt her in all these years...

Once Zack was out of her life again, she would be able to return to that.

Wouldn't she...?

CHAPTER TEN

'I KNOW I shouldn't, Mum, but I feel really nervous,' Dani told Merry as they stood outside the huge oak door that fronted the imposing house.

Merry shot her daughter a sympathetic glance. She couldn't claim to be feeling exactly relaxed about this herself. But it wouldn't do for *both* of them to admit to feeling nervous!

Zack had been proved correct in his observation that Karen appeared to him to be a woman who liked to create trouble! He had been right about several other things too, Merry had realised in the week since he'd left her, but those other things she had pushed to the back of her mind, deciding that what they were dealing with now was more important for the moment. After all, tomorrow *was* another day...

Not even a day had passed from the time she had met Karen again to when she'd received a telephone call from her father—she had vowed at that moment to become ex-directory! But the call had to come from her father, of course, because, as they all knew, Merry would have simply replaced the receiver on hearing the sound of her mother's voice. And would have still gone ex-directory!

Her father was another matter completely; Merry had always been close to him during her childhood, and had received no ultimatums from *him* when she'd told her parents of her pregnancy. What her mother hadn't known then, and probably still didn't know, was that her father had visited Merry shortly after she'd given birth to Dani, that he had helped her financially too, during those first few difficult years of studying and being a single mother. It was as much as he'd been able to do when her mother had refused to even have Merry's name mentioned in the house.

She knew her mother had put her father up to the telephone call inviting herself and Dani to dinner; he wouldn't have dared to do it without her mother's consent.

Dinner. Just the four of them, her father had assured her. With no hidden agenda. She had never known her mother *not* to have one, but this time it wasn't so hidden; Dani was the only Baker grandchild, and her grandmother wanted to meet her.

In which case, in total agreement with Zack over this, Merry had felt it was Dani's choice…

Which was the reason they were now standing outside the front door of the Baker residence. Merry hadn't made the same mistake this evening of wearing the classic black dress that had earned her such ridicule from Karen last week! Her dress tonight, newly bought, was the same deep emerald colour of her eyes, and it fitted the tininess of her slender figure perfectly. It might be so in real life, but Merry wouldn't look like the poor relation this evening!

'Your grandfather is wonderful, Dani,' she told her daughter softly. 'My mother—' She stopped, at a loss for words where her mother was concerned—where *any* mother who could reject her own daughter under such circumstances was concerned. She had tried several times during the last week to describe Mrs Baker to Dani, but the truth simply wouldn't do; she owed her mother nothing, but Dani's relationship with her was a completely different matter.

'Don't keep worrying about it, Mum.' Dani squeezed her hand reassuringly. 'I simply want to meet them both. I'm curious, that's all. I don't expect to feel much else,' she added.

Merry's first thought, on seeing her mother again for the first time in nineteen years, was that time hadn't been kind to her. The face that had once been regally beautiful had become pinched and bitter; Eleanor Baker looked all of her sixty-three years!

Merry's father had fared slightly better, tall, and still strikingly handsome in his black dinner suit, wings of grey at his temples in hair otherwise as dark as Merry's own. It was so good to see him again!

'Merry, darling.' He moved forward to hug her. 'You look wonderful,' he told her warmly.

She blinked back the tears, proudly pulling Dani to her side. She *was* so proud of Dani, felt she was the single most perfect thing she had ever done in her life. 'This is my daughter, Dani— short for Daniella.' The last was added slightly defensively as she looked across the room to where her mother stood, looking at them all so aloofly.

The house itself hadn't changed at all since Merry's childhood, still the show-piece of the woman who owned it, the deep red and gold decor somehow seeming to reflect Eleanor Baker's coldness rather than casting the warm effect that it should have.

'Named for your father, of course.' Her mother spoke for the first time since their arrival, a voice well-remembered from the last time Merry and

her mother had spoken: cold and slightly conde-
scending.

How her mother must hate having to do this,
Merry realised sadly, almost feeling sorry for that.
Almost... Too much had been said and done in
the past for her ever to completely forgive
Eleanor.

Merry's head went back. 'Of course,' she confirmed in a clipped voice, remembering the proud
look on her father's face the day he'd realised she
had named her daughter after him.

'In that case, my dear,' Eleanor spoke directly
to her granddaughter, 'I shall call you Daniella.'

Dani returned her look with unblinking eyes. 'I
would rather you didn't. My name is Dani,' she
replied clearly.

Merry looked at the two women, the one so
much older now, but having lost none of her im-
periousness, the other poised on the brink of
womanhood—and her expression turned to one of
amazement as she saw for the first time that Dani
had her grandmother's regal bearing, if none of
her snobbery, and a definite will of her own! Her
mother, Merry realised with some amusement as
she began to relax for the first time in days, had
met her match in her granddaughter!

'Very well,' Eleanor accepted after several

stunned seconds. 'I'm sure it's a very pretty name.'

'I've always thought so,' Dani agreed.

The initial clash between grandmother and granddaughter, in which Dani had undoubtedly been the winner, set the tone for the rest of the evening, with Merry's mother avoiding any subjects that might be cause for controversy. Including that of Merry's supposed engagement to Zack Kingston... Karen was sure to have mentioned that little fact to the family as well, Merry was sure. But it was never mentioned.

In fact, the whole evening was more pleasant than Merry could possibly have hoped for. What had seemed to her like a huge mountain to climb had turned out to be nothing more than a small molehill. She would never forgive or forget the way her mother had let her down all those years ago, in fact she might never see her mother again after this evening, but it really didn't matter to her any more. She had faced her mother and felt nothing but a slight sense of pity—for all that her mother could have had, which instead she had so wantonly given up.

'Whew, what a dragon.' Dani's chuckled remark, on their way home shortly after ten o'clock, seemed to echo Merry's thoughts. 'Grandpa is a poppet, though,' she added with real affection, having fallen quite easily into calling him such, while Eleanor had very firmly remained Eleanor!

Merry eyed her daughter ruefully. She needn't have worried on that score either; Dani knew exactly who she was—and wasn't! 'You do realise what tonight was all about, don't you?'

'Of course.' Dani wrinkled her nose inelegantly. 'They wanted to look me over, see if I'm good enough to be a Baker.'

Merry laughed at her daughter's forthright summing up of the evening. Dani was right, of course; Merry probably just wouldn't have put it quite that bluntly. 'Do you think you passed?' she teased.

'Who cares?' Dani dismissed.

Exactly—who cared any more? That particular Nemesis was well and truly faced as far as Merry was concerned, and Dani wasn't about to let it become one for her.

Dani reached out and squeezed her arm briefly. 'You've been a wonderful mother to me,' she told her huskily. 'The best family anyone could ever wish for.'

Merry swallowed hard. 'Thank you.'

'I'm glad you decided to name me after

Grandpa, though. He loves you, and you obviously love him very much.'

'Not as much as I love you,' Merry told her softly.

'What a lucky pair we are,' Dani pronounced with satisfaction. 'And as for my surname; that's going to be totally irrelevant once I'm married to David,' she said happily.

Dani had remained firm in the announcement she had made almost a week ago. Having now met David several times, Merry agreed with Zack that his nephew looked nothing like him, but in other ways he was so like his uncle it brought a lump into her throat just to be in the same room with him.

'Have the two of you decided on a date for the wedding yet?' she probed gently.

Dani shrugged. 'Some time after we've both got our degrees, and before we start medical school.'

Merry had been included in several conversations with the young couple, and she knew that their ultimate aim was to open up a medical practice together—Kingston and Kingston. They seemed to have progressed a long way in a week, but, as Merry knew only too well herself, it *was* possible to fall in love in the space of a second, not to mention in three days…!

'Isn't he sweet,' Dani murmured dreamily at her side. 'I told David how nervous I felt about this evening,' she explained at Merry's questioning look, 'and he's sat here and waited for me to come home.' She pointed to the colourful Mini parked in front of their home.

Merry's own gaze went past the Mini to the Jaguar stationed in front of it. *She* hadn't told Zack she was nervous about seeing her parents again—in fact she hadn't spoken to him for six days—but it looked as if he had guessed her feelings for himself, and decided to follow his nephew's example. He had waited for her to come home, too!

CHAPTER ELEVEN

How Merry's heart ached just at the sight of him!

She had inwardly acknowledged to herself this week how much she was missing him, but face to face with him like this—! She ached, too, to know the warmth of his smile, the deep huskiness of his laugh, the warm strength of his arms, to hear him tell her again that he loved her...

'Zack,' she greeted him tensely, having locked her car door and turned to find him standing on the pavement beside her.

But she had known he was there, had felt him there.

'Mum, David and I are just going for a drive,' Dani called out to her as she got into the car beside David.

Zack looked at Merry closely, searchingly. 'Is everything okay?' he prompted softly as his nephew and Dani drove away.

'Why shouldn't it be?' Merry dismissed flippantly. 'Dani and I have just come back from dinner, that's all.'

His deep blue gaze remained fixed on her face.

'I know where you've been, Merry,' he confirmed gently. 'David told me. I had to come; I feel responsible.'

Responsible? She didn't want him to feel that—it was the last emotion she wanted from him!

She had thought so much about him this last week—had hardly been able to think about anything else. Thoughts of Zack, and how she felt about him, had even lessened the importance of dinner with her parents this evening. But she had known she had to get that out of the way, for Dani's sake, before she made any move to see Zack.

And now he had come to see her...

What did they do now? If Dani and David had stayed then they could all have gone into the house for coffee, but—

'Invite me in, Merry,' Zack demanded gruffly.

Now that he was here this was all going too fast for her. What if—?

Zack barely waited for the door to close behind them before gathering her up into his arms. 'I've missed you!' he groaned, his face buried in the scented softness of her hair.

She had missed him too. God, how she had missed him. He was deep inside her heart now, and she couldn't seem to get him out. In fact, she had decided in these last days without him that she didn't want to!

'What did you say?' Zack had become very still, raising his head to look down at her with eyes that had gone cobalt blue.

What had she said? She hadn't— She couldn't have—

'I love you, Zack.' The words came out clear and firm this time.

And she was the one who had said them. Not once, but twice!

'You love me...?' He seemed totally astounded by her admission. *He* was astounded; she didn't even seem to have control over what she said any more!

'Yes,' she confirmed with certainty. 'And there is no responsibility to be felt about this evening by anyone. I realise now that I should have done it years ago.' She shook her head. 'All I can see them as now is two elderly people who have lived their lives by a code, imposed by other people as well as themselves. And because of that they missed out on their granddaughter growing up. I...' She hesitated momentarily. 'I've lived my own life by a certain code these last nineteen years too. It's a code that hasn't allowed people close enough to be able to hurt me. ''Emotionally skimming'', I think you called it,' she remembered ruefully.'

'Merry—'

'No, let me finish, Zack?' she asked softly. 'Because I've stopped skimming. What's left is a very emotional woman, a woman who wants that white wedding, the walking down the aisle *and* the ''till death us do part'' bits.' The tears in her eyes blurred her vision, but she knew Zack was still there, could feel him there. 'But only if *you're* the man waiting at the end of that aisle for me. Zack, will you marry me?' Oh, *help*. She quaked inwardly as she heard herself say those last four words.

His arms tightened about her. 'I'll even let you plan the wedding—as long as you make it soon!' he grated.

She didn't care how soon it was. She had been without him this last week—and she had absolutely hated it. She loved this man, every caring inch of him!

'Do you mind if we convert the top of my house into a studio for you *after* we're married? I really don't want to wait until the work is completed—' Zack looked down at her as she gasped. 'I remember you once told me that no one has everything they want, so I asked Dani what it was *you* wanted—and she told me you had always wanted a place of your own where you can paint full time.' He paused and smiled. 'Your wish will be granted, my love.'

Candid, *wonderful* Dani!

'I would like us to have a child of our own, too,' she told him almost shyly. To finally be given the studio she had always wanted would be wonderful, but at the moment she could imagine nothing more exciting than the two of them having a baby of their own to love and care for.

'Remembering your inability to take the pill— I told you I would store that away for future reference!' he joked '—and the way I find it difficult to keep my hands of you, I think that it's highly likely!' he said. 'There's absolutely no reason why you can't paint *and* have our baby, my darling,' he assured her lovingly. 'Together we can do anything!'

Together... It wasn't something she had ever known before. But it sounded and felt wonderful!

And she knew, with Zack, it always would be...

THEY'RE WED AGAIN!
by
Penny Jordan

Penny Jordan has been writing for more than fifteen years and has an outstanding record: over 100 novels published including **Power Play** which hit the *Sunday Times* and *New York Times* bestseller lists, and most recently, the phenomenally successful **To Love, Honour and Betray**. With over 60 million copies of her books in print worldwide and translations in more than seventeen languages, Penny Jordan has established herself as an internationally-acclaimed author. She was born in Preston, Lancashire and now lives with her husband in a beautiful fourteenth-century house in rural Cheshire.

Recent titles by Penny Jordan:

The Mistress Assignment, April 1999
The Perfect Lover, February 1999
One Night in His Arms, November 1998

CHAPTER ONE

'AUNT BELLE! You look *wonderful*, positively glowing...'

'Shouldn't that be *my* line to *you*?' Isabelle smiled as she hugged her newly married niece, and then stepped back to admire her wedding dress.

'I'm sorry about the mix-up with the invitations,' Joy apologised. 'But Great-Aunt Alice insisted on helping Mum to write them, and you *know* what she's like.' She pulled a wry face. 'She completely forgot that you and Luscious Lucius got divorced simply ages ago, and sent you both joint invitations to his address...'

'"Luscious Lucius". You still call him that, do you?' Isabelle teased her niece, smiling a warm look at Joy's new husband.

'Oh, Andy doesn't mind,' Joy laughed back. 'After all, Luc *is* his cousin, and besides—' she gave her new husband a mock stern look '—Andy has always thought that *you* are gorgeously sexy—for an older woman...'

As the groom went pink, and tugged at his cra-

271

vat, Isabelle raised her eyebrows. She was thirty-four, almost thirty-five, to Joy's twenty-three—not yet in her dotage, surely?

At Joy's age she and Luc had already been married for close on two years. They had married far too immature—a girl whom marriage had hot-housed into a woman. And while Luc might have loved the girl he had married, he had certainly ceased to love the woman that girl had become.

As she had told Luc at the time, she'd thought it grossly unfair that he had refused to acknowledge and appreciate the stresses that her career had placed on her, the anxiety that being the main breadwinner in their household had caused her. And then, on top of that anxiety, to have Luc complain that she was never at home, that she valued her job more than she did him, had been just too much for her to endure, and had ultimately caused the series of destructive rows which had eventually led to their divorce.

'Luc, I have hardly any time to myself,' she had pointed out to him during one of their arguments. 'When I *am* at home, I have housework to do, food to buy—this house doesn't clean itself, you know. I'm the one who has to worry about paying the mortgage and keeping the cupboards filled—all you have to worry about is your precious studying. Sometimes I think that is all you do think about—care about!'

Belle could still remember how his face had darkened, his eyes clouding as he'd turned away from her, his head seeming to hang a little. At over six foot he was much, much taller than her, but as he'd moved away from her then he'd looked oddly shrunken and defeated, humiliated and humbled somehow, and along with her anger she had felt a sense of anguish and pain, a sharp flash of panic which she'd quickly pushed to one side.

If she had thought about the subject at all before they had married, she had assumed naively that their marriage would be an idyll, a continuation of the hours, and days, and the very occasional stolen weekends they had managed to snatch since their first meeting earlier in the year when she, newly graduated and working for the high-powered city firm of financial analysts where she had been lucky to get a job, had been introduced by a friend to the brilliant young mathematician who had turned his back on the profitable world of commerce and finance and who, idealistically, had opted instead to devote himself to further study and ultimately a career as a university lecturer.

It had been a private joke between them in those early days that she was the one with the large salary and the company car, whilst he was the one still eking out a meagre living on a grant. But there had been no doubt in Belle's mind about her feelings, her love for Luc, and she had admired him intensely for his dedication and his idealism.

'I want to marry you…' Luc had told her longingly a few months into their courtship. 'I want us to be together for always. But I can barely afford to support myself, never mind a wife…'

'We could live on my salary,' Belle had told him sunnily, far too deeply in love with him to care how they financed their lives, just as long as they shared them.

If anyone had warned her then that her job, her earnings, which had made it possible for them to be together, would one day be the cause of them breaking up, she would have laughed in immediate denial. Her love for Luc and his love for her had been so strong, so meant by fate, that she'd been sure nothing could ever make them part.

She might have been in the vanguard of a movement that had women taking on a much more prominent role in financing their own and their partner's lives, but striking a blow for equality had been the last thing on Belle's mind when, a few years into their marriage, she had persuaded Luc that it made more sense for them to buy a house now that they were married than for her to go on sharing his cramped rented accommodation. They could afford the mortgage after all. She had just been promoted and had received a good rise.

'You mean *you* can afford it,' Luc had corrected her gently, but Belle hadn't really heard him. She had been far too busy excitedly studying the house details she had brought home with her, dreaming already of how she would decorate their new home.

And in the end Luc had gone along with her wishes, and they had bought the pretty village property they had both fallen for in the small, and in those days undeveloped village within reasonably easy commuting distance of London and close to Cambridge, where Luc eventually hoped to get a university post.

'I won't be able to use my bike to get to college any more,' Luc had protested when they had first gone to see the house.

'You can travel by train, like I do,' Belle had pointed out. 'We can travel to the station together in my car.'

'What about the days when you leave at six and don't get back until nine or ten?' Luc had reminded her, but Belle had been so desperately in love with the house, so sure it was perfect for them, that eventually he had given way—as she had known he would.

They had celebrated their first night of owning the house in the big double bedroom in front of the fireplace, lying on their duvet on the bare floorboards.

Luc, always romantic, had insisted on lighting a fire in the hearth, and the room had smelled of woodsmoke and candles. There had been a problem getting the electricity turned on, Belle remembered, and she had gone to try to sort it out. In her absence Luc had been out and bought candles—hundreds of them, or so it had seemed. They had lit her way up the stairs where Luc had carefully and formally ushered her into their bedroom.

In their soft glow Luc's face had taken on a sternness, a maturity which had both startled her a little and thrilled her. She'd become so used to his gentle, easygoing acceptance of whatever plans she made, that to see him looking so purposeful and determined had touched a little feminine nerve inside her that had made her ache with longing for him.

'This house is our home,' Luc told her as he started to undress her. 'Our home, Belle. We'll work on it, shape it, share in it together… I know it's *your* salary that's made it possible for us to buy it, but it takes more than money to make a home, and I want our home to be something we've *both* worked for…'

There was a warning there for her to heed, but she neglected to do so, shivering a little in the cool evening air, despite the warmth of Luc's smoky fire, snuggling up close to him as he removed the last of their clothing, opening her mouth eagerly to the hungry passion of his as he started to kiss her.

The physical attraction between them had been immediate and intense right from the start; Luc, three, nearly four years her senior, had technically at least been the more experienced of the two of them, but, as he had freely and adoringly admitted to Belle, she had brought to their relationship and to him a sexual intensity and an emotional openness that made him feel that everything he had experienced before, everything he had thought he knew, had been merely a pale shadow of their shared reality.

Now, with their kisses growing deeper and deeper, and the warm, silk-rough glide of Luc's hands over her eager body, Belle forgot how cold it was, how cheerless the empty, unfurnished room; she forgot, too, the hassle she had had over their unconnected electricity supply, the irritation she had experienced with Luc because he had been so engrossed in his studies that he had forgotten to notify the authorities in time to have the supply reconnected before they moved in. What did that kind of electricity matter when the variety *they* created between them was so intense that it could fuel a whole universe?

The duvet was soft and inviting, even if at the back of Belle's mind lay the knowledge that it would have to be washed before it could go anywhere near the new bed she intended to persuade Luc to agree to her buying; the glow from the candles was doing wonderful things to the soft curves of her body and Luc's, and the glow in Luc's eyes was making her burn so hotly for him that her tremulous, almost panting breath was threatening to blow those candles closest to them out.

'Luc…'

Wantonly she reached for him, pressing her open mouth to each hollow and curve of his can-

dlelight-shadowed body, feeling him tense and
shudder in wild reaction to her sensuous caresses.

Her tongue-tip teased the dark arrowing of hair
that spread with delicious invitation down the
length of his torso, a rich, fertile valley all excitingly male, yielding a harvest that Belle already
knew full well more than lived up to its promise.
There was an idealistic intensity about Luc that
he brought to everything he did, but most especially to his love for her.

She was his first real true love. He had once
told her in the early days of their relationship that
she would always be his one true love.

Belle loved him just as intensely, but there was
a practicality about her nature which made her
sometimes feel just a little impatient of Luc's idealism and his total lack of interest in anything
material.

Of course, like him, she agreed that no amount
of money or material possessions could make up
for a lack of love; that what they had, what they
shared, was worth more than a king's ransom, a
hundred kings' ransoms, but… But just think how
wonderful it would have been tonight if they had
been making love in their new bed, the handsome
king-sized one she had seen in the small exclusive
handmade furniture shop just outside Cambridge,

a bed with a wonderful hand-carved headboard. They could have their initials carved into it, and some special symbol to represent their love…

And then, as Luc's tenderly roving hands touched those most secret, sacred places of her body, she forgot all about the new bed and the mess the dusty floor would be making of their duvet, as a small moan of blissful pleasure escaped her lips.

She remembered about it the following day, though, as she complained to Luc about the dust-marks on the duvet and the candle wax that had fallen on it.

'It's a duvet—a piece of fabric. It will wash,' Luc had defended.

'Oh, yes, it will wash,' Belle agreed, tight-lipped. 'But not here and not by me. For one thing we don't possess a washing machine, and for another, even if we did, we don't have any electricity supply to run it.'

'Look, I'm sorry about that. I've already explained, Professor Lind wanted to ask my opinion about…'

Professor Lind was something of an idol to Luc, who desperately wanted to emulate the older man's academic achievements. Belle had met him several times but sensed that, like Luc, he was rather contemptuous of her much more materially based world. She also rather suspected that the professor felt Luc had made a mistake in marrying her, and when she had taxed Luc with this he had looked a little embarrassed and finally admitted that the professor *had* counselled him against getting married.

'He doesn't think any man should get married until he's over thirty,' he had told Belle ruefully, adding huskily, 'But then he's obviously never met a woman like you...never been in love...'

Discussing the duvet reminded Belle of the bed she had seen but, predictably, Luc objected the moment she had told him where she had seen it.

'It will be far too expensive for us,' he told her, his voice suddenly unusually curt and hard.

'Oh, Luc...I want us to have something special, passed on not from either of our parents, something that's ours...' she told him softly, moving towards him, intending to snuggle into his arms.

But to her chagrin he turned away from her, his face unexpectedly grim as he told her sharply, 'I thought we already had something special.'

'The house...' Belle agreed. 'Oh, yes, but I want it to be furnished as specially as it deserves, and—'

'No, Belle, *not* the house,' Luc told her distantly. 'I was referring to our love itself...'

They made up the quarrel on that occasion, but the issue of the new bed remained unresolved—until Belle thought she had found an ideal way of circumventing it.

Christmas was less than six weeks away, and the bed she coveted was tantalisingly on display in the small Cambridgeshire store where she had first viewed it.

One night, after they had made love and then were lying sensually entwined in the cramped space of the old three-quarter bed Luc's parents had given them, Belle tentatively raised the subject of a new bed again.

'I really loved that one I told you about,' she told Luc softly. 'And it would look wonderful here in this house...this room...'

Their house was old, eighteenth century and cottagey, and it cried out for sturdy, hand-made proper furniture, but of course such furniture was expensive.

'It would make a wonderful Christmas present to ourselves,' she wheedled softly in Luc's ear. He had proved increasingly stubborn of late about her contribution to their household, refusing to allow her to spend her unexpectedly high bonus on furniture, telling her that it was her money—not theirs.

'Don't you understand…? Can't you see…? I've seen the look on the faces of your friends, your family, when they come round here. They know there's no way *we* could afford to live somewhere like this, to buy a house like this, whilst *I'm* still virtually having to live on a grant…'

'You earn extra from the private tuition you give,' Belle protested.

Luc gave a harsh laugh.

'*Extra!* A pittance…*peanuts* compared to what you're earning. Look, I know what you're saying about the bed, and I do understand… But Belle, please, just this once, please indulge me. There's something… Trust me, Belle.'

'Well, if you insist,' Belle agreed, but secretly she was already planning to surprise him on Christmas Eve with the delivery of the new bed and the headboard. She would tell him that it was a present to both of them—which it was, of course. And he would understand. She knew he would.

When she went in to order the bed a week later, she soothed her conscience by telling herself that it was just silly male pride that was making Luc so difficult over it, and that he would soon forget all about his veto once he had seen how beautifully it suited the house.

At work the run-up to Christmas was hectic, a frenetic mixture of deadlines and glittery, no-expenses-spared client parties.

In Cambridge Luc's college was empty of students for the Christmas break, enabling Luc to take full advantage of the college library and its other facilities for his own studies. But in order to help out with the mortgage he had taken on more and more private tuition, leaving him less and less time for his own work.

'Pure maths at Luc's level requires a devotion and commitment which is almost on a par with that once required by the priesthood,' Luc's mentor told Belle severely when she gave in to Luc's quiet insistence and accompanied him to Professor Lind's pre-Christmas drinks party—a sedate affair, held in the chilly monastic starkness of his college rooms, the only food and drink on offer his housekeeper's home-made and deeply unpleasant mince pies and a sherry which made Belle grit her teeth.

'You know I only drink champagne,' she told Luc plaintively. After the luxury of vintage champagne and the delicious nibbles provided by her wealthy clients, Mrs Oakes' mince pies and the professor's sherry, like the high-minded academic conversation, were not to Belle's taste at all.

She *did* notice, though, how one of the professor's other students, a quiet, demure young woman with unexpectedly critically cool blue eyes, reacted in a way that was a good ten degrees *less* frosty when it was *Luc* who was addressing her and not Belle herself.

Not that Belle felt remotely threatened by or jealous of Harriet's obvious attraction to her husband. Why should she? Luc loved *her*, and would love her even more when they were cosily tucked up together in their lovely new bed with its wonderful headboard, she promised herself, and she happily contemplated writing a cheque to pay for it.

It had taken bribery and cajolery on a heroic scale to get her boss to agree that she could skip the firm's Christmas Eve get-together so that she could be at home with Luc when the bed was delivered. She had hardly seen anything of him over the previous month, or so it seemed, and she was looking forward to spending her few precious days off with him.

They were going to his parents for dinner on

Christmas Day, and hers on Boxing Day, but they would have at least one night together in their new bed.

When she woke up on Christmas Eve morning Belle was so excited that she couldn't eat her breakfast. The house they had bought, their home, was everything that she wanted. It had the potential to make a wonderful home, and there was even the prospect of converting the loft above the garage into a self-contained bedsit, should the day arrive when they needed the services of a nanny.

Certainly, they both wanted children, but they had agreed that they were too young for them as yet. Luc wanted to wait until he had finished his studies, and from the tone of his conversation Belle had guessed that he would want her to give up her own job once they did have a family. She was not so sure that was something she would want to do, but there was plenty of time for her to talk Luc round to her point of view.

It was a pity that the bed had been so expensive, otherwise she might have been able to treat them to a visit to the January sales...

They desperately needed a decent sofa, and Belle rather liked the idea of them having two instead of the traditional one and a couple of armchairs. The cottage had a good-sized sitting room-cum-family room, as well as its large kitchen-cum-dining room, and on the other side of the entrance hall there was, much to her delight, a very respectably sized and pretty drawing room which ran the full length of the house. Plenty of scope for her home-making talents there. And the fact that the previous owners had been elderly meant that none of the attractive original features had been removed.

'You're looking very pleased with yourself,' Luc commented as he bent to kiss the top of her head and reach past her for the coffee pot.

'Mmm...' she agreed lazily, arching her neck and inviting him without a word to nuzzle the soft warm skin there.

'What have you got me for Christmas? I hope it's something very special,' she teased him, knowing full well that the only thing she really wanted from him, the gift she valued above everything else, was the one she already had: the gift of his love for her, his commitment to her.

'Well, I might just...' he began, and then stopped theatrically, his eyes sparkling with love and happiness as he teased her back. 'No guessing, though. You're just going to have to wait until tomorrow.'

'Tomorrow.' Belle pouted. 'But I thought

we'd... I'm going to give you *my* present *today*. Tomorrow we're going to your parents...'

'Not until lunchtime,' Luc reminded her.

'It's going to be a very busy time,' Belle sighed. 'First dinner with your family, and then we're going to my parents on Boxing Day.'

The two families, who had not known one another before Luc and Belle had met, had become firm friends, and they lived close enough to make visiting one another quite easy, often sharing their homes with each other's families at special times like Christmas. On Christmas Day night Belle's parents, her elder sister and her husband and their two young children were joining Luc's parents and other members of his family. As a country vicar, Luc's father lived in a vicarage more than large enough to house everyone overnight, even if his small stipend meant that he could never afford to comfortably heat the vast Victorian church property.

Belle liked Luc's family, even if she sometimes found them a trifle unworldly compared with the people she mixed with in her working life. Certainly their values and beliefs were very much in tune with those of her own parents, and she particularly liked Luc's uncle and his wife, and their thirteen-year-old son who shared so much of a family resemblance with Luc that Belle had not been surprised when Luc's mother had told her that Andy looked just the same as Luc had done at his age.

Luc's father had studied theology at Cambridge, and there was a tradition in the family of its male members being Cambridge men.

Because they were spending so much time away from home over Christmas, Luc and Belle had agreed that it would be a waste to have a real Christmas tree, and one of Belle's clients had presented her with an artistic and very expensive Christmas arrangement from one of London's top florists, made up of bare twigs and glass baubles, which had caused Luc to raise his eyebrows a little.

'Don't you like it?' Belle had asked him.

'It's…it's very artistic,' Luc had replied cautiously, and then had added a rueful admission, 'At home we always have a huge tree loaded with masses of stuff. Not very arty, I suppose, but it always seems…right. Vicars' wives always have to recycle everything, and Ma used to encourage me to make my own decorations when I was small… Not very aesthetic, I know, but for me the real spirit of Christmas is the thought behind the gift, not its material value.'

He was right, of course, and Belle knew it, shared his sentiments, but somehow he had made her feel that her values were glossy and worthless and even, in some belittling way, that *she* was glossy and worthless too.

Today, though, was Christmas Eve, and very soon their own special Christmas present was going to arrive. And every Christmas from now on, when they woke up in their special bed, when they made love in it, they would remember this, their first Christmas in their new home. Belle couldn't wait to see the bed with its special headboard in situ, to polish and admire it.

It was almost lunchtime when the van finally arrived in the narrow country lane outside their house.

'What's this?' Luc frowned as the driver got out. 'They must be looking for somewhere else. We haven't ordered anything…'

'Yes, we have,' Belle corrected him excitedly, craning her neck so that she could see out of the window as the men went to the rear of the van. 'Well, *I* have. It's our Christmas present…well, mine to you…to us…to the house. It's the bed, Luc, the one I told you about…with the wonderful headboard,' she hurried on.

'The one we agreed we wouldn't have because it was too expensive?' Luc asked her quietly.

But Belle was oblivious to the cold undertone to his voice, too busy watching what was going on outside the window to be aware of the hurt look in his eyes as she agreed flippantly, 'That's the one.'

'You went ahead and bought it without telling me, despite what we'd agreed...'

Now Belle did look at him, alerted to his feelings by the ominous tone of his voice.

'I thought you'd be pleased,' she told him. 'It's a present...a surprise. Luc...what is it? Where are you going?' she demanded frantically as he turned his back on her and started to walk towards the back door.

'Luc, come back,' she pleaded, but it was too late, and she couldn't run after him because the delivery men were already coming up the path with their new bed.

Luc would come round when he saw how wonderful their bedroom looked with the bed and its headboard proudly adorning it, Belle decided two hours later, when the men had gone and she was standing in the doorway of their bedroom admiring her new acquisition. They would need to get some different bedding now, she acknowledged, frowning a little as she studied the pretty floral set they had been given as a wedding present. Somehow it just didn't do the new bed justice.

Luc had sanded and polished the old floorboards shortly after they had moved in, and they certainly set the bed off perfectly. It was, she knew, the kind of bed that demanded heavy Irish linen sheets scented with lavender, old-fashioned bed linen, all the traditional touches.

Luc would love that, waking up smelling of lavender... Luc...where was he? He had been gone a long time. She hoped he'd...

It was almost half an hour later when another van pulled up outside the house, a much shabbier, older one than the one which had delivered their new bed and its accoutrements, and, to her astonishment, she saw Luc climbing out of the driver's door.

'Luc.' She went to the front door and opened it, calling out anxiously to him. 'Where have you been?'

'To get your Christmas present,' he told her grimly.

Her Christmas present. In that old van... What on earth...? Warily she walked to the front gate and opened it, staring into the back of the van as Luc unlocked and raised the shutter door.

'What is it? What have you got in there?' she asked him uncertainly.

'I've already told you. Your Christmas present.'

As the last of the fading daylight filled the van and she saw inside it Belle's heart gave a shocked bound. There, in pieces, inside the van, was an old-fashioned bedframe, an obviously newly bought mattress and, tucked along one side of it, covered in a piece of old sheeting was the unmistakable shape of a wooden headboard.

'Luc…what have you done—' she began, and then stopped as he turned round and she saw his face.

She had never seen him look so bleak…so distant…so alien from her and to her.

'Very much the same as you've done. I've bought us a Christmas present. A new bed. For us…for you…' he told her in a voice that was icily polite and icily distant.

'That isn't new…the frame's old…' Belle began defensively. 'It looks…'

'It looks what?' Luc challenged her. 'It looks as though your colleagues…and your clients…would laugh at it, turn their materialistic

designer noses up at it. Well, for your information, this bed belonged to my grandparents. They
slept in it…cherished it…cared for it and valued
it, just as my parents have done.'

'It's… It's…' Belle just didn't know what to
say, and then, as Luc climbed into the van, the
sheeting slipped off the headboard and the colour
left her face completely. Unlike the frame itself,
the headboard was quite plainly new. She could
tell that because of the pretty carving on it, en-
twining their initials and the date of their marriage.

'Luc… You bought…' she began, but Luc was
already shaking his head.

'I bought *nothing* apart from the mattress,' he
told her grimly. 'The wood, good solid English
oak, belonged to the father of one of my pupils.
He gave it to me in exchange for his son's tuition.
I did the carving myself. It isn't as fancy nor, I
dare say, as desirable as the one you've bought,
but…'

'You carved it…' Belle stopped him. '*You*
carved it…'

'Yes.' Luc told her curtly, pushing the cloth
back over it. 'But of course I realise that it won't
come anywhere near to matching the one you've
bought. The one *I* couldn't afford to buy you. It

doesn't matter what I do or what I say, what I give you...how much I love you. The fact remains that you're the one who's supporting us both, financing us both...'

'Luc, what does *that* matter?' Belle protested. 'And besides, that's only temporary. When you get your fellowship...

'Oh, Luc, I love you so very much, and I love the headboard as well,' Belle told him tenderly—and she meant it.

Luc's gift to her, his bed, was installed in their bedroom whilst the one she had bought was relegated to one of the guest bedrooms. They made up their quarrel, and the ones that followed it, but with each one the fabric of their marriage grew a little thinner, until eventually the day came when neither of them could be bothered to repair the worn patches any longer.

The crux came one weekend, when Belle arrived home early from an overseas conference to find that Luc, who had attended a dinner party in Cambridge the night before, had stayed over in Harriet Parish's rooms.

Luc protested in vain that it was all completely innocent, that he had simply had too much to drink to want to risk driving, that he loved her

and that Harriet was simply a fellow student…a
friend…

In the row that followed they said so many ugly
and hurtful things to one another that Belle knew
there was no going back. Not this time…

'You're so damn materialistic, you wouldn't
know real value if it hit you on the head,' Luc
accused her at one point during their argument.
'Money, money—that's all that matters to you.'

'Perhaps it would matter more to you if you
were the one who earned it,' Belle retaliated. 'It's
all very well for you, sitting up there above the
rest of us in your ivory tower, Luc, but you seem
to forget that without my earnings there would be
no ivory tower for you to live in…'

And so it went on, the pair of them tearing at
the precious fabric of their vulnerable marriage,
rending it, ripping it, destroying it, in a frenzy of
bitterness and petty resentments.

Belle moved out of the house that weekend and
she never moved back.

Six weeks later she filed for divorce, refusing
to even discuss with Luc any possibility of them
getting back together. Ironically, the only thing
she took from their marital home was the bed and
headboard—not the one she had bought, that she
had left behind, and for all she knew it was still

there in the house with Luc, who had bought out her share of their marital home.

No, the headboard, the one that still graced the head of the bed in her small London home, was the one that Luc had made for her. Not that she had intended that to happen. The men she had sent to collect the other headboard and bed from the spare room had made a mistake, and somehow or other she had never bothered to correct it.

CHAPTER TWO

'I MUST admit that Mum was stunned when you said that Luc had come round to deliver the invitation to you himself,' Joy, the happy bride, was saying now. 'I mean, we realised soon enough about the mistake. What on earth did he say? You must have been so surprised to open the door to see him there...'

'Mmm...'

'Luc, I was just saying to Belle that she must have been really surprised to open her front door and find you there,' Joy repeated breezily as her new husband's cousin suddenly materialised at Belle's side, apparently oblivious to the interest the fact that the two of them were standing amicably together was causing amongst their fellow wedding guests.

Luc's dark river-green eyes met Belle's honey-gold ones, exchanging a silent message.

'What on earth did you say to her? I mean, you hadn't spoken to one another for years...'

'Joy...' Andy cautioned his new bride, explaining to Belle and Luc, 'I think it must be the cham-

pagne on top of an empty stomach. She told me
when we walked back down the aisle that she'd
had three glasses whilst she was getting ready this
morning...'

'No, four...' Joy corrected him, and then gig-
gled.

'Darling, the photographer wants you,' her
mother announced, coming up to the newly married pair and urging them to follow her.

'Oh, no more photographs,' Joy was complaining as her mother led her away.

'Saved by the flashbulb,' Luc commented hu-
morously to Belle after they had gone.

'Mmm... You could hardly have told her what
really happened, could you?'

'What? That you took one look at me, went
white and practically fainted into my arms,' Luc
commented.

'I'd been in bed with flu. I hadn't eaten anything for three days...' Belle defended herself.
'Besides,' she added slyly, 'I don't think *you'd*
have wanted *me* telling Andy that you carried me
upstairs to bed and started to undress me...'

'I did no such thing...'

'Yes, you did. My robe—'

'Your robe came off when I trod on the belt
you had left undone as I picked you up. And I

had to take you upstairs. All you have downstairs is your garage and an entry hall... And besides, if you will go completely naked under your robe... It was a freezing cold February day. I just wanted to get you somewhere warm. You frightened me to death, passing out like that. Mind you, I wasn't surprised. You were far too thin and frail...'

'I told you, I'd been ill. Which is why—'

'Goodness me, you two look very cosy. How long have you been married now? It must be over ten years, and still no children! Well, they say, don't they, that if you've none to make you laugh then you've none to make you cry?'

Great-Aunt Alice...

Belle gave Luc a speaking look above the elderly lady's head. There was no point in trying to explain her error, especially not when....

'Aunt Alice...there you are...' Carol, Belle's sister and the mother of the bride, came hurrying back, looking harassed as she put her arm around their elderly relative.

'Darling, I'm so sorry about all of this. You'll never guess what she's done now,' she hissed in a whisper to Belle, but before she could elucidate, David, her husband, was hurrying up to her telling her that the caterers wanted to speak urgently to her.

'Shame,' Luc commented, giving Belle a small smile as he watched his ex-sister-in-law's departing back. 'Now we'll never know just what it is that Great-Aunt Alice has done...'

'You mean what *else* she's done,' Belle corrected him drolly, returning his smile with a look in her eyes that caused a passing waitress, who was not aware of their divorced status, to reflect rather ruefully on the enviable ability of some couples to keep a passionate intensity in their relationship which was now only an increasingly blurred memory in her own. Mind you, she had to acknowledge fairly, it would be a very odd woman indeed who did *not* feel a twinge of sensual female excitement at the sight of a man as attractive as Luc. Her own husband, kind man though he was, was not exactly charismatic.

'Mmm... I must say I was rather taken aback when I received the wedding invitation addressed to both of us.'

'It *was* very thoughtful of you to take the trouble to deliver it by hand,' Belle responded mock demurely, her honey-gold eyes dancing with laughter—and something else, something deeper and warmer that made Luc's breath catch slightly in his throat. Belle had always had that special something about her, a warmth and energy, a vibrancy. He had noticed it about her the very first time they had met.

'I was in London anyway,' Luc reminded her, attempting to make light of the incident, but, like hers, his eyes glowed hot with remembered emotion, giving him away.

'It's rather warm in here. What do you say to us taking the opportunity to get a little fresh air before we go in for the wedding breakfast?' Luc suggested.

'People will talk,' Belle pointed out to him. 'They'll wonder what's going on…'

'Mmm…' Luc agreed, placing his hand on the back of her waist and gently guiding her towards the exit to the hotel's gardens.

'I'm glad to see that you've put some weight back on.'

'I'd been ill,' Belle reminded him.

'You were skin and bone,' Luc continued. 'I thought…'

'That I'd been pining away for you over the years?'

Luc gave her a direct look.

'No. I didn't think that, Belle. I've got my

faults, I know that, but suffering from delusions has never been one of them.'

'Who says it would have been a delusion?' Belle surprised them both by admitting a little gruffly. 'There was a time when we first parted...' She paused, and then, her face clouding, told him, 'Oh, Luc...I was so dreadfully unhappy then, and—'

She stopped abruptly. It wasn't like her to admit to any kind of vulnerability, and she could see that Luc was as surprised by her admission as she herself was.

'If we weren't here...' he began, and Belle shook her head chidingly. But that didn't stop a tiny thrill of excitement running dangerously down her spine.

It *had* been a shock to open her front door that day and discover that her unwanted visitor was no less than Luc, her ex-husband, to whom she had neither spoken nor seen since their divorce seven years before.

The sight of him standing there, so tall and darkly handsome, so excessively and alluringly male and mature, had been more than her already overloaded weakened defence system had needed to send it into complete chaos.

As she'd clung to the front door she'd been

able to literally feel the blood draining down through her body at the same time as a weakening rush of dizzying faintness poured swiftly through it.

She had known what was going to happen, *known* she was going to faint, but at the same time she had known too that she simply did not have the strength or the will-power to halt it. Her last thought as Luc had masterfully reached out to catch her up in his arms had been how good he smelled, how good he *felt*...how good it was to be held so protectively and so safely in his arms.

Her faint had only lasted a couple of minutes, but that had been long enough for Luc to close her front door and carry her upstairs, through the living room of her small mews house and into her bedroom.

She had come round to discover that she was lying on her bed completely naked, with Luc leaning anxiously over her calling her name.

Even now, more than three months later, she still couldn't quite account for the effect, the erotic charge, the sheer inconsistency of the emotions which had allowed her to experience a previously unknown rush of intense female sensuality at the knowledge that she was naked whilst Luc was fully dressed. It was so out of character for her, so alien to what she might have expected to feel, that for several seconds it had robbed her of the ability to make any kind of response to Luc's presence other than to simply lie there watching him with widened golden eyes.

Later he had told her that it had been that look of dazed wonderment in place of the angry rejection and bitterness he had expected that had encouraged him to put aside his own protective defences and show her his concern and anxiety.

'Luc...' had been all she had been able to say, in an unfamiliarly weak and hesitant voice.

'You fainted,' he told her gently, his fingers stroking her forehead in reassurance.

'I know... I haven't been well,' she responded. 'I've had some kind of flu bug...'

'Which you no doubt refused to acknowledge and fought off until it *really* made you ill,' Luc countered a little grimly.

For a moment Belle was tempted to deny what he was saying, but the strong core of self-honesty she had developed since the failure of their marriage refused to let her.

'I had an important client meeting to attend,' she admitted. 'I should really have put it off, but this is such a cut-throat business I felt I couldn't afford to do so...'

Five years ago Belle had left the firm she had originally worked for and had set up in business on her own. Financially the rewards were not perhaps quite so high as they had been, and certainly the demands on her time and her energies were far greater, but so was the sense of satisfaction she gained from being her own boss.

Just recently, though, she found that she was deliberately ignoring opportunities to further her business and add to her client base, that she was beginning to respond to a previously unacknowledged need to allow things into her life other than her work, beginning to admit to a sense of awareness that there were certain things she was missing out on, certain emotional needs in her life which were not being met. But of course these were admissions she could not make to Luc, not when all those years ago Luc had accused her of putting her career above their marriage, when Luc had warned her that one day she would find herself lonely and alone.

'You always did make far too many demands on yourself,' Luc told her wryly, his criticism turning to concern as she suddenly started to shiver. 'You're freezing,' he told her almost accusingly.

This caused her to flash back at him, her eyes

brilliant with a mixture of fever and pride, 'And whose fault is that? I'm not the one who took off my robe.'

Immediately she wished she hadn't spoken, because now Luc, who before had only been looking at her face, watching her eyes, suddenly switched his gaze to her body.

Instinctively Belle tensed her muscles.

She had been a girl when she and Luc had first met. Now she was a woman. As a girl she had taken for granted the lush femininity of her body, the luminous sheen to her skin, the softness of her female flesh. Now she was older, her body shape different.

She could see the way Luc was frowning at her. No doubt she didn't compare well to whoever was currently sharing his bed. After all, a man in his position, a man with all his sexual assets, his charisma, his good looks, not to mention his powerful position as a leader in his scholastic field, was bound to be able to have his pick of all the best of his female students.

She, on the other hand... But, no, she wasn't going to start thinking about how empty her life was, how empty it had been since their divorce... Why should she? That had been her choice. There had been men, offers, opportunities; she had simply been too picky to accept any of them.

Luc was still frowning.

'You're too thin,' he told her abruptly. 'Are you eating properly?'

'It's fashionable to be thin,' Belle returned sharply, even though she knew perfectly well that her body weight was normally a good half-stone heavier than it was right now, and that she personally had thought herself a little on the thin side before this bout of flu had brought her weight down even further.

'Fashionable!' Luc's eyebrows rose.

'Yes,' Belle persisted. 'Just because *you* don't find my body attractive, that doesn't—'

'I didn't say I didn't find you attractive. I simply said you were too thin,' Luc interrupted softly. 'As a matter of fact—'

Quite what might have happened if he hadn't abruptly stopped speaking she didn't know, but he continued, his voice oddly hoarse, 'You need something to eat. Get into bed and don't you dare move so much as a muscle whilst I go downstairs and get you something.'

But she could hazard a very strong guess, Belle reflected with self-honesty after the door had closed after him. After all, whatever might have been the cause of their final quarrel, and her pride-fuelled abandonment of their marriage, it had had nothing to do with her not finding him physically attractive, or with her not wanting him...as a man...

Her face hot, she reminded herself that she was a woman in her mid-thirties, a woman whose body, whose emotions, whose most private physical needs had never once betrayed her in all the time she had been on her own.

It must be her weakened state that was making her so vulnerable, she reassured herself. Yes, that was it. That and the shock of seeing Luc so unexpectedly, of finding herself in such an unexpectedly dangerously intimate situation with him.

Thinking of which, where on earth *was* her robe?

She had just reached the bedroom door when Luc opened it from the other side, frowning severely at her when he saw that she had disobeyed his edict.

'You shouldn't be out of bed. You've already passed out once,' he reminded her severely.

'I was looking for my robe,' Belle informed him, trying to summon what dignity she could. No small task when one was standing shivering and nude in front of the man who had every reason to find the sight of one's naked form less than physically appealing.

'Get into bed. I'll go and find it for you,' Luc told her with unexpected gentleness. 'At least you've got the sense to keep this place properly heated, even if you *don't* seem able to feed yourself. What on earth do you live on, Belle? There is hardly anything in your fridge or cupboards.'

'That's because I prefer to buy fresh food,' Belle returned quickly and loftily. 'And I've been too ill to feel like going out shopping for the last few days.'

'Mmm... Well, I've managed to find a can of soup and some eggs. Drink your soup whilst I go back down and make you an omelette.'

He was certainly behaving very masterfully, Belle acknowledged as she tucked hungrily into her soup when he had gone back to the kitchen.

But hadn't that always been one of the causes of their problems? The fact that it had irked his male pride that *she* had been the main provider. Not that he had tried to dominate her. No. She could never have loved him the way she had had he been like that. But she had always felt that he had subtly punished her for not being more helpless, more financially dependent upon him.

The warmth of her bed now that she had snuggled under the duvet and the blissful comfort of the hot soup in her stomach combined to make her feel relaxed and sleepy. So much so that by the time Luc returned with the promised omelette she was already half asleep. The sight of the amount of food he had piled onto the plate brought her sharply awake, though. Indignantly she stared at it.

'I can't eat all that,' she protested. 'It's indecent. There must be at least a dozen eggs there…'

'Not quite,' Luc told her cheerfully, without any apparent remorse. 'Actually we're *both* going to eat it. I don't care to miss out on my meals even if you do,' he told her severely. 'And since I could only find one plate, we shall have to share.'

'The others are in the dishwasher,' Belle informed him, and then added defensively, 'I'm a single woman living alone, Luc. I don't have either the space or the need to own a full twelve-place dinner service.'

'Surely you entertain sometimes?'

'Not really. I prefer to take business clients out, it's much easier and more professional. And besides—' she chewed a little betrayingly on her bottom lip '—it isn't always a good idea to invite male clients into one's home…'

'You've had problems with men…clients… behaving badly towards you?' Luc demanded fiercely.

'Er…it was a long time ago, when we first divorced and it was probably my own fault. I didn't realise the false message I could be giving inviting a client home.'

'He frightened you? Hurt you? Who…?'

'Nothing like that,' Belle hastened to assure him. 'It was just that there was a rather… embarrassing episode. A misunderstanding, really, that was all.'

'You mean one of your clients tried to…?'

'I've told you, Luc, it was all a long time ago, and fortunately he accepted that there'd been a misunderstanding. But after that I made the decision not to invite clients home—not that the way I run my life, either private or professional, is any business of yours.'

'Don't you ever find it lonely living alone?' he asked her, completely throwing her. But before she could make the defensively protective denial that was hovering on her lips he further confounded her by admitting quietly, 'I know that I do…'

'You…you live alone…?' Belle raised her eyes to his face.

'I've lived alone since you left,' he told her simply.

Belle's appetite had completely deserted her, and oddly Luc didn't seem to be particularly hungry either.

'Belle…'

'Luc…'

'I'm glad to see you kept the bedhead,' he told her huskily, and then he lifted his hand and reached past her to trace the initials and the date he had carved into it. 'I have to admit it isn't anywhere near so handsome, though, as the one you bought.'

'Nor so expensive,' Belle said quietly, dropping her gaze from his so that he wouldn't guess that the cost she *was* referring to was not in terms of the money she had spent on the bedhead, but the reckless wastage, the dreadful continuing payment with increasingly heavy interest she was still having to make in terms of broken dreams and lost love.

'Belle…'

As he withdrew his hand from the bedhead and straightened up, Belle lifted her head.

His gaze met hers and held it. Her whole body started to tremble, her heart beating far too fast.

Luc started to lower his head towards hers. He

was going to kiss her. Belle just knew it. Her heart
was racing so fast that she thought it might ex-
plode. Automatically she closed her eyes. She
could almost feel the warmth of Luc's mouth
against her own, taste the wonderful familiarity of
his kiss, breathe in his special scent, feel...

'I must go...'

Abruptly her eyes snapped open. Luc *wasn't*
going to kiss her after all.

'It was very thoughtful of you to call,' she told
him stiffly. 'I'll get in touch with Carol and tell
her about Great-Aunt Alice's mistake.'

'It's quite a coincidence that your niece and my
cousin should be marrying...'

'Yes...I suppose it is.'

'Andy was telling me the last time I saw him
that he's applied to finish his training in the same
town where Joy has just been appointed a junior
registrar at the local hospital.'

Immediately Belle guessed what he must be
thinking.

'And of course you don't approve of that. No
doubt you think *she* should be the one to follow
him?'

'On the contrary,' Luc replied evenly. 'I think
that he's a very fortunate young man to have a
woman who loves him so much that she's pre-

pared to take on the burden of being the major wage-earner until he's fully qualified. After all, if Andy hadn't changed his mind about the career path he wanted to follow, he would be qualified himself by now.

'I still think it's ironic that it takes longer to train to be a vet than a doctor, but I hope that Andy will appreciate both Joy and her love, and that he doesn't allow his male pride—'

He broke off and looked away from her. 'Fortunately his generation has a far healthier and more flexible attitude towards interchanging the traditional roles than ours perhaps did.'

Belle tried to speak, but found that she couldn't articulate a single word because of the lump in her throat.

This was the first time Luc had ever acknowledged that he could have been wrong. She *knew* that *she* had made mistakes, gone about things the wrong way, been rather less careful of his male pride than she might have been, but this was the first time she had felt that Luc, too, might have regrets, doubts about the things he had done, the way he had behaved…reacted. Perhaps if she had known that then…if they had sat down together like this then and talked… But Luc wasn't sitting down now; he was getting up. He was going away—leaving her—his Good Samaritan duties done.

Belle watched as he walked towards the door.

'Thank you for…for the soup,' she told him gruffly as he opened it, and then she looked away, closing her eyes, unable to bear watching him go out of her life…again…

When several seconds went by and she hadn't heard the final click of the door she opened her eyes again, widening them as she saw how close Luc was to the bed. How close he was to her.

'You don't have to thank me Belle—not ever— not for *anything*,' he told her, and then he did what he hadn't done before. He bent his head and kissed her.

A brief, non-sexual, amicable little kiss—or so he'd said it was supposed to be, when he'd told her later—but somehow their lips, their mouths, their senses had other ideas, and the brief brush of his cool mouth against hers became something warmer, deeper…longer…and far, far more intimate as their mouths clung together.

'I shouldn't be doing this. You're not well,' Luc groaned, but he still took her in his arms, holding her tightly against his heart so that she could feel its fierce thud as he cupped her face in his hands and looked deeply into her eyes.

Very tenderly Luc caressed her lips with his. Somewhere in the distance Belle could hear a noise, shrill, intrusive, unwanted. Her telephone was ringing. Reluctantly she broke the kiss.

'It's Carol,' she told Luc as she recognised her sister's number on the visual display unit.

When she picked up the receiver she could hear her sister's voice announcing frantically, 'Belle, something dreadful's happened. Great-Aunt Alice has sent...'

Belle could see Luc walking towards the door. She wanted to call out to him to stay...not to go...not to leave her. But she was a grown woman, and grown women did not give in to such foolish urges, such foolish emotions.

Covering the receiver, she called out instead, 'I'm afraid I'm going to have to ask you to let yourself out...'

'Belle? Belle, is someone there with you?' she could hear Carol demanding curiously.

'It was just...an unexpected visitor...' Belle responded as casually as she could as Luc closed the bedroom door very gently behind himself.

And it was, after all, the truth.

Carol, at any rate, seemed perfectly happy with her explanation, continuing urgently, 'I don't know *how* to tell you this, but Great-Aunt Alice has only gone and sent your wedding invitation to Luc. Belle! Belle, are you still there?'

'I'm still here,' Belle confirmed.

Ten minutes later, after her sister had rung off, Belle warned herself sternly that there was no point in wondering or dwelling on what might have happened if her sister hadn't rung up, if Luc had continued to kiss her, if she had actually dared to give in to the emotions, the sensations that had been flooding her.

With Luc's lips caressing hers it had been extraordinarily easy to forget their quarrels and the harsh words they had said to one another in the final, agonising dying throes of their marriage and oh, so easy to remember instead the love they had once shared.

Had *once* shared?

Shakily Belle closed her eyes. It must be the weakening effect of her flu that was making her feel like this, making her remember…regret… wish… But the way she had felt just now, when Luc had kissed her, had been the reaction of the woman she was now to the man he was now, she acknowledged with painful honesty. She had wanted him as the man he was, had felt that age-old female response to his nearness and his touch as the woman she had grown into.

Not wanting to pursue such a dangerous train of thought, Belle punched her pillow and told herself that she ought to be trying to sleep and get herself better.

Belle was asleep when Luc let himself back into her small house several hours later. He had found her spare keys hanging on a hook in the kitchen, neatly labelled. He had been reluctant to leave her on her own, having seen how ill she looked. She was far too thin, far too pale, and no doubt she was working far too hard and neglecting to look after herself properly.

A wry smile curled his mouth. One of her complaints about him had been that he fussed too much.

'When I'm hungry, I'll eat,' had been her standard response to him in the old days, when he had complained about their lack of ordered meal times.

These days he could sympathise more with that view. He certainly found no pleasure in going home to an empty house and cooking for himself, and as a consequence he found that he tended to snatch meals on the run between lectures and meetings. But at least he could dine in hall if he wanted to—the academic's version of the businessman's 'business lunches', he acknowledged ruefully as he climbed the stairs and went into Belle's kitchen to unpack the groceries he had bought whilst he was out.

No doubt she would be furious with him for what she would undoubtedly consider to be his unwarranted interference. But, deny it though she would, there was still, on his part at least, a sense of there being a bond between them, a relationship, and he could no more have returned to Cambridge after his meeting with fellow academics without returning to check that she was all right than he could have walked away when she'd opened the door to him and he had seen how ill she looked.

It was true that all those years ago, after the initial shock, and his instinctive attempt to deny what was happening, he had been forced to acknowledge that, given the growing frequency and intensity of their quarrels, and the disharmony between them, he'd had no option but to accept Belle's decision that she wanted a divorce. Certainly it had seemed impossible at the time for them to be able to reconcile their growing differences, but in the years since then his position had given him plenty of opportunity to observe and consider the changes taking place in the way the sexes related to one another and ran their relationships.

It was no extraordinary thing at all now for a female student to take on the financial responsibility of helping to support her partner, or to go on to become the main breadwinner whilst he opted to continue his studies; why, even some of his female colleagues were openly outspoken about the fact that they, as highly qualified women earning good salaries, actively *preferred* to have a partner who was happy to take a more passive but nevertheless extremely important and supportive role in their relationship.

'It's just too exhausting battling to accommodate two major egos,' one female colleague had told him frankly, when they had been discussing the subject. 'Quite honestly, whilst there's a part of me that will always be drawn to the high-powered "Alpha"-type male biologically speaking, as a thinking woman, I *know* that I have a far better chance of happiness and a far pleasanter life with a man who is prepared to let me take the lead role.'

Not that he and Belle's relationship had been quite like that.

He personally had *always* considered Belle to be his equal in *every* way, although sexually she had tended to look to him to initiate their love-making, at least in the earlier stages of their relationship. If he was honest, Luc had to admit that his own inflexible old-fashioned male attitude to money had been the maggot which had eaten away at the foundations of their marriage. Although he had always been too proud to admit it to her, it *had* irked him, *hurt* him, that she had been the one to provide the major part of their income, and because of that he had been less than generous in sharing the pleasure it had given her to buy things for their home…and for him.

Yes, there had been faults on both sides, but…

But it was too late now to go back and rewrite the past. Not the past, maybe, but there was still the present…and the future. Luc paused in the act of closing the fridge door.

Holding Belle in his arms earlier, he had been overwhelmed by an impulse…a need…to take things further. Very thoughtfully he made his way to Belle's bedroom. She was asleep, lying curled up like a small child, looking very alone in the large bed. And she had let her guard down enough with him to imply she had not shared that bed with anyone else.

Which put them both on an equal footing.

Luc knew men who complained that the sexual

frustration of being without a partner drove them to irrational excesses of behaviour and unsuitable relationships... But, desperately though he had missed Belle, and the intimacy of their lovemaking, he had never experienced any desire to fill her place with another woman, another body... any body...just to ease the sexual ache of her absence. And yet earlier today, holding her, he had been sharply and shockingly reminded of just how powerfully potent the male sex drive could be, of just how determinedly and dangerously it could overrule reason and logic.

If the intensity with which he had once wanted Belle, and loved her, had dimmed over the years, then being so close to her had certainly given him a sharp reminder of just how it had once been.

Luc sat down on the bed beside her, watching her, remembering.

The first time he had held her, really properly held her, she had literally trembled with excitement in his arms. When he had kissed her he had felt as though he had instantly become Master of the Universe, Lord of Eternity, no mere mortal any longer, at once so strong and powerful that there was nothing, no goal beyond his reach, and at the same time so achingly vulnerable that she could have reduced him to emotional dust simply by refusing him her smile.

It had been the love of poets and sages, beyond reason, beyond logic, and certainly beyond the control of a mere mathematician, and miraculously she had felt the same.

It was, they had both sworn, a love that would last for ever; they were soulmates, two perfect halves of an even more perfect whole. So why and how had they managed to destroy it? Not so much, perhaps, through human frailty, but rather through human strength, pride, arrogance, mistaken belief on the part of both of them that they were wholly in the right.

It was no doubt fitting that he should be examining the flaws which had led to the destruction of their marriage now—if not on the eve of his cousin's marriage to Belle's niece then certainly on the runway approach to it. Not that Andy was likely to ask him for his advice, or his admission on where he had gone wrong.

He was still deep in thought when Belle opened her eyes. At first she thought she was seeing a mirage. She had seen Luc leave with her own eyes, but here he was, sitting on the side of her bed as he looked towards the window, his expression, in repose, both stern and sad.

Instinctively she reached out to touch him.

Instantly he turned towards her.

'Belle, you're awake. How are you feeling?'

'Better,' she told him, dismissing the subject of her health in favour of something which interested her far more.

'What are you doing here? I thought you'd gone.'

'I had…I had a meeting to attend, otherwise… I was concerned about you. You shouldn't neglect your health, you know. You're…'

'Not getting any younger. I know,' Belle agreed dryly.

'I've bought you some groceries,' Luc informed her. 'If you're hungry.'

I'm not… Belle had been about to say, but instead—as she would be the first to admit to herself later—a little deviously she fibbed.

'Well, yes, I am a little, but I really don't feel like getting up and cooking. My head still aches and…'

'You stay right where you are,' Luc commanded her, getting up. 'I'll do the cooking.'

'Are you sure? Don't you have to get back?'

'Yes and no,' Luc told her promptly, holding her eyes as he added quietly, 'After all, what is there for me to go back to other than an empty house?

'I'll go and make us both something to eat, and then, if you feel up to it, Belle, I'd like us to talk.'

'Talk?' Steadily Belle returned his gaze, her own never faltering as she read the message he was giving her with his eyes. 'I feel up to it,' she responded huskily.

CHAPTER THREE

'BELLE, Carol says it's time for the wedding breakfast. Carol's got the reception line organised to go in. It's a shame that you won't be on the top table, but…'

'Mum, I really don't mind,' Belle reassured her mother. 'After all, I'm only Joy's aunt, not her mother or her bridesmaid…'

'I can't believe the last wedding we had in the family was yours and Luc's. I saw him earlier. He made a point of coming over to talk to your father and me…'

Belle smiled and waited patiently, knowing what was coming next. Her mother had never made any secret of the fact of how much she had liked Luc.

'I hate to say it, Belle,' she had told her younger daughter unhappily after the divorce, 'but this is what happens when a woman puts her job before her husband.'

'Mum…*I'm* the one who wanted the divorce, not Luc,' Belle had reminded her mother sharply. 'And as for putting my job first—'

She had stopped, knowing that there was no point in arguing with her mother and upsetting her. She was a woman of her time and had what Belle considered to be antiquated, old-fashioned views about a woman's role in life. She had worked as a secretary until Carol had been conceived, and after that she had stayed at home to look after her daughters and her husband. Not out of any sense of duty, but because that was what she had wanted to do.

'Carol's put you on a table with—'

'Great-Aunt Alice. I know,' Belle acknowledged, dutifully smiling at her father as he came over to join them.

Joy had opted for informal round tables for seating her wedding guests. Belle's was in the middle of the room, commanding an excellent view of the other guests, but as she approached it her eyebrows lifted slightly in amused surprise as she saw Luc standing beside the chair next to her own—the chair which should have been occupied by Belle's Great-Aunt Alice.

As she joined him, Belle cast a discreet look at the place-cards. They read 'Mrs Isabelle Crawford' and 'Mr Lucius Crawford.'

'Another demonstration of Aunt Alice's handiwork,' Belle murmured to Luc as the other guests sharing their table reacted to their joint presence with varying degrees of astonishment and confusion.

'Well, let's just say that she was certainly the inspiration for it,' Luc responded in an amused undertone.

Her eyes brimming with laughter, Belle looked at Luc. 'Where *is* Aunt Alice, by the way?' she asked him.

'Er…I *was* to have been seated with my godfather….'

'Admiral Rogers?'

'Mmm…'

'Well, I hope you aren't going to regret your moment of Machiavellian interference with Joy's table plan,' Belle warned him, 'because I'm certainly going to. People are going to think it very odd to see us seated together in apparent amity…'

'Mmm… But after all, it isn't as though this is the first time lately that we've shared a meal on…amicable terms…is it?' Luc reminded her.

'No,' Belle agreed, shaking her head at him as a secret amused smile passed between them.

It had been late in the evening when Luc had eventually left. They'd talked, but by mutual agreement they'd avoided going too deep into painful areas on this occasion. He'd cooked them both a meal, and then insisted that the two glasses of red wine he had coaxed Belle to drink would be good for her and help build her up.

'Red wine *is* good for you,' he had insisted when she had raised her eyebrows.

'And chocolates,' she had semi-mocked him as she'd popped one of the delicious hand-made truffles that were her favourites into her mouth.

'The Aztecs considered chocolate to be an aphrodisiac,' he had continued blandly. 'And I've certainly no reason to argue with that.'

Belle remembered how she had blushed—and why. Long, long before the current fad for chocolate body paint there had been a certain occasion when, as a result of a cosy winter evening spent in front of an open fire, Luc had insisted on licking away the remnants of the melted chocolate she had dropped first from her fingers and then from the vee of flesh exposed by her robe where it had fallen open.

The sizzling sensuality she had experienced beneath the lazy, deliberate brush of his tongue against her skin had driven her to a frenzy of need which had resulted in her punishing him for his slow, lingering tantalisation of her body and her senses with an equally intimate exploration of his body with her own fingers and lips.

After that, the gift of chocolates between them had possessed a special intimacy and meaning, although she had assumed when he produced them this evening that he must have forgotten this.

Now, as he looked from her mouth to her fingertips, and then back to her mouth again, Belle knew that whilst he might not have bought the chocolates to remind her of that occasion—why, after all, should he have done so?—she *had* been reminded of it, *was* being reminded of it, and extremely forcibly, by a body and a set of emotions which, no matter how strictly she had fought to control them, had never truly forgiven her for denying them, and certainly had never, ever forgotten just how intense and magical the sexual rapport between her and Luc had been.

Every day for a week after that Luc rang her to see how she was feeling.

By the third day she was back at work, unofficially, at least, working from home, her body tensing every time the telephone rang in case it was Luc calling and then, abruptly, seven days after his initial visit the calls ceased.

Belle couldn't believe how bereft she felt, or

how much she missed the sound of Luc's voice, as warm and rich as dark melting chocolate, touching her senses and unleashing emotions, longings, needs, she had thought long ago safely banished.

By the end of the second day without a call from him she was reduced to virtually willing him to ring, snapping unforgivably at both her mother and her sister for telephoning her and not being him.

'You need a holiday,' her mother chided her. 'You work far too hard, darling. Which reminds me. Your father and I were wondering if you could possibly manage to house-sit for us whilst we go away. Carol would do it, but with the wedding so close...'

'Don't worry, I'll do it,' Belle confirmed. She had been thinking for some time of relocating, moving herself and her business outside London. After all, her parents weren't getting any younger. Her sister and the rest of her family were all based in Cambridgeshire, her roots were there, and certainly with the aid of modern technology she could easily work from there. Besides which...

Belle wasn't sure when she had realised she was tired of opening her eyes in the morning and only being able to see a small patch of clear sky, or when she had first had that sharp yearning for the familiar flatness of the fens, the wideness of its skies. She just knew that her city life had somehow or other lost its appeal.

It was ironic to remember now how she had berated Luc, before they had found their pretty cottage, for refusing to transfer to the LSE so that they could both be based in London.

'I'm not a city person, Belle,' he had told her quietly, looking at her. 'I want our children to grow up in the same country environment that we both enjoyed.'

Their children... It had been on the tip of Belle's tongue to remind him just how impossible it was for her to even *think* of taking time out to have one child, never mind children... But instead she had demanded tartly, 'You're running ahead a little, aren't you, Luc? I can't afford to finance a nanny as well as your studies.'

It was a comment that she had bitterly regretted once she had made it. It had shamed both of them, and she had hated herself for the look she had seen in his eyes, but the thought that Luc was already planning ahead for their family, when she felt under so much pressure at work, when she had so little time and so many responsibilities, had panicked her into lashing out verbally at him.

Now things were different. Now career women

of her age, all too conscious of the fast ticking of their biological clocks, were choosing the option of children without even a permanent partner, never mind the burdens on their careers, rather than miss out on the maternal boat. She envied them the single-mindedness that enabled them to make such a decision. Perhaps her own deep-rooted belief that a child thrived best surrounded by the love of both its parents sprang from the nurturing she had received in her own very happy childhood.

But that hadn't stopped her thinking sometimes that if she and Luc had had a child—children—it might have compelled them both to work a little harder at protecting their marriage. Or, conversely, it might have led to her being a single parent, struggling to bring up a child and manage her career as well.

She had surprised herself two years before when she'd discovered how easy it was to make the decision to downsize her business life, to leave behind the hectic life she had lived for so long and set up in business on her own, on a much smaller scale, with only a handful of carefully picked clients—clients who shared her own view that with wealth came a certain moral responsibility not to abuse those who did not possess such assets.

She was proud of the way she was guiding her clients to combine sound investment and financial management with an awareness of the moral issues involved in making profits, an awareness of other people's poverty, and, increasingly now, prospective clients were approaching her because they had heard of her humanitarian beliefs and record.

Three days after Luc had last rung her, he finally telephoned.

'I don't know if you've received a copy of the wedding present list or not yet,' he began, 'but it occurred to me that if we were to club together we could potentially remove one of the larger items from the list.'

'We could, but—'

'Why don't we discuss it over dinner?' Luc interrupted her.

'I...' Belle opened her mouth to refuse, but discovered instead that her voice seemed to have deserted her.

'I've got to come down to London to see a colleague the day after tomorrow. If you're free that evening I could call for you...'

'I... Yes. Very well,' Belle agreed weakly.

Luc took her to San Lorenzo which, in itself, surprised her. Not so much because of its reputation as one of the best and most expensive restaurants in London—after all, as a Fellow he was now hardly the struggling young academic he had been when she had first met him—but because she hadn't really thought that such a high-profile society place would be to his taste. What surprised her even more, though, was the discovery that the staff knew him well enough to have remembered his name.

Sensing her surprise, Luc waited until the wine waiter had gone before explaining easily to her, 'One of my students used to insist on bringing me here for her tutorials.'

'Really?' Belle gave him an icy little smile. 'I though it was the tutor who dictated where a tutorial would take place, not the student.'

'Mmm…but this student was rather special.'

'Oh.' Belle's voice had grown even icier.

'Mmm…' Luc smiled reminiscently, apparently unaware of the frigid atmosphere Belle was generating. 'She was a second or third cousin to the owners of the restaurant, and she was working here to help finance her way through university as a mature student—'

'She was a *mature* student?' Belle interrupted him sharply.

'Well, yes…'

'How mature?' Belle demanded instantly.

'Oh…pretty mature… Around fifty or so…'

Immediately Belle started to relax, unaware of the look of wry comprehension mixed with tenderness that Luc was giving her. She had always been very passionate and, whilst not possessive, certainly inclined to be very protective of their relationship. He, on the other hand, as he openly had to admit, had been rather immaturely jealous. He re-angled his chair so that the darkly handsome young waiter who was currently studying her with burning admiration was blocked out of her view.

It was late when they finally left the restaurant, and it was Luc who commented wryly as he hailed a taxi, 'We still haven't decided about the wedding present.'

'No,' Belle agreed.

They had been too busy talking about themselves to discuss anything so mundane as the rival attractions of a washing machine or a dishwasher, the two items they had narrowed their choice down to.

'I must have made you so angry sometimes,'

Belle had commented at one point during the evening, when they had been discussing the breakdown of their marriage.

'Not angry, no,' Luc had countered quickly, shaking his head and reaching across the table to take hold of her hand in both of his.

'Hurt, rejected, and even at times demeaned, yes. But angry, no! It hurt me that I couldn't afford to provide you with the material things you wanted, that *I* wasn't the one paying the mortgage, that *I* couldn't go out and order that bed you wanted…'

'You were a proud man, and I should have realised how much what I was doing was hurting you,' Belle had groaned remorsefully, but once again Luc had shaken his head.

'No. If I was proud then it was a false pride. My pride should have been in *you*, in what you were doing for both of us, in what we were achieving by working together.

'I made a lot of mistakes, Belle, but so far as I am concerned the biggest mistake of all was the one I made when I let you go.'

'I made mistakes as well,' was all Belle had been able to whisper in response.

Now, on the way home in the taxi, she was mentally examining what he had said. Uncertainly she darted a glance at him. His face was turned towards the window, so that she could only see his profile. To say he regretted their divorce was one thing; to say that he still loved her was something else again.

'Have you got time to come in for a cup of coffee?' Belle asked him uncertainly as the taxi drew up outside her home. 'We ought to make a decision about the present.'

'Yes, of course,' Luc agreed immediately.

The flowers he had given her when he'd picked her up were in water in the kitchen. As she waited for the coffee Belle breathed in their scent, touching the petals with gentle fingers.

Luc was standing in the sitting room removing his jacket as she walked in. He glanced at his watch and then cursed.

'What is it? What's wrong?' Belle asked him.

'I've just realised that it's half past twelve, and not half past eleven as I thought,' he told her. 'That means I've missed the last train. Never mind. I'll book myself into a hotel.'

'You can't do that,' Belle protested. 'Not at this time of night. I...you could stay here...the sofa converts into a bed and...' Uncertainly her voice trailed away. Staying here with her was probably the last thing Luc wanted to do.

But just as she was wishing that she had not spoken so impetuously, she heard him saying warmly, 'Well, if you're sure you don't mind, I *would* be very grateful.

'This reminds me of the first time you stayed over with me,' Luc told her five minutes later, when they were drinking their coffee.

'You mean the night you'd taken me to a college ball and your car wouldn't start so we had to spend the night together in your rooms?'

'Mmm...that's the one,' Luc agreed reminiscently.

As she looked hurriedly away from him Belle hoped he hadn't noticed the way she had to wrap her hands tightly around her coffee mug to stop her fingers from trembling.

That had been the first night they had actually been lovers. She had known how she felt about Luc then, of course, and she had been pretty sure that he shared her feelings, but that night had been the first night she had allowed herself to give way to those feelings.

She could still vividly remember how nervous she had felt when she had walked with Luc to his rooms. There had been no question of him deliberately contriving to have his car break down— they had discovered later that the part in question

had been slowly wearing away for some time—
but there had been something about the way he
had held her earlier when they had been dancing,
the way he had kissed her, the passion with which
he had whispered to her that she was the most
beautiful girl at the ball, the most beautiful girl in
the whole world, that had warned her how potentially dangerous it would be for them to be alone
together.

He hadn't touched her at first, explaining almost formally that since there was only one bed
he would sleep on the floor, but then she had
started to shiver, as much with nerves as cold, and
he had come over to her, slipping off his dinner
jacket to place it on her shoulders. The moment
she had felt the warmth of his fingertips against
her skin she had been lost.

The sexual tension between them even in the
short time they had known one another had become increasingly hard to ignore each time they
touched, kissed...*breathed*... It had been there,
that night, and as her body shuddered helplessly
and visibly at his touch, Belle had known that the
moment had come to succumb to it.

As she'd turned towards him his jacket had slid
disregarded to the floor. She'd raised her face towards him, her eyes misting with emotional tears

as he'd reached out and cupped it with hands that trembled just as much as her body had done. He had started to kiss her, softly, gently, and then, abruptly, he had stopped, withdrawing his mouth from hers.

Deprived of its warm, sensuous contact, Belle had opened her eyes to stare with uncertain questioning into his.

'I can't...' he'd begun hoarsely, and then stopped. 'I don't...'

He had closed his eyes and leaned away from her, the moonlight picking out the arch of his throat and the tensing of his jaw. His eyes had closed in some kind of male anguish. Opening his eyes, he'd looked directly at her and told her thickly, 'Belle, if I touch you now...kiss you now...it won't...I can't...it won't be gentle,' he had finally told her rawly. 'I want you too much to be able to...'

Instinctively Belle had known what he meant, what he was trying to tell her. Boldly she'd stepped towards him, and away from her virginal girlhood.

'Show me,' she'd commanded him softly. And then she had simply stood waiting, watching him.

She had known, felt the difference the moment he touched her. His fingers had burned against her skin, almost as hotly and excitingly as the look she'd seen in his eyes. But that had been nothing compared to the tension, the need, the hunger she'd felt in him when he had kissed her, his mouth almost bruising the softness of hers as he'd given way to the intensity of his passion before lifting his mouth to apologise disjointedly, touching her lips with his fingertips, telling her that he was thoughtless, selfish, that he had no right...

'Stop talking and kiss me again,' Belle had interrupted him huskily. This time she had returned his passion measure for measure, biting wantonly at his bottom lip, running her tongue-tip excitedly along the shape of his mouth, opening hers to the hot thrust of his tongue when he'd reacted to her sensuality. How long they had stood like that, kissing one another, *devouring* one another, *consuming* one another in the fierce passion of their mutual need, Belle had had no idea. She'd only known that when they finally broke apart it was with one accord, as though their every movement had been perfectly choreographed. As they'd undressed one another she'd had no sense of shyness or uncertainty; there had been no clumsiness or awkwardness, only the soft slithering sound of their clothes falling away from their bodies and then that fierce, primitive moment of mutual, visual examination, of studying one another as they'd stood clothed only in the soft shadows of Luc's room.

It had been seeing the way Luc had looked at her that had made her lift her head in pride and joyous recognition of the full power of her femininity, glorying in Luc's reaction to it and her own sense of pleasure and strength in the message his reaction had given her. She was beautiful, desirable, *loved*. She had seen all that and more in his eyes.

And she'd felt the same way about him. Very gently she'd reached out and touched him, carefully placing her lips to the hollow at the base of his throat, her hands spread out across the breadth of his chest.

Very delicately she had breathed in the scent of his skin, and then very deliberately she had tasted him.

Her touch had had the effect of smashing the barrier holding back an oceanic dam, but she had given herself willingly, gladly, voluptuously and joyously to the tumult, making herself a part of its power. Later, exhausted, beached, bleached dry, light-headed with the release and emotionally intoxicated with the euphoria of their love, they'd promised one another that this was just the beginning, the explosive starburst of a whole new universe of love that they would share for ever.

The following morning she had woken up in Luc's bed with Luc's dinner jacket draped over her naked body. On the empty pillow beside her had been a red rose, and attached to its stem had been an engagement ring…

She glanced instinctively now at her left hand, and realised to her chagrin that Luc had done the same.

'You're still wearing it,' he told her softly, not just echoing her thoughts but showing, too, that he had guessed just what she had been remembering.

'It's a little bit on the tight side, and I'd have had to have had it cut off,' she told him, not quite truthfully. But there was no way she was going to admit to him just *how* she still came to be wearing it, no way she was going to tell him about that night, less than a year after their divorce had become final, the night which had been the anniversary of the night he had given the ring to her when, overcome by sentiment and longing, she had slipped it back onto her finger and had left it there. No need, either, to mention just how often in times of anxiety and stress she touched it, twisting it, gaining comfort from its presence and from the memories she had learned to cherish.

'Besides, *you* still wear your wedding ring,' she pointed out, gesturing to the plain gold band on his left hand.

'*I* wasn't the one who wanted a divorce,' he told her sombrely.

'It's getting late,' Belle told him hurriedly. 'We ought to go to bed—' She stopped, and bent her head so that the thick cascade of her hair fell across her face, concealing its hot colour.

'I…I haven't anything I can offer you to wear, I'm afraid,' she apologised. 'I'll just go and get some clean towels and some bedlinen.

She kept the duvet for the sofa bed in the top of the wardrobe in her own bedroom. It was, after all, seldom used. She was standing on her dressing table stool trying to get it down when Luc saw what she was doing and came in to help her.

'Let me do that. You might fall,' he chided her.

'No, I won't,' Belle denied, and of course promptly did, bringing the duvet with her, so that as Luc rushed forward to catch her it unfurled, engulfing them both.

She was wearing a silk jersey black dress she had bought in Italy, very plain in design and very fluidly sexy. As she tumbled it rode up, revealing the soft flesh of her thigh and the wispily brief briefs she was wearing underneath.

Luc, who had put out his hand to steady her, discovered that instead of touching her waist his hand was actually resting on the smoothly naked flesh of her leg.

Were his fingertips actually stroking her skin, not just touching it? Belle wondered dizzily. Or was she just imagining it, *wanting* it…

'Belle.'

She heard him whisper her name, and instinctively she looked up at him.

'You haven't changed,' he told her softly. 'You still do things to me that…' He groaned rawly under his breath as he leaned over her. Belle felt her stomach muscles clench as she recognised that he was going to kiss her. But she didn't do anything to try to stop him. On the contrary…

'Belle…'

'Mmm….' Dreamily Belle opened her eyes at the same time as she snuggled deeper into Luc's arms.

'You know what's going to happen if we stay here like this, don't you?' Luc warned her.

'No,' Belle fibbed untruthfully as she delicately nuzzled the deliciously Luc-scented skin just below his jaw. 'But you could always show me,' she added helpfully, and encouragingly, just in case he hadn't quite got the message.

'Don't tempt me,' Luc told her throatily as he tasted the soft sweetness of her lips, deliberately lingering over them, teasing the warm outline of them with tiny little kisses.

'No, I won't tempt you,' Belle agreed obediently as she opened her mouth to the delicate probing of his tongue-tip.

Some time later, as he carried her to her bed…*their* bed…Luc reproved her, 'Didn't your mother ever tell you that it's wrong to tell lies?'

But Belle's only reply was a long, shuddering sigh of pleasure as he placed her naked body onto the bed and then covered it with his own.

'Oh, Luc… *Luc*… I've missed you so much,' she whispered to him as she held him tightly.

'Nowhere near as much as I've missed you,' he told her. 'Nowhere near…'

CHAPTER FOUR

'PEOPLE are talking about us. I warned you that they would,' Belle told Luc, shaking her head reprovingly at him as he offered her the last of the petits fours. 'Your parents have been watching us very suspiciously for the last hour.'

'Mmm...' Luc responded. 'And so have yours.'

'Well, you've got to admit it *is* rather unusual for a divorced couple to be so...'

'Intimate with one another?' Luc suggested as she finally gave in and took the sweet he was lifting to her lips.

'*Friendly* with one another, I was going to say,' Belle corrected him sternly.

'Friendly!' Luc gave her an extremely wicked look. '*You* were rather more than friendly last night...'

Quickly Belle placed her fingertip to his lips.

'Don't you dare,' she warned him. 'Don't you *dare*.' But there was laughter and warmth in her eyes, rather than disapproval, and there was a matching warmth in Luc's.

* * *

'Darling…what on earth is going on? Luc's mother has just asked me how long you and Luc have been back on speaking terms, and I must say…'

'We decided it was time we put aside our differences,' Belle told her mother calmly, half an hour later.

'Well, yes…that's very sensible, darling, but I must say…'

'Carol wants you, Mum,' Belle warned her mother as she saw her elder sister frantically beckoning to their mother, smiling to herself as she quickly escaped from her parent's anxious questions. There was no doubt about it, she and Luc *had* created quite a stir. She could see the open speculation in people's eyes as they watched them. Only Joy, the bride, seemed oblivious to the undercurrents and speculation sweeping through the room.

'Aunt Belle, there you are. I just wanted to tell you again how grateful Andy and I are to you and Luc for your wonderful wedding present. I never expected…'

'You like it, then?' Belle asked her niece with a smile.

'Like it? We are over the moon. I never…I didn't even know you knew I wanted…'

'Your mother happened to mention that you'd

seen it and fallen in love with it,' Belle informed
her niece fondly.

'Yes. I had...*we* had. But for you and Luc...'
She stopped and fell silent as Belle raised a quizzical eyebrow.

'Well, I suppose in a way it made sense for the
two of you to give us a *joint* present,' Joy acknowledged breezily. 'After all you were once...
Well, anyway, we're both thrilled with it. 'I'd always loved the one that you and Luc—' She
stopped awkwardly. 'Oh, dear!!'

'It's all right, darling, I fully understand what
you're trying to say,' Belle reassured her.

'Oh, Andy,' Joy exclaimed thankfully as her
new husband walked up. 'I was just telling Aunt
Belle how thrilled we are with the present she and
Luc gave us...'

'The bed? Too true. Joy had been dragging me
over to that shop virtually every week.'

'I was so upset when the shop told me that it
had been sold, even though I knew *we* couldn't
afford it, and then when Luc came round and told
me...'

'What was all that about?' Luc asked Belle,
arriving back at their table as the bridal couple
moved on to talk to some of their other wedding
guests.

Whilst he handed Belle the drink he had gone to fetch for her she explained.

'They were thanking me…*us*…for their wedding present.'

'The bed?'

'The bed,' Belle agreed.

As he bent towards her Luc murmured provocatively, 'Well, if they get as much…pleasure out of using it as we have recently done ours…'

'Luc,' Bell warned him, and then added dryly, 'And you certainly weren't saying that when we divorced seven years ago.'

'That was then. I've come to see that shop-bought bed in a different light since then,' Luc told her suavely. 'A *very* different light… especially since you've bought those new curtains for the cottage. What was wrong with the old ones?'

'They were looking worn and tired. They were the same ones I put up before we divorced…'

'They reminded me of you,' Luc told her tenderly. 'That's why I kept them…'

'Watch out, here comes your mother,' Belle warned him.

'Luc…and Belle. You're looking wonderful, my dear…'

As she bent to kiss her ex-mother-in-law, Belle acknowledged that she had always got on well with Luc's mother, even if originally she had been a little in awe of her.

'What's this about you both giving Joy and Andrew a bed? And from the same place where—I should have thought...but then...'

'We've decided the time has come to forgive the bed its sins,' Luc told his mother mock gravely. 'After all, it wasn't entirely to blame.'

'Oh, Luc...if you're going to be flippant. I simply meant that I thought it was rather odd you should have chosen to give them something that wasn't even on their wedding list...and to give it to them jointly.'

'We decided that we could give them something a little more substantial if we combined our resources,' Belle told her gently.

'Well, yes, of course. But people do keep asking questions.'

'Perhaps we made the wrong decision,' Belle suggested.

There was a small, intimate pause, and then Luc responded obliquely, 'Oh, I don't think so.'

Belle remembered them making the decision to buy the bed, and the phone call which pre-dated it...

'Belle, I've had an idea...'

As she cradled the telephone receiver Belle felt

a small frisson of pleasure begin to curl through her body. She had been away on business for three days, and it had been heaven to come home to find Luc's messages on her answering machine. And now here he was, ringing her to welcome her home.

'Mmm…?'

'About the wedding present…'

'Mmm…?'

'You did say you were coming home to house-sit for your parents this weekend, didn't you?'

'Mmm…'

'Well…'

When he'd finished telling her his idea, she exclaimed, 'You're saying that we should buy them a *bed*? Like the one we…I… It wasn't on their list.'

'No, I know, but Andy let slip that Joy would love to have one.'

'Well, yes, but, Luc! You don't think it would be tempting history to repeat itself, do you…?'

There was a small pause before Luc replied, 'Don't be silly. Besides, I thought we'd agreed.'

'It will cause talk—you know that, don't you? You and I giving them a joint gift.'

'I don't mind—let them talk,' Luc told her softly, adding persuasively, 'Andy says Joy's set her heart on the bed. It would be a wonderful surprise for Joy if we gave it to them. Andy's promised to keep it a secret from her.'

'Well, yes, I know what you're saying, and it would be lovely to surprise Joy with it.' Belle gave in.

'Yes, it would,' Luc agreed, and then asked her softly, 'What time this weekend are you expecting to arrive?'

'Belle, it's Carol. Look, I was wondering, since you're in Cambridgeshire for the next week, if you'd like to come round and have supper with us on Saturday evening. I'm not sure what time you're due to arrive, but I know that Mum and Dad are planning to leave for the airport at two in the afternoon. It would give us a chance to talk. I've been so busy with the wedding arrangements—'

'Carol, I have to go,' Belle interrupted her sister firmly. 'I'd love to see you whilst I'm down at Mum and Dad's house-sitting, but I'm afraid that Saturday night is going to be out.'

Deliberately she didn't offer any further explanation, swiftly ending the call before her sister could question her any further. There was no way she was going to tell Carol that the reason she couldn't accept her invitation was because she had already accepted an earlier one—from Luc.

And fortunately her sister was too preoccupied to question the deeply unusual circumstances of Belle and Luc giving Joy and Andy a joint wedding present.

From the sitting room window of her parents' house, Belle could see a car pulling into the drive. She drew in a sharp breath as she saw Luc climbing out of it and walking towards the front door.

'What are you doing here?' she demanded as she opened the door to him. 'You said you'd pick me up at eight o'clock tonight…'

'I know, but I couldn't wait any longer to see you,' Luc confessed as she let him in. 'Oh, Belle…'

Not since they had been a courting couple had they behaved like this, Belle acknowledged as Luc barely waited until he had closed the front door behind them to take her hungrily in his arms and kiss her with a passion which she admitted she had no difficulty whatsoever in matching.

'It's less than a week since you saw me,' Belle managed to find the logic to remind him when she was finally able to talk.

'A lifetime,' Luc told her mock solemnly, his tone belying the look of sparkling humour in his eyes.

This was a side of him she had never truly appreciated in the past, Belle acknowledged, as she shared his laughter, his sense of fun and teasing good humour. Perhaps because she had taken herself so seriously in those days, she had never allowed herself to appreciate it, but, as she was now discovering, shared laughter was a very, very potent aphrodisiac.

'Carol rang the other day. She wanted me to have dinner with *them* this evening.'

'What did you tell her?' Luc asked as he followed her into her parents' kitchen.

'I said that I'd got a prior engagement,' Belle informed him wryly.

'A prior *engagement*…mmm…'

There was no mistaking the way Luc reinforced the word 'engagement', and followed it with a meaningful look at her left hand.

'Luc, honestly!' Belle reproved him. 'What on earth would people think if they could see us…hear you…?'

'I don't care what other people think…only what *you* think…what *you* feel,' Luc told her extravagantly.

'Oh, Luc…' A little shakily Belle went into his arms. 'Are we right to be behaving like this? We made a mistake once…'

'Look, we promised ourselves that we wouldn't question what was happening, that we'd just take things…and each other…on trust,' Luc reminded her.

'Yes, I know,' she admitted. 'It's just… Mmm… Luc, someone might see us,' she protested half-heartedly as he started to kiss her.

'Mmm…but at least this time it won't be your father,' Luc responded reminiscently. 'Remember that evening when he came down?'

'Mmm…he hadn't realised that you'd come in with me, and he walked into the kitchen, where I'd gone to make us both a cup of coffee…'

'And I'd followed you to help you.'

'Oh, that was what you were doing, was it?' Belle asked darkly.

'Well, at least this time there's no chance of your father walking in,' Luc commented, taking her back in his arms.

Several bliss-filled seconds later, Belle was just snuggling deeper into his embrace when the back door suddenly opened.

'Belle, it's me, Jane…' she heard her mother's friend and neighbour calling out cheerfully.

Any hopes that she and Luc had managed to spring apart without being seen were squashed when she heard Jane's voice change completely as she started to apologise in a flustered voice. 'Oh, dear, I'm sorry, I hadn't realised…' And then it changed again as she recognised Luc. 'Luc... But what...?'

'Luc called round to see Mum and Dad,' Belle fabricated quickly. 'He hadn't realised that they'd gone away.' Heavens, it was amazing how very creative one could be with the truth when the need arose, and she wasn't even blushing.

'Oh, I see...'

Uncertainly she looked from Belle to Luc, and then back again.

'How's your eye now, Belle?' Luc asked solicitously. 'She'd got an eyelash in it,' he told Jane straight-faced.

'Oh...I see... Well, I only called round to say hello,' Jane explained. 'Er...I'll er...leave you to it...'

'Now the whole neighbourhood is going to know that you were here,' Belle groaned after she had gone. 'Oh, Luc...'

'Oh, Belle...'

'Now what are you doing?' she demanded a little breathlessly as he took her back in his arms.

'Looking for that eyelash,' Luc told her.

'I just hope that Jane hasn't seen us driving away together,' Belle worried half an hour later as Luc backed his car out of her parents' drive.

'We've got a perfectly legitimate excuse for being seen together. We're buying Joy and Andy a joint wedding present—remember?'

'Yes, I know that, but we're not doing that now, are we?'

'No, we're not doing it now,' Luc agreed urbanely.

'So where *are* we going?' Belle asked him curiously ten minutes later. 'It's too early for dinner and…'

'Wait and see.'

As they passed the country church where her niece was to be married, Belle leant forward in her seat.

'Does it bring back memories?' Luc asked her.

'Yes,' Belle admitted.

They had been married there themselves, and her eyes blurred briefly with emotional tears as she remembered how deliriously happy she had been, how filled with excitement mingled with awe at the thought of marrying Luc.

Not that she had originally wanted a big white wedding with all the trimmings. She had wanted something far quieter and more intimate.

It had been Luc who had persuaded her otherwise, pointing out to her that the vows they made to one another would be just as precious no matter where they made them, and that it would be unfair of them to exclude their families from the occasion.

'You wanted to be married somewhere private and out in the open air—remember?'

'Yes, I do,' Belle agreed, her voice a little husky with emotion at the way he had picked up on her own thoughts. 'An island, or the top of a hill... I wanted our marriage to be different, special...romantic, a private memory we could cherish for ever...'

'I know.'

'Instead it was a full family affair with me in a dress like a meringue and eight bridesmaids.'

'You looked beautiful.'

'You could barely get close enough to kiss me after the vicar had said you could because of the width of my dress hoops. Remember?'

Luc started to laugh.

'It wasn't funny,' Belle protested indignantly. 'A bride whose groom can't kiss her is no laughing matter.'

'I wasn't laughing at that,' Luc told her. 'I was just remembering the panic we had when no one could find little Timmy and then he crawled out from underneath your skirt.'

Belle laughed too.

'Yes, he'd been under the table whilst I was

talking to his parents and he'd crawled under my hoops without any of us noticing.'

Silently they exchanged reminiscent looks, and then out of the corner of her eye Belle saw a familiar signpost.

'You're taking me home?' she asked Luc incredulously, not realising until it was too late just how betraying her choice of words had been.

'I'm taking you home,' Luc agreed huskily.

This time the silence between them was deeper, closer, and potentially tense with unspoken emotion. Belle could feel her heart starting to beat far too fast as they drove through the village and Luc took the narrow country lane that led to the house they had bought together.

Belle had fallen in love with it at first sight, and the feelings that swamped her as they rounded the bend and she saw the house through its framing protective canopy of trees made her press her lips firmly together to stop her chin from wobbling and trembling. They had bought this house with such love and she had left it in so much pain that she could hardly bear to remember just how she had felt.

'It hasn't changed,' Belle whispered as Luc stopped the car.

Originally two separate farmworkers' cottages, the pair had been knocked through into one when they had bought it, and the whole building carefully renovated.

It was surrounded by a large garden overlooking the lane at the front and running down to a stream at the rear. Inside the front door was a long, narrow stone-flagged hallway and a flight of steep stairs. The stone mullioned windows gave the house character and an air of timelessness.

'Oh, you've still got the same curtains,' was the only thing she could think of to say as Luc helped her out of the car.

She had bought the material on impulse one wet afternoon when Luc had been studying and she had driven into Cambridge to do some shopping.

She had found the heavy damask fabric by accident on a market stall. It had come originally from one of the colleges, the stall owner had told her.

Uncertainly Belle had fingered the rich heavy fabric. Even at the stall holder's price it was still horribly expensive, but it was also perfect for the house.

She reminded herself that only the previous week she and Luc had rowed about money, and in retaliation for his claim that their expenses were far too high she had immediately accused

him of spending far too much on the books he
had claimed he needed to study.

'I thought that's what college libraries were
for,' she had told him scornfully, still smarting
from his reference to the fact that she had spent
more on a pair of luxury tights then he had done
on a whole week's lunches.

'It is, but they don't carry a set of these,' Luc
had countered quietly.

So she had walked determinedly away from the
stall, only to walk back again ten minutes later,
closing her eyes as she told the woman she would
have the fabric.

She had made the curtains herself. How could
she preach economy to Luc and then pay someone
else to make them?

'They're beautiful,' Luc had told her quietly
once they were hung, but the lack of genuine en-
thusiasm in his voice had hurt and angered her.

If she wanted to spend the money she had
worked so hard to earn on expensive curtains,
then she had every right to do so. And she had
told him so.

Remembering the incident now, Belle winced
at her own careless disregard of Luc's feelings,
her lack of wisdom and foresight.

'The shop has sent me a brochure with photographs of the different styles of beds they do,' Luc

explained as he unlocked the front door and ushered Belle in in front of him. 'Since they don't
carry a stock of each design, I thought you might
want to look at it.'

'Do they still do our bed?'

'"Our" bed?' Luc gave her a slow, teasing
smile. 'It's *my* bed now—remember? The removal men took the one I made when you moved
out. Of course it's not too late for us to—'

'No, no, I don't want—I'm keeping the bed
I've got,' Belle told him quickly, and then added
a little defensively, 'I like it, I'm used to it—
it's…'

It's a tiny bit of you, she could have said.

Belle shot Luc a slightly self-conscious look,
but he was already ushering her towards the drawing room.

'Come and sit down. I'll make us both a cup
of tea and then you can look at the brochure.'

The sitting room was just as she had left it. The
covers on the sofas a little faded, perhaps, and the
rust carpet's original colour softened by the sun,
but the classic timelessness of the furniture Belle
had chosen because the house had demanded it
had stood the passage of time very well, she acknowledged.

Luc might not have changed anything, but she
could see that the room had been repainted at

some stage and its surfaces were dust-free and well polished.

'Sorry about the delay,' he apologised ten minutes later, when he reappeared with their tea and the catalogue. 'I couldn't find this. Mrs Leyton, who comes in from the village to clean for me a couple of times a week, had "tidied" it away.'

Being in the house which had once been her home, the home she had once shared with Luc, who was here beside her, whose home it still was, was causing her to feel so many conflicting emotions that Belle could barely concentrate on the brochure he was showing her.

Certainly the company had extended its original small range of furniture, and the four-poster beds they had added to their list were works of art— and had she been looking for a new bed—

But they weren't looking for a bed for the master bedroom here; they were looking for one for Joy and Andy. And since they already knew exactly which one they wanted...

'I really ought to get back,' Belle told Luc hurriedly, closing the brochure. 'But first I need to go upstairs and wash my hands...'

One of the drawbacks to the house had been the fact that it had not possessed a downstairs cloakroom. They had had plans to add one at the same time as they added an extra bedroom suite. Confidently Belle made her way upstairs whilst Luc carried their tea things back to the kitchen.

Up here, too, nothing seemed to have changed. The dried flowers she had arranged were gone from the deep window on the landing, but the curtains were the same, and... On her way to the bathroom she suddenly paused, stopped, and then retraced her steps.

The door to the master bedroom was closed. Very gently she turned the handle and then stepped inside.

It was like stepping back in time to another world. Once inside the bedroom she had shared with Luc the memories came flooding back with such force that she had to cling to the door for support. It was in this room that they had loved, laughed and fought. Belle could hardly bear now to think of the sacrilege it had been to fight in a room which should have known only the intimate content of their love.

Shakily she let go of the door and walked over to the bed, her hand trembling as she automatically smoothed the creases out of Luc's side of the duvet.

Luc's side...

Unwanted and unheralded the tears came hot and fast, a silent glissade of pain and regret. Her body shook with the force of her sobs, but still she didn't make a sound.

'Belle?'

Shocked, she stiffened her body in rejection of the warmth of Luc's arms. She hadn't heard him come in, didn't want him to see her like this.

'You're crying,' he told her, begging rawly as he turned her round to face him, 'Don't...please, don't.'

'Oh, Luc, I feel so ashamed when I remember the things I did...the things I said,' Belle wept, unable to conceal what she was feeling. 'I was so thoughtless, so selfish...'

'No more thoughtless or selfish than I was stubborn and unreasonable,' Luc comforted her.

'It's all such a waste,' Belle cried heartbrokenly.

'Love is never wasted,' Luc told her softly. 'Just like it never dies...'

Belle looked up at him.

'It's not too late for us, Belle, we still have the future...*our* future...together—if we choose to take it...'

'What are you saying?' she whispered. 'We said that we wouldn't rush things or make promises, that we'd take each day as it comes...'

'I know, but I know as well that each day isn't

going to be enough for me. I want all your days. All *our* days.'

'Remember Cheringham House?' he asked her obliquely.

Belle nodded her head. The stately Georgian property was owned by the local council and had been painstakingly renovated and opened to the public. She had always loved it, often coaxing Luc away from his studies to go round it with her.

'Under the new law, it's now been given permission to hold weddings. It has an island…'

'In the middle of the lake with a pretty mock-Gothic temple… Yes, I know,' Belle agreed.

And then, as she looked at him, she breathed, 'Oh, Luc, we couldn't…could we?'

Ten minutes later, when she had finally extracted herself from his arms, she reminded him, 'We're supposed to be going out to dinner, remember?'

'I've got a better idea,' Luc told her masterfully. 'Why don't we eat here…?'

'Here?'

Belle looked at him.

'What are we going to eat?' she asked him shakily.

'I know what I want to eat,' Luc responded sensually. 'All right, all right,' he acknowledged as he fielded the look she gave him. 'Let's go down and see what we can find in the freezer.'

'Mmm…champagne and lobster. You really are spoiling me,' Belle told Luc contentedly as she licked her fingers.

'Well, I have to admit it was a lucky find. I'd forgotten all about the lobster. It was a present…'

'From one of your students?' Belle asked a little possessively, a warning glint in her eyes.

Luc laughed.

'No, from my mother, as it happens.'

Belle allowed herself to relax. His mother was a wonderful cook, and loved nothing better than passing on the results of her skills to her friends and family.

'Mmm…that was wonderful,' Belle declared, stretching sensuously.

'Mmm…wonderful,' Luc agreed, reaching across to slide his hand into the tempting vee of flesh exposed by the borrowed shirt she was wearing and bending his head to kiss her.

'Just think,' he murmured as he covered her mouth with his, 'if we bought a four-poster, we could close the curtains and eat in bed in true Tudor fashion.'

'Throwing the bones out for the dogs and serfs, you mean?' Belle teased back, wrinkling her nose as she disagreed. 'Yuck, I don't think so. Although I must admit the idea of a four-poster does have a certain amount of appeal...'

'Mmm...although I have to say that there is something deliciously sensual about the way the light from the window touches your skin which I couldn't enjoy through closed curtains.'

'Luc...' Belle reproved unsteadily as he gently pushed his shirt back off her shoulders, exposing her breasts to the early evening sunlight streaming in through the windows, and then moved back to enjoy the results of his handiwork.

'Your skin looks as though it's been sprinkled with gold dust,' he told her softly. 'You have the most beautiful skin, Belle, the most beautiful body...'

'I'm thirty-four,' Belle protested, but in truth she thought that Luc's body looked even more sensually exciting now than it had done when they were younger. Perhaps Luc was right in what he had said to her earlier, that it took pain and loss and despair to make one appreciate love properly.

Well, she had certainly experienced all of those. They both had.

She trembled a little with excited anticipation as Luc's hands cupped her breasts. Her body was so intensely responsive to him it frightened her a little.

He kissed her throat and then her nipples, his eyes darkening as he looked back into her face.

'I don't know how I managed to live without you,' he told her rawly, and then added, 'But it wasn't really living; it was simply existing.'

His mouth returned to her breasts, teasing their hard crests. Belle moaned eagerly beneath her breath and reached for him. Her need for him overwhelmed her, urgent, immediate and hotly demanding. The feel of his weight against her body, between her thighs, made her shudder wildly. Her hands clasped his back, her nails pressed hard against his skin as she clung passionately to him. She cried out as he entered her, a wild, elemental cry of love and need mingled with pain and regret for all that they had lost, all that she had thrown away, and then the past was forgotten, the future just a shadowy vision, the only thing that mattered the thrusting movement of his body within hers.

Luc cried out fiercely against her as his own need peaked and her body exploded into a frantic spiral of orgasmic pleasure.

Damp, panting, her heart still racing, Belle looked up into his eyes.

'Great-Aunt Alice could have an awful lot to answer for,' she warned him meaningfully. 'This wasn't something I'd planned for...'

'All the more reason to take that trip to Cheringham House just as soon as we can, then,' Luc responded.

'I might not—' Belle began, but Luc shook his head, and then bent it and kissed her tenderly.

'With or without child, I want you back in my life, Belle.' Belle snuggled closer to him and then tensed.

'Luc, I don't want to have to tell anyone about us...not yet...it's too soon. What we have between us is too...precious. I...'

'I understand,' Luc confirmed as he kissed her again.

'Belle.'

Belle gave Luc an answering smile as he called her name and cut a swathe through the busy fellow wedding guests to reach her side.

'What happened?' he asked her quietly, adding with a rueful look, 'I was just beginning to wonder if I ought to send my mother on a search party to the Ladies for you.'

'It's just as well that you didn't,' Belle whispered, glancing warningly at where his hand rested, just a little too possessively and potentially betrayingly on her arm. 'Body language, Luc,' she reminded him under her breath. 'People are watching us.'

'Mmm...what do you mean, just as well I didn't?' Luc demanded, ignoring the second part of her comment.

'I never actually got as far as the cloakroom,' Belle informed him as they were caught up in the throng of people moving excitedly towards the exit so that they could watch the bride and groom leave.

'Why, what happened?' Luc asked her anxiously.

'My mobile started to ring,' Belle answered him, 'and once I realised who was calling I decided that it might be an idea to make sure I took the call in private. So I went out to the car.'

'In private?' Luc started to frown.

'Look over there at Luc and Belle,' Luc's mother sighed disappointedly at her husband as she caught sight of her son's frowning face.

'Just when I thought that the pair of them seemed to be getting on so well. I suppose I should have known it was too good to be true. And to think I'd actually begun to hope...' She shook her head ruefully. 'They always seemed so right for one another, and I can't help wishing...'

'Leave them to lead their own lives,' her husband advised her gently.

* * *

'In private,' Luc repeated with concern.

'Mmm…' Belle responded dreamily.

Belle's face was slightly flushed and Luc could almost feel the excitement bubbling up inside her. Her eyes, when he looked down into them, shone with barely concealed happiness. So much so that he could almost feel it radiating from her. She looked, Luc decided wryly, buoyed up with a secret—and with love.

'It must have been a very special call—and a very special caller.' Luc couldn't resist challenging her.

Belle's smile deepened, and so did her pretty pink colour.

'It was,' she admitted candidly.

'Belle, quick. She's leaving. Here…'

A handful of rose petals were pushed into Belle's hand by her mother, to shower onto the bride. Obediently, Belle turned her attention away from Luc and towards her niece and her new husband.

'Belle looks wonderful, doesn't she?' one of Belle's female cousins commented to another.

'Positively glowing…'

Belle, who had overheard their comment, waited until they were out of earshot before turning to Luc and remarking in a very, very soft whisper, 'Positively *blooming* might have been a more *appropriate* description—under the circumstances. Doubly so, in view of the fact...' She added mock coyly.

She stopped and waited for the penny to drop.

'My call was from the doctor's surgery,' she added helpfully, her own face breaking into a wide grin of excited happiness as she saw the enlightenment dawn in Luc's eyes.

'It's quite definitely twins,' she told him breathlessly.

'Twins... Two babies...' Luc gazed at her in adoring awe.

'Yes, twins does mean two babies,' Belle agreed teasingly, tongue in cheek.

She had had her suspicions for a while that she might be pregnant—she had even gone out and bought herself a home pregnancy test. But Luc had been away at the time, and in the end, she had wanted him to be there to share the moment with her. After all, he had been there—very much there—when their baby had been conceived, and they had agreed that this time round they were going to share their lives as true partners, true lovers.

Luc had been with her when she had first been told that she might be carrying twins, and today's phone call was the formal confirmation of the news they had already unofficially been given.

'Luc—Luc, stop it,' Belle protested as Luc suddenly wrapped her in his arms and gazed deeply into her eyes before starting to kiss her.

'Luc, people are watching us,' Belle protested huskily beneath his mouth. 'Luc… Luc… Mmm… Mmm…'

'Let them watch,' Luc whispered back hoarsely.

Around them Belle could hear the astonished whispers of the other guests as they turned away from the departing bridal car to stare at Belle and Luc.

'I think we'd better tell them, don't you?' Luc whispered lovingly. 'Otherwise, if we don't…'

His hand covered her still flat stomach protectively, and even though she knew technically it was impossible as yet Belle could have sworn the two beings they had created with their love were kicking their assent to their father's suggestion.

'Well, they're going to have to know some time,' Belle agreed philosophically as she glanced down at her body. 'But a lot of them might not approve,' she warned him. 'After all, it's not exactly conventional.'

'We have the right to live our lives the way we

want to live them, unconventional or not,' Luc argued softly.

And then, still holding her in the protective circle of his arm, he cleared his throat and began, 'Ladies and gentlemen, family and friends. Belle and I have an announcement to make.'

As he looked down at her, Belle looked back up at him, all the love she felt for him showing clearly in her eyes. A shaft of light touched the gold of the new wedding ring she had just removed from her purse and slipped onto her wedding finger—they had had it made from the gold of her old ring and Luc's, a symbolic fusing of the old to create new in a bond that could never be broken.

Her sister saw it first, pre-empting Luc's announcement by screaming excitedly,

'Belle, you're married—you and Luc have remarried! Oh, how could you, without saying anything. Oh, Belle...Luc... Oh, this is so wonderful...'

'Wonderful,' Luc echoed as he raised Belle's hand to his mouth and gently kissed her fingers.

Through the excited hubbub that followed, Belle could hear her great-aunt Alice saying quite clearly to her mother, 'There you are, Mary, I knew I was right. They *are* married...'

As their relatives pressed happily around them, Belle could feel the joy bubbling up inside her.

Oh yes, they were married—had remarried. In a small, perfect, private ceremony on the island on the lake at Cheringham House, two weeks ago.

She had wanted to keep it a secret for just a little longer but... She patted her stomach tenderly.

Some events had a way of precipitating their own celebrations.

Above the heads of their excited audience Luc mouthed softly to her, I love you—and them.

Blissfully Belle returned his smile. One day—not this time, perhaps, but one day—they would have a little girl, and when they did, when they did, she rather thought they might call her Alice.

MILLS & BOON®

This Month's Romance Titles

♡

Each month you can choose from a wide variety of romance novels from Mills & Boon®. Below are the new titles to look out for this month from the Presents™ series.

Presents™

THE MISTRESS ASSIGNMENT	Penny Jordan
THE VIRGIN BRIDE	Miranda Lee
THE SEDUCTION GAME	Sara Craven
ONE WEDDING REQUIRED!	Sharon Kendrick
LUC'S REVENGE	Catherine George
THE MARRIAGE TAKEOVER	Lee Wilkinson
THE PLAYBOY'S BABY	Mary Lyons
HIRED WIFE	Karen van der Zee

MILLS & BOON®

This Month's Romance Titles

Each month you can choose from a wide variety of romance novels from Mills & Boon®. Below are the new titles to look out for this month from the Enchanted™ series.

Enchanted™

BOARDROOM PROPOSAL	Margaret Way
DR. TEXAS	Debbie Macomber
THE NINE-DOLLAR DADDY	Day Leclaire
HER HUSBAND-TO-BE	Leigh Michaels
THE FATHERHOOD SECRET	Grace Green
A WIFE AND CHILD	Rosemary Carter
A REAL ENGAGEMENT	Marjorie Lewty
WIFE WITHOUT A PAST	Elizabeth Harbison

Available at most branches of WH Smith, Tesco, Asda, Martins, Borders, Easons, Volume One/James Thin and most good paperback bookshops

MILLS & BOON®

Makes any time special™

By Request

Bestselling themed romances brought back to you by popular demand

Each month By Request brings you three full-length novels in one beautiful volume featuring the best of the best.

So if you missed a favourite Romance the first time around, here is your chance to relive the magic from some of our most popular authors.

Look out for
***Trials by Marriage* in April 1999**
featuring Carole Mortimer,
Jacqueline Baird and Elizabeth Oldfield

MILLS & BOON®

Makes any time special™

The Regency Collection

*Mills & Boon® is delighted to bring back,
for a limited period, 12 of our favourite
Regency Romances for you to enjoy.*

*These special books will be available for
you to collect each month from May, and
with two full-length Historical Romance*™
*novels in each volume they are great
value at only £4.99.*

Volume One available from 7th May